The Lord of Milan

Robert Nieri

The Lord of Milan

Originally published by RN Art Products Limited (company number 10098872)

Registered office: 143 Exchange Road, Nottingham, NG2 6DD

Cover design and art work by Christopher Nieri.

This is a work of fiction based on the life of Herbert Kilpin.

www.lordofmilan.com

This book is dedicated in loving memory to
Peter Alfred Nieri.

With profound thanks to Luigi La Rocca
for his generosity.

THANKS

Louise, Olivia, Jacob, Mamma

Jared & Left Lion, Andy & Lisa Black, Dee & Pete,
Brandon, Gary, Rachel and Kathleen, Brian Granville,
Gavin, Henderson Mullin, Moby Farrand, Colin Slater,
Richard Bullock, George Taylor, Richard Williams,
Danny Taylor, Pete Vallelly, The Boot Family, Tobias
Jones, Nigel Garlick, Nottingham Conference Centre
(Abi), Jen Hudson, Nigel Cooke, Ajda Vucicevic…and
anyone else I've forgotten. It's not a slight, trust me.

Biggest thanks to lil bro, Chris for turning these words
into what you have in your hands and for his fab artwork.

HELLOS

Martin, Kerry, Skyla, Albie.
Mick, Sue, Chris, Ali, Sam & Caitlin
Ray, Emma, Joe and Orla
Scoffer, Ariel, Steve, Fiona.

The woman lay groaning on the sweaty bed, pale hands gripping the head rail behind her matted hair and whispered through gritted teeth to the older woman above her:

'Tell him to drop his bloody cleaver right now and come upstairs!'

The midwife turned briefly to the massed female company standing silently in the corner of the cold bedroom and hurled a brisk 'Please fetch Edward' in their direction, causing one of the gaggle to dislodge and hurry out of the room, brisk little footsteps fading down the stairs, leaving the bedroom in a near silence punctuated only by the soft tick-tocking of a clock on the wall and the cries of pain of the expectant woman, constantly shifting under the ruffled bedspread.

Minutes passed with no one making the next move. Then, murmuring voices rose from downstairs before a door creaked open, followed by the sound of ascending feet, this time heavy but slow and Edward Kilpin entered the room.

His wife relaxed when she saw him but Edward stiffened in the presence of so many women, awkwardly approaching the bed to kneel in front of his woman before lifting a lock of hair plastered to her cheek with his freshly scrubbed hand and softly stroking the side of her head.

'I'm here now, me duck. You know the drill by now!'

Sarah Kilpin raised a weary smile, acknowledging her

gruff husband's attempt to lighten the mood.

Edward looked at her for a while longer, then gently slipped his hand away, pushed himself to his feet and took a vacant seat next to the wall, unrolling his sleeves and buttoning his cuffs, as he looked out of the window at the snow continuing to fall on Mansfield Road.

THE BOY WHO
WOULDN'T GROW UP

1

p13

EXODUS

2

p33

THE
YOUNG COUNTRY

3

p57

HARD TIMES

4

p91

THE RED AND
THE BLACK

5

p114

THE
GLORY

6

p152

EVERYTHING IN
ITS RIGHT PLACE

7

p170

GOLDEN
YEARS

8

p194

THE
DARK WOOD

9

p216

RESURRECTION

10

p273

EXTRA TIME

11

p294

THE BOY WHO WOULDN'T GROW UP

'Pan, who and what art thou?' Hook cried huskily.
'I'm youth, I'm joy,' Peter answered at a venture,
'I'm a little bird that has broken out of the egg.'

—— *JM Barrie, Peter Pan*

I

Baby Herbert announced himself to this world on 24th January 1870 with a burst of short, loud cries to fill the silence following the moans and groans of his mother's long labour.

The women took over with the well-practised routine, busying themselves in a silent operation to remove the cord and clean the baby before reuniting him with his mother.

Edward sat apart, hands clasped on knees, powerless in his own household. He was used to dealing with blood and guts every day of his working life, preparing the meats of the animal kingdom he supplied to the good folk of Nottingham, but not with this warm bundle of life caked in placenta, even though this was the ninth surviving child Sarah had borne him.

Patiently he waited for the women to complete their tasks and then, when given the sign, almost apologetically he approached the bed to kiss his wife's forehead and peer over the blanket at his newborn son.

'Edward, that's the last one. I can't go through that again.'

'You said that last time, love. Just rest now.'

'How many more boys do you need to help you run your shop?'

'Hush now, it's done… He has a fine pair of lungs, that one!'

During their brief exchange the silent women had

slipped out of the bedroom to busy themselves downstairs, leaving the couple with their baby. The boy was sleeping soundly after his first liquid lunch and now Sarah too drifted off into exhausted slumber.

Edward sat still, listening to footsteps and trying to make out muffled conversations elsewhere in the house. Intermittent tinkling of a bell announced the arrival and departure of customers downstairs but, he mused, with not nearly enough regularity to keep feeding his still growing family of six boys and three girls.

The snow had stopped falling, deadening the sounds of man and horse outside, but the clock continued to tick.

II

Born in the village of Stoke Goldington near Newport Pagnell in 1825, Edward had arrived in the bustling town of Nottingham in the 1840s with dreams of bettering himself and offering his own family more than his parents had been able to give him, scratching a meagre living from the Buckinghamshire land. Sucked into the East Midlands by the lace boom, for a time he had tried his hand in the mills and factories before working out that he should stick to what he knew best, working as a butcher to feed the workers with whom he had been competing for a daily wage.

Edward had saved and saved what little money he'd earned as a butcher's boy, sending some back to his parents and hiding the rest under a floorboard in his lodgings before he'd accumulated enough to set himself up in business in a modest way. He started out in a narrow alley in the slums of The Rookeries, stocking carcasses and cuts that butchers to the wealthy merchants of the Lace Market passed over, placing his stall outside his small shop early in the morning and staying open until late at night to catch any remaining trade as the last tired workers made their way home.

He took time to arrange as artfully as possible all his joints, giblets and entrails. Working men and women of Nottingham were increasingly able to afford meat for the family all year round, not just at Christmas, but Edward did not have a free run at the available business. Mounds of tripe did not sell themselves and his competitors hawked their wares with insistence, standing in the Market Place or by their trestle tables, cajoling passers-by, inviting them to look beyond the flies and to imagine what wonders could be made of cuts with a little clever seasoning.

Edward was a shy, straightforward soul. He could not and would not advance by guile or bluff and took pride in selling edible meat at affordable prices, discarding the putrid joints that not even the most pungent spices of Arabia or a glass of Nottingham ale could mask. After closing its doors he scrubbed and swept his shop late into the night by candlelight and the smell of freshly laid sawdust contrasted with the more interesting odours of less conscientious rivals as the doors were opened again for business early the next morning and the more discerning housewives made their way in increasing numbers to Mr Kilpin.

Gradually he built up his custom and in time found more upmarket premises just north of the city centre, up on Mansfield Road, close to new housing built in a more genteel area on the Sand Field.

In the same quiet, methodical way Edward had chosen well his partner for life and together they were raising a large family.

Sarah Smith was Nottingham born and bred. As a young woman her mother had sent her to buy some meat. She decided to try the new butcher who had just opened on the main road and came home with a rabbit for the pot and a fondness for the earnest man who had attentively served her. Her mother approved of both and within a year her parents' dowry had been put to good use in extending the range of meats on offer at Kilpin's the butchers.

Edward was soon renting all the available rooms above his shop, with the arrival of the first of the fifteen children Sarah would bear him over two decades until she reached the age of forty-three and was done with being pregnant.

The Kilpins naturally wanted the best for all their children, but with Edward straining to support his burgeoning family and Sarah nurturing each baby to childhood as the next one came along, all the children had to play their part in keeping this busy household together, helping father in whatever way they could or looking after younger siblings to ease their mother's load.

Childhood is our age of wonder and discovery when we soak up our world and it colours us. Responsibility came early to the Kilpin children who, as the offspring of a butcher living above chilled carcasses, adopted a more unsentimental, matter-of-fact approach to life than playmates growing up in neighbouring confectioners' shops, taking it for granted that there is an end to life and realising pretty quickly that it can be nasty, brutish and short - and not just for pigs, geese and chickens.

But children of all eras need to breathe, to dream, to play.

During the summer months in particular the choice smells of the shop, of the road of a hundred horses and the all-pervasive malty odour from the Nottingham brewery just down the road provided what little additional encouragement little Herbert needed to leave the dead meat behind and explore his neighbourhood in search of adventure.

The rear entrance to the Arboretum was a minute's walk from the Kilpin home. Herbert would slip away from the hubbub of Mansfield Road, turning right into Chatham Road to walk across North Sherwood Street and in through a gateway onto a tree-lined pathway which brought him, after a two minute dash, to a short tunnel under Addison Street before which he paused, hands on knees, to catch breath.

Then he walked slowly and deliberately through the darkness to emerge seconds later into the light of a magical, wooded landscape, created twenty-five years earlier for the relaxation and repose of the good folk of Nottingham, as the town had spread across the Sand Field.

This was Herbert's glimpse of a world beyond his view and, literally, a breath of fresh air.

The Arboretum had opened on 11th May 1852. Plants and flowers had been labelled with information about their country of origin and details of their size. Originally the park had been accessible to the public only on Sundays, Mondays and Wednesdays and for the rest of the week on payment of a subscription but there had been an outcry, and within five years the Arboretum's gates were flung open to all, for free, every day.

It proved difficult to maintain the idea of the Arboretum as a place of educational improvement; it was with some dismay and mild disgust that well-meaning, upstanding members of the Victorian establishment noted at the time that the Arboretum seemed to be merely a huge playground for young girls and boys.

How very regrettable.

Over a thousand trees in rolling parkland provided plenty of cover for hide and seek and games of rough and tumble, far away from the tut-tutting of controlling adults. But it wasn't just a park. It was a free world of adventure in, but not of, the surrounding town. Very few other children were lucky enough to live so close or to have the time to play at pirates and storm the mount guarded by a Chinese Bell Tower and four great cannon, booty grabbed by the mighty British Army and gifted to the people of Nottingham; the bell taken during the Opium Wars with China and the cannon at the siege of Sebastopol during the Crimean War.

On the far western side of the Arboretum lay an ornamental lake, enveloped in high summer by trees and vegetation under cover of which the local kids would slip into the cool, slimy waters while the killjoy park keeper Bumpdul was away from his lodge, using it as Nottingham's first (unofficial) open air swimming pool.

Here, unlike in most other places in town birdsong prevailed, of the wild and free type – followed, some time later, by the more poignant cheeping of the unluckier residents of the Circular Aviary.

In the Nottingham of the 1870s and 1880s when space was increasingly at a premium as more and more warehouses, factories, shops and houses sprang up and surrounding villages coalesced, the open spaces of the Arboretum gave Herbert a great love of the outdoors and for adventure. This was his enchanted garden: a special place, no more than five minutes from his terraced home on a busy road, to nurture and fortify his spirit.

But as he grew older Herbert ventured slightly further from home, carrying on up Mansfield Road away from town towards Mars Hill, formerly Gallows Hill. Until 1827 public executions had taken place here, the condemned brought to meet their fate on the back of a cart along the road Herbert now climbed.

As a child Herbert's older brothers told him of the unfortunate soul who had refused the customary offer of one last drink at the Nag's Head public house, just across the road from their house. The distraught man had declined with the shake of a head, just wanting to hasten the dreaded deed. But as soon as he'd been left dangling in the wind and the crowd had begun to disperse a breathless messenger had arrived from the town with a cruelly timed reprieve.

'So, Herbert, the moral of this story is that when you're all grown up there will always be time for a stiff drink - and don't you forget it!' beamed James one day, just before taking a clip around the ear from his passing father, who told him not to get into bad habits, nor lead his younger brother astray.

Passing the Nag's Head, Herbert carried on up Mansfield Road to the top of the hill, crossing the road that ran from east to west along the summit on which thirteen windmills had once stood.

On his right was St Andrew's Church, built in the Gothic Revival style on the site of the old gallows, visible on the skyline of Nottingham for miles around and from which he could look back down over the town towards the Trent river and to the fields beyond.

And facing him, the entrance to Rock Cemetery, carved out of the sandstone on which Nottingham was built.

Except that this gothic landscape wasn't the result of some grandiose architectural scheme, but a discarded testament to the destitute of Nottingham who in decades past had quarried sand out of Gallows Hill and lugged and carted it down into town to pay for food. Sand that was used for mortar to bind together the houses for the huddled masses or thrown onto floors in homes and shops to collect dirt and dust.

The cemetery had opened in 1856. The mines became catacombs and a large natural hollow was reserved for the town's illustrious corpses as an exclusive place of burial. As Herbert and his friends grew through childhood and tired of hide-and-seek in the tranquillity of the Arboretum, they dared each other to accept an altogether edgier challenge among the gravestones of the Rock, as the sun went down, the shadows lengthened and the silhouettes of seraphims, mourning virgins and triumphant cherubs cut into the reddening sky, before all light was doused and every slightest sound took on heightened meaning.

The boys spooked each other with the tale of the poor man who when digging the sand seventy years earlier had been buried alive as the rock fell in on him, an incident that had led to the closure of the quarry before it had been reinvented years later as a place to bury those who had already died. Legend had it that the man's restless soul still wandered the place at night, still looking for a way out.

Who dared spend longest in one of the catacombs, mimicking the eternal repose of the putrefying bodies buried just a few feet below the porous earth, until everyone else had given up the ghost and decided to go home – to slip in the back door before fretting parents had time to realise that one or more of their numerous brood was missing and unaccounted for (and with school the next day)?

Herbert gathered all his willpower to do what came least naturally to him, to remain stock-still as bats flitted above and unidentified creatures scuttled in the undergrowth, while the last horse-drawn trams passed up Mansfield Road towards town and imaginations ran riot.

For a child whose first impulse was action, how great his powers of resolve proved, as he held his breath and curled up tight as a foetus in a hollow below a headstone, while his playmates crept along the path on the other side.

And all just to win a game.

It was worth the reproachful glance from his silent mother - much harder to take than the sharp clip behind the ear from his father - after Herbert tried to enter his home undetected, as the clocks struck ten.

But it wasn't all about life and death. It was about something much more important to Herbert. In the early 1880s his special place wasn't home, school or church. On the other side of the cemetery walls, at the bottom of the slope leading down the other side of Mars Hill, lay the vast expanse of the Forest Recreation Ground.

Back in the day of Robin Hood this site had been the southern most extremity of the royal hunting forest of Sherwood. Over the centuries the trees went, chopped and sold off for buildings, furniture and the ships of the Royal Navy and by the nineteenth century it remained a forest in name only, standing on the Lings, an expanse of open land.

Crowds gathered to watch the horse races on the Forest, a handsome grandstand providing wealthy spectators with a better view and refreshment facilities. Cricket matches were another draw for the people of Nottingham and sometimes they would also gather to hold political demonstrations.

As a result of the Enclosure Act in 1854 the Forest Recreation Ground was preserved for the delight and delectation of the emerging middle classes as they promenaded on a Sunday afternoon serenaded by brass bands.

Since the 1860s the wide, open space had also hosted football matches. The new sport was quickly catching on. In the streets surrounding the Forest dozens of players in kit all made their way in the same direction to compete.

Herbert had first noticed groups of older lads walking up North Sherwood Street one Saturday morning in spring as he and his mates crossed the road heading for the Arboretum to taunt Bumpdul. Herbert had taken some pig's blood from his father's shop and his gang was off to daub all the tulips in the park keeper's immaculately kept flowerbeds around the Bell Tower.

They'd kicked a ball around the Arboretum for years, but without much intent, the rolling slopes putting paid to any proper contest. But these older boys and young men, kitted out in colourful shirts, shorts and stockings heading off to the Forest aroused the miscreants' curiosity. Kilpin dropped his bucket of blood in the still sparse undergrowth by the park gate and beckoned his mates to follow the stream of human traffic up the hill.

The gang sat on the grass slopes above the huge field and watched transfixed for hours as twenty games at a time were played before them, each pitch marked out by lines of spectators urging on their teams.

When all the games had ended and everyone else had left to go home or to the pubs the boys ran down the slope and began kicking their ball around the flat turf, mimicking the moves they'd just witnessed and forgetting about the bucket of congealed blood in the Arboretum, leaving Mr Bumpdul's tulips to flower in all their multi-coloured glory without a stinking red gloss.

III

Monday 5th June 1882 was the start of a new week towards the end of the school year at the Bluecoat School on Mansfield Road when everyone was beginning to go through the motions.

The pupils were happy enough sitting indoors during the dark, cold winter months but summer was now on its way. The chatter of birds, the fresh smell of budding greenery, the clippety-clop of horses drawing their loads up and down the road, together with the greetings and shouts of traders and the gossip of housewives, all decanted into the classroom through its open windows.

The children's interest wandered, but quickly they turned from the views and sounds outside to face the teacher who now addressed them, picking up the thread of the instruction and the question being asked with the help of murmured promptings from friendly neighbours.

In truth, the teachers too had had enough by now, but years of dissimulation had made their application to the task in hand seem more genuine.

Mr Brownleaf repeated the question.

'Do you all remember when we talked about Charles I and the English Civil War?'

'Sir, was that the king with the twirly tash and pointy beard up at Castle?'

'Quite right, Elsie. On 22nd August 1642 King Charles raised his royal standard on the highest tower of Nottingham Castle, to declare war on his own people and so begin the English Civil War. You will recall we learnt how Charles urged the people of Nottingham to follow him into battle against those who supported the parliament, which had refused to raise taxes to pay for his foreign wars and expensive works of arts. But they refused...'

'He should have known what was coming sir, because his big red banner flapped in the wind against the black skies before it was blown away. That was a very bad sign...'

'Yes, that's right, Leonard. Charles left Nottingham without popular support because although he was a king, he was not a leader of men. He could not win their hearts and minds. Well children, news has now reached us of the death of a man just before the weekend who was not a king but who was a leader of men and united his land. This is he.'

Brownleaf held up a newspaper showing a photograph of a man who looked like Jesus, but with a side parting and quite a bit older. Maybe a cross between Jesus and God. And he wore a funny hat and a striped cape.

'Boys and girls, this man is Jooseppy Gary Baldy, which means 'Joseph' in Italian.'

This was impressive. So he was the foster father, as well as the Father and Son...

'From an early age Gary Baldy's dream had been to unite Italy as a country. He was sentenced to death as a young man for taking part in an armed revolt against the land's Austrian rulers and he fled to South America where he sailed in the merchant navy and led a life of adventure, fighting for the freedom of Uruguay...'

By now, more children - even Herbert - were turning away from the flight of the birds in the clear blue sky towards Mr Brownleaf, red in the face from the excitement he felt at what he was recounting and revelling in the knowledge that finally, after all this time, he had his class's attention.

'He married a local girl called Anita and they fought side by side. In time he returned to Europe and just over twenty years ago he led a group of a thousand men (and one woman) to Sicily to take the island from the Bourbon army and navy. His army was a mix of students, criminals and those without work and they wore the redshirts of the abattoir workers in Uruguay which didn't show the blood of the animals they butchered. No one gave Gary Baldy a chance of success but he was a brilliant commander and he had luck on his side.

'He landed on the western side of Sicily and led his men on an uphill bayonet charge against an enemy with twice the number of men, shouting 'Here we either make Italy or we die!' The Bourbons were defeated and Gary Baldy led his men across the island and then over to the mainland, moving with speed to the great city of Naples where he was given a hero's welcome.

'He had conquered the southern half of the Italian peninsula but he had no thoughts of personal power or glory. Instead he met his king - who was Victor Emmanuel II from the House of Savoy - at a small place in the centre of Italy called Teano.

'The two men rode up to each other, Gary Baldy took off his hat, shook Victor Emmanuel's hand and then raised his voice: 'Hail, the King of Italy!'

'Then two weeks later and without fanfare Gary Baldy sailed back to the plain stone home he had built on a rocky little island near the coast of another big island called Sardinia.

'After his successes Gary Baldy travelled all around the world, meeting kings and queens, prime ministers and presidents, who were honoured to receive him.

'Children, listen to this, written when he travelled around England in 1864,' and at this point Brownleaf peered closely at the obituary in front of him, his eyesight not being as sharp as it had once been, cleared his throat and read out the marked text to his captive audience:

> **All England rose to do him honour; the City of London stopped in its immense and busy life to greet him; the Prince of Wales called on him; the nobility and gentlemen, the mechanics and factory workmen, all paid him their own mark of respect.**

> **Gary Baldy is the most heroic figure in Europe. A simple, true, brave man, enthusiastic for Italian unity and for human liberty, having won a kingdom for his sovereign, but who contented himself with a cabbage garden on a little island. Flattered by kings and statesmen, but never yielding a hair's breath of his principles, or even softening a word, where right and truth are at stake. When people cannot honour such a character, they have become corrupted below the appreciation even of virtue and manhood.**

Herbert had not listened so intently to anything Brownleaf had ever said. His mate Walter leaned over and whispered in his ear, as Herbert continued to stare at Brownleaf.

'That's incredible. When I'm older, I'm going to have adventures like Gary Baldy!'

The lesson was ending and Brownleaf surveyed his

classroom with a triumphant air, rightly feeling for the first time in many years that he had a rapt audience and that, after all this time of unfulfilled dreams and thwarted ambitions, he could finally take pride in the job he did. Herbert turned to face Walter, who noticed his friend had a far-off look, like he wasn't really in the room:

'But Walter, why on earth wait until you're older…?'

IV

By the following spring the 'Garibaldi Reds' had their own shirts, supplied by a friend of Herbert's older brother William who worked for a tailor in town.

He had pestered his friends for half a crown, which they managed to scrape together over the winter, doing odd jobs; lugging coal, sweeping floors and running errands.

Every day after school, even in the dark, he had forced them to follow him, running up Mansfield Road to Mars Hill and down into the Forest and then back again. Now they were ready to take their place in the *'halfha crown round'* and compete in the youth championship against boys' teams from all around Nottingham.

As the chestnut trees came into leaf and platoons of daffodils poked through the grass on the slopes above the flat expanse of grass, throughout the course of one rainy Saturday the Garibaldi Reds overwhelmed every team they faced.

They began each game slowly, assessing the opposition and working out where their weaknesses lay. Then, when the Reds were in position and at Herbert's sign from the right side of the pitch, they all yelled *'Charge!'* and surged forward together towards the opposing end, carrying all before them and kicking the ball into an often empty net.

With their bloodcurdling shouting, superior stamina and daring, the Garibaldi Reds vanquished all comers. Even though the teams they faced in the semi-final and final knew what was coming, still they had no answers and Herbert and his mates left the field of play as sodden victors, bloodied warriors, the red dye of their shirts running down their hands and legs.

Cold, wet but elated, Herbert had run all the way back up Mars Hill and then down the road to home. He'd entered the shop gasping for air, clutching his medal but his father had just stared at him with a puzzled look before telling him to go and wash, as a customer followed him in.

Confiding in his mother that evening, in one of those rare moments of leisure when her attention was all his, he had asked why father could not be proud and pleased for his success.

'Oh, but he is son, I'm sure of that… he just doesn't show it. He never had the chance to go to school, or to have much fun, and he doesn't really understand the games you play.

'Just before you came back that nice Mr Barrie came in the shop, you know, the young Scottish gentleman who lives on Birkland Avenue. He had been walking in the Forest this afternoon and saw you all win the cup. He recognised you and told father about your victory and how it had been quite a sight to behold, all you boys running together with your red shirts and limbs.

'Even if it was only for the slightest moment I swear I saw your father's eyes twinkle and a little smile light up his face before he turned away to cut Mr Barrie his leg of lamb and muttered that it was about time you grew up!'

EXODUS

When I was young I thought I had my own key,
I knew exactly what I wanted to be.
Now I'm sure you've boarded up every door.
While we're living, the dreams we have as children fade away.

—— *Noel Gallagher, Fade Away*

Left your tired family grieving,
And you think they're sad because you're leaving.
But did you see the jealously in the eyes,
Of the ones who had to stay behind?

—— *Stephen Morrissey, London*

I

Nottingham was one of the cradles of modern football. Its players and clubs came to national prominence and were involved in many developments which modernised the game.

In 1862 a group of Nottingham businessmen and cricketers had formed Notts County Football Club at a meeting held in the Lion Hotel on Clumber Street. Football was a public school game, played by the wealthier members of society.

When the Nottingham Forest club committee met for the first time in 1865 at the Clinton Arms Hotel on Shakespeare Street, half a mile away from the Lion Hotel, all the players were amateurs. No entrance fee was charged for games and a collection box was passed around, the players paying one shilling subscription every week, far more than an ordinary working man could afford. The first friendly match between the teams was played before four thousand spectators on the Forest Recreation Ground in 1866. Billed as *'The Garibaldi'* versus *'The Lambs'* the game had ended in a 1-0 victory to Forest.

County had been playing to the Football Association Rules since they had been drawn up in 1863 following a historic meeting at The Freemasons' Tavern in London, but in 1868 Forest became a member of the Sheffield Association so they could play more teams. The new rules differed only slightly but the hacking of shins banned by the Football Association remained a feature of the northern game, leading to many cuts, bruises and even broken legs.

Samuel Weller Widdowson had an answer. An all-round sportsman playing cricket for Nottinghamshire in the summer months and football for Forest for twenty winters, as well as the odd game for County when they needed him, and who even represented his country on one occasion, Widdowson was one of the game's great innovators, turning out for a Forest game in 1874 with a pair of cricket pads cut down to size and strapped to the outside of his stockings.

The mirth was short-lived because soon the rest of his team and all other players had followed his lead, but not before he had shrewdly taken out a patent on shin pads.

Widdowson was a player for Forest in a game against Sheffield Norfolk in 1878 when a referee's whistle was first used and as Forest captain he introduced the pyramid line-up of goalkeeper, two full-backs, three half-backs and five forwards that was to prevail for decades to come.

In 1881 Notts County were hit by a financial crisis but in the 1882-83 season they managed to reach the semi-final of the Football Association Cup where they lost to Old Etonians, a sign that football was still not a working man's game. They made the same progress the following season, before bowing out to Blackburn Rovers.

Then finally, in 1885, football went professional: amateurism had been betrayed the previous year, not by thirty pieces of silver but by five shillings a week paid by

Preston North End to their players, with an additional two shillings for each away match.

But Herbert Kilpin didn't become one of the first footballers to play for money on leaving school.

Following his early success with the Garibaldi Reds Herbert had continued playing football, now turning out for Notts Olympic in their all white strip in the Midland Alliance League. But he simply wasn't good enough to play football for a living and, deep down, underneath all his disappointment, he knew it.

When he finished school he didn't follow his father and a couple of his older brothers into the butcher's trade. Instead he found a job in the booming lace industry. As Manchester led the world in the manufacture of cotton, so Nottingham became an internationally important centre of lace manufacture in the second half of the nineteenth century.

Herbert entered employment as the town was reaching the pinnacle of its success and in these boom times he went to work for the company of Thomas Adams, a philanthropic industrialist who had commissioned the architect Thomas Hine to build one of the largest and finest lace warehouses in all of England.

Herbert's journey to work down Mansfield Road and into the Lace Market, no more than fifteen minutes on foot, took him first past the Bluecoat School, then the Nottingham Brewery, the *'Filo da puta'* (Son of a Whore) pub named after a prize racehorse, past the Holy Trinity Churchyard and then across Cow Lane Bar into the centre.

The way to the warehouse and then back again in the evening was also the route in and out of town for a carriage bringing a dapper middle-aged man to and from his own place of work.

Kilpin kept seeing this odd character and one day mentioned this to his big sister Lucy, who was a housekeeper for a well-to-do family nearby.

'That'll be the architect Watson Fothergill, he lives on Mars Hill just behind the church in a big house he's had built for his family.

'He's designed lots of all those fancy new buildings in town. You must have seen his style: all towers, turrets, carvings of animals, plants and strange beasts. He uses a lot of red brick and black timber.

'I know Louise, one of his servants, and by all accounts he's ever so strange. A stickler for punctuality, his timekeeping extends to half minutes and he's so fussy about his designs and the quality of the materials used to build them that he's driven more than one poor tradesman into bankruptcy.

'Louise says he's ever such a cold fish. The silence at the dinner table. His wife gets Louise to ask Mr Fothergill if he would like another helping of meat!

'It's a wonder they've ever been close enough to start a family.'

Herbert recalled the red and black colours of the buildings that greeted him every morning on his way to work as he passed the Nottingham Express and Midland Counties

Courier Office on Upper Parliament Street before cutting down Thurland Street past the Nottingham and Notts Bank.

The Fothergill townscape was now as much a part of Herbert's immediate world as the smell of the brewery and the local pubs it supplied. Fothergill may have been every inch the upstanding Victorian gent, perhaps hoping to bolster his credentials by knocking down the *'Son of a Whore'* public house and replacing it with the *'Rose of England'*, but a pub remained a pub and alcohol in all its tempting manifestations was on tap wherever Herbert looked.

Saturday nights in Nottingham town centre in the 1880s were wild; machine girls wearing the latest fashions from Paris flirting with the boys as the band played selections from the latest opera here, and an organ ground away there. The clocks struck eight, nine, ten, as the cafés and public houses filled until eleven o'clock, the *'hour of the cross'* as reeling men, noisy women and giggling girls jostled with one another and fights, brawls and policemen marked the end of the day.

The spirit of Nottingham certainly flowed freely, as had the ale in the times of Robin Hood to keep the outlaw and his men very merry. The town was awash with pubs and Herbert passed a dozen or more every day.

As young workers had more money in their pockets, to impress the opposite sex and to enjoy a little or a lot of the tipple on tap, so they had more leisure time, especially to indulge in the new sport that had been sweeping the nation for the last twenty years.

In 1887 twenty seven thousand people had attended the FA Cup Final at the Kennington Oval between the Birmingham clubs of Aston Villa and West Bromwich Albion and the following year the Football League was established, with Notts County, but not Forest, a founder member and with six paid players on its books.

So, Herbert was young, free and single. He had a decent job within fifteen minutes' walk of his home, played football in his free time five minutes down the road. His father and brothers and sisters were around him. His universe was contained within a mile's radius of his father's shop. Nottingham was awash with pubs and was renowned for its pretty girls.

Wine, women and song - or at least when his team won a game.

What more could a man possibly want? Herbert could see his life ahead of him for years to come, with nothing to break a pleasant but hardly demanding routine.

But foreign merchants visited the Lace Market all the time, giving the area a cosmopolitan air and in 1887 one young man arrived at the warehouse to give Herbert a fresh perspective.

His name was Edoardo Bosio and he was a textile merchant from Turin.

One lunchtime Herbert was kicking an old ball around the courtyard with his pal Jacob. Out of the corner of his eye he'd caught the sight of the Italian who'd recently arrived to work with the business walking out of the warehouse into the Lace Market. Herbert guessed he'd be in his early twenties, four or five years older than him. He seemed nice enough, but operating in different circles to Herbert and his pals who remained stuck in the warehouse; not someone with whom he would be getting on speaking terms any time soon. Herbert had noticed how the young women had blushed as the educated man walked past in his dapper, well-cut suit and how he greeted each person in turn with impeccable manners. He also spoke decent English, for a foreigner.

Receiving the ball back with some venom from Jacob, Herbert struggled to control it and spun round to give chase, surprised to see the gentleman had stopped walking and was watching them with curiosity, but somewhat hesitantly, without the poise he exuded within the building.

'Good afternoon. Please may I join you?' he asked politely.

Herbert exchanged a puzzled look with Jacob, both wondering why one of the bosses would want to kick a ball around the courtyard of a lace warehouse with a couple of assistants on their lunch break.

'Of course, feel free…I'm Herbert and this is Jacob.'

'Thank you, that's very kind. My name is Edoardo, Edoardo Bosio.'

The three of them formed a triangle and kicked the ball first one way and then the other, using both feet. The foreigner was clearly untutored in the drill but he was enthusiastic and had some innate skill to make up for his lack of practice.

Soon it was time for them to get back to work but this gentleman seemed oblivious to the passage of time. More quizzical looks between the English boys as they wondered whether in humouring this important person they were somehow gaining exemption from their after-noon's labours in the warehouse. But after another fifteen minutes Herbert decided enough was enough and politely manoeuvred the drill towards a conclusion.

'We see sir, that you are keen on football. Would you like to come and watch a game we are playing at the weekend, on Saturday morning, twenty minutes' walk from here?'

'I would like that very much, and please call me Edo-ardo - or just Edward.'

'Good...Edoardo. If it pleases you we could meet at the warehouse gates at nine in the morning and walk up Mansfield Road together?'

'You are very kind, Herbert. I would be right to under-stand you will be playing at the Forest, no? I've watched some games there but to support a team will be much more enjoyable. I would be happy to meet you there, let's say at nine thirty, if that is good for you?'

Bosio turned up as he'd promised and cheered on his new friends. Despite Herbert assuming Edoardo Bosio would have better things to do at the weekend, perhaps enchanting the admiring daughters of the directors over afternoon tea or escorting them for a walk in the sunshine along the banks of the Trent, the young Italian chose to come back every Saturday to watch from the sidelines and then, when asked, jumped at the opportunity to play a game, when one of the lads had not made it out of bed following a heavy night in the pub on pay day. Bosio was a quick learner and kept his place in the team on merit.

This involved more than holding his own on the pitch. As well as training twice a week in the evenings and turning out to play a game every Saturday, Bosio joined in with the merrymaking after work on Fridays at Talbot's Gin Palace, with evident gusto.

'Bona cervisia laetificat cor hominum.'

'Beg your pardon, Edoardo?'

'That was the Latin motto of my ancestor, Giacomo Bosio, who founded the first brewery in Italy, over forty years ago: 'Good beer gladdens the heart of men.' Beer has given our family its good fortune by making men happy!'

'We'll drink to that, Edoardo. Cheers!'

'You should do more than that. When I return to Italy you must all come to visit me and you can compare for yourselves the beers of Bosio & Caratsch with those of Hardy & Hanson. But they are still nothing in comparison with the many wonderful red wines of my region and our fantastic food.'

The group readily accepted Bosio's invitation, with a bonhomie easily engendered by the end of a working week, good company and plentiful supplies of pale ale and stout.

But Bosio was serious. 'Gentlemen, I mean it. You have shown me great kindness and friendship and I intend to reciprocate.'

'Edoardo, we don't know what that is but we'll still drink to it...'

All was forgotten the following morning as sore heads turned out on the Forest to play a team of ruffians from Shirebrook who had left home at dawn to travel over twenty-five miles into Nottingham just for a fight on a football pitch. Despite being hung over, Notts Olympic refused to give in to the relentless provocation of the visitors, passing the ball around with such speed and accuracy that the Shirebrook players ran themselves into the ground, eventually turning on each other to engage in a testosterone-fuelled scuffle as the referee abandoned the game with the score at 8-0 and awarded victory to Olympic.

Bosio's time in England soon came to a close. He was to return home to Turin, much to the regret of the fair young ladies of Nottingham and to his football pals, for different reasons.

On his last day in the town the staff at Thomas Adams presented Bosio with gifts to show their appreciation of his kindness and courtesy. The eldest daughter of the managing director presented Bosio with a beautiful piece of worked lace, while the board gave him a rather amateurish painted view of Nottingham Castle. Bosio received both with good grace and gratitude.

Then, unscripted, Herbert stepped forward and handed his friend an old leather ball, scuffed from being constantly kicked around the cobbles and against brick walls. The directors were aghast, fearing a joke that was about to go badly wrong, but Bosio's face lit up.

'This I shall treasure for as long as I draw breath. You cannot imagine how much this means to me.'

It was a warm summer's day and the directors could only surmise that the heat had gone to Bosio's head.

II

Life carried on as normal for Herbert after Bosio's departure. He worked diligently enough at Thomas Adams and made progress of sorts, from the warehouse to fixing the machines. He left Notts Olympic to join the team at St Andrew's, the church that lay a stone's throw from his home and loomed over the Forest.

In 1889 Nottingham Forest was a founder member of the Football Alliance and in the same year the referee assumed full control of the game. The following year goal nets were introduced by Mr Brodie of Liverpool after a game at Goodison Park, home to Everton, when nobody could agree on whether the ball had crossed the line and a riot almost broke out as a result.

That year County finished third in the League and reached the final of the FA Cup where the side lost to

Blackburn Rovers at The Oval cricket ground in Kennington in front of twenty three thousand spectators.

The club also became a limited company in 1890. The board of directors held their first meeting on the evening of Tuesday 19th August at the Lion Hotel on Clumber Street and ratified the contracts of sixteen professional footballers for the 1890-1 season, under which each was to receive a princely sum of between one hundred to two hundred pounds per year. By contrast each of the twenty-six amateur player members had to pay a yearly subscription of five shillings.

County had three teams: a Nottinghamshire League team to compete in League matches, English Cup ties and other matches; a second to compete in the Midland Alliance League and in other matches; and a third one to play matches on a Thursday, as arranged.

Even in this early age of football intrigue was rife. After receiving instructions to order seven hundred and fifty season tickets and to place them on sale at ten shillings and sixpence, the club secretary read out a letter to the board from the Forest Football Club, in response to an allegation that one of Forest's officials had approached a member of the Notts first eleven with an offer for the 1891-2 season and denying that anyone on behalf of Forest FC had approached or engaged any Notts players.

Then, one day in the early summer of 1891 life suddenly changed for Herbert Kilpin when an old friend returned.

'Edoardo, it's great to see you again!'

'Ciao, Herbert. I find you very well. How is life in Nottingham?'

'Can't complain, Edoardo, can't complain at all. We've changed teams but we're still winning on the pitch and enjoying ourselves off it.'

'Yes I see you are no longer the slight young man I met some years ago and I have even less wish to be tackled by you on a football pitch. But I have a question for you. Could I tempt you to follow me back to Turin to come and try the fantastic beers of Bosio & Caratsch, or the wines of the Langhe?'

'That's very kind of you Edoardo, but I don't have the time or money to visit you this summer.'

'I'm not talking about a visit, Herbert. I've opened my own factory in Turin. Beer is something I shall always drink for pleasure, not brew for my living. Textile production is how the Bosio family will continue to prosper in the years to come. I need good men to help me, who understand the technology and who can teach my workforce to use it.

'My dear Herbert, would you like a job in Italy?'

III

It was July 1891. Herbert lay on his bed dragging at a cigarette in a bedroom he shared with his older brother James. The house in which he now lived was cramped; the Kilpin family had outgrown 129 Mansfield Road as the siblings had become adults and, in the case of another brother Edward Clement, married and had children. Herbert and James now lived with Edward, his wife Fanny and their two young daughters at 170 Chatham Place, just around the corner from 129 Mansfield Road, even closer to the Arboretum, while head of the family Edward, Harry, the three unmarried sisters Lucy, Ann and Maria, and Lucy's young son Joseph were now sharing the family home with an elderly lodger.

Herbert knew that playing football for his living was beyond his capability and in any case that it was a short and uncertain career. Continuing to work in a warehouse in the Lace Market was unlikely to bring anything other than his weekly pay and, at best, promised a lifetime of respectable sameness. He only needed to look at James who, along with William and Harry, had followed their father into the butcher's trade or at Edward Clement, a jobbing gardener with a family to support.

Herbert was painfully aware that life was short. At the age of ten he had already seen his sister Sarah and brother Arthur die in the same year; Arthur aged just thirteen and Sarah at twenty. And the previous year, his mother Sarah had died at home of chronic asthma and heart disease: perhaps the only person who might have persuaded him to do the sensible thing and settle down after finding a nice girl.

As the sounds of laughter and song and the occasional fight from the taverns on Mansfield Road drifted in on the breeze through the open window Herbert was thinking that the small world in which he had spent his childhood and his early manhood was no longer so magical and full of promise and that its confines were ever more apparent.

He wasn't used to thinking this hard and needed some air. He slipped out of the house, not wanting to engage in conversation and headed towards the Arboretum.

The hour was late and couples and groups of children were leaving the park as he entered through the short tunnel, sauntering against the flow of the human race.

The mingled bouquet of the thousands of flowers in bloom, trees in leaf and of the lush grass was the smell of his childhood and instantly brought back memories of running around with his friends, climbing trees, playing hide and seek and clowning around to annoy Elijah Bumpdul, the park keeper.

Old Bumpdul was still around, zealously guarding the contents of the park from the onslaught of successive generations of wayward children, in particular from those lost boys who appeared to have no fear of God nor respect for municipal property.

Herbert saw the lights on in the lodge by the gates

beyond the lake, steadily burning brighter, sucking in the fading daylight from the park as dusk fell.

By now Herbert was almost alone, even the ducks had waddled and quacked enough for the day and had shut up shop. Soon Bumpdul would be leaving the lodge, a heavy bunch of keys jangling in his plump hand, to survey his kingdom one last time, to straighten wayward plants and pick up discarded objects and waste, before closing all the gates for the night.

Facing the lake and gazing down at the fiery reflection of the twilight sky in its still waters Herbert noticed the birdsong was more intense, more melancholy, in this spot. He turned and saw an aviary that couldn't have been here long.

Outside the park a man was heading down Goldsmith Street for the public houses of the town, late for a rendezvous with his drinking companions. He glanced left, through the iron bars of the Arboretum railings and in the deepening gloom he made out the outline of a young man standing stock-still, facing the Circular Aviary.

Keeping an eye on the pavement ahead to avoid the last workers heading out of town the thirsty straggler returned his gaze to the motionless figure in the park. By the time the man had passed the main gate and the park lodge and reached the edge of town, his thoughts turning to the lovely cold mug of ale that was awaiting him after his day of toil, still Herbert hadn't moved.

Two minutes later, a light went out over in the lodge,

instantly casting the patch of grass next to Herbert into darkness, followed by the opening and slamming shut of a door, as old Bumpdul started on his final tour of duty for the evening.

Herbert stepped over the aviary railings, took a penknife from his pocket and began forcing open the cages. The birds inside stared at him, confused by the entry of someone so late when they had already been fed and, in the case of the more domesticated residents, nonplussed by this unexpected interruption. It wasn't until the man started waving his arms and running around the aviary that they got the message and flew their coop.

Bumpdul was near the Bell Tower when his attention was caught by swift movement above. He looked up to see a group of the most fantastic birds, all different, flying ever upwards, silhouetted against the deep pink sky. A beautiful sight at the end of a beautiful summer's day.

Elijah Bumpdul felt privileged to do the job he did, in the great outdoors, unlike many of his generation who had toiled all their working lives in mills and factories or had emerged blinking into daylight from their days of hard labour in the caves' tanneries. He went on his way, back towards the lake, to enjoy his final minutes of contentment and oneness with nature.

Herbert looked around the abandoned perches and at the mass of brightly coloured feathers lying on the straw. He'd be in big trouble if he hung around.

But he already knew there was no chance of that happening. He had decided he was going a long, long way away.

IV

Herbert said his goodbyes to his brothers, sisters, nephews and nieces at Nottingham railway station one sunny morning in August 1891.

After Sarah Kilpin had died Herbert's older sister Lucy had assumed the role of mother to the Kilpin brood in general as well as to her own son Joseph, born out of wedlock when she was only sixteen. It was she who cooked, scrubbed, worried and dreamed and to whom had been left the task of registering the death of Sarah, sat by her bed when her dear mother had breathed her last. Lucy did all this in her spare time, working by day as housekeeper to a family living near the Arboretum.

Lucy had a good idea she might not see her younger brother again. She was sad to see Herbert go. But there were other feelings too.

Although not unattractive she was already twenty-nine, with a thirteen-year old son and fast losing hope of finding a good man. It wasn't just her two younger sisters Ann and Maria who particularly depended on her. Old Edward said little, but was clearly struggling without his beloved Sarah.

Lucy carried on, giving of herself while Herbert decided to take off, without a thought for anyone else. Not just to another town but to another country; to Italy of all places. She had received some schooling as a child and into adulthood had continued to read books by candlelight until she fell asleep, exhausted after another day's toil, and so she had an inkling of the beauty of this land to which the wealthy ventured on their Grand Tour.

Lucky sod. She was jealous and knew it, but dutiful to the last she hugged Herbert on the platform and told him to write back when he could.

Herbert had already bid farewell to his father at the shop. If Edward Kilpin had ever had enough time to think about it, destined as he was to slave away as a self-employed butcher lugging carcasses and hacking at meat until he dropped dead at the age of seventy-six, deep down he would have understood his youngest son's decision to escape, as he himself had done nearly fifty years ago, leaving the land to chance his luck in this expanding lace town.

He would tell his family that his wayward son would be back soon and wouldn't find foreign lands to his liking, especially if Herbert had no chance of running after a ball all day, which was how he seemed to waste all his waking hours when he wasn't working in the warehouse.

Herbert wasn't to travel alone to Italy. Bosio had recruited a couple of other lads from the Adams warehouse to work in his factory, who had hung back when Herbert said his goodbyes to his family. Finally, they all clambered aboard and the last carriage door was shut. The station-master's whistle blew, the train jerked into motion and Herbert and his companions were on their way.

First of all, to the gothic grandeur of St Pancras Station and the Midland Grand Hotel which greeted them as they arrived in London, even more daunting in comparison with the cramped and decrepit Midland Station they had left earlier that day.

Blown away by the scale of this great cathedral to modernity, they stepped onto the platform with their luggage, oblivious to the serene flow of more seasoned travellers around them, gazing upwards and momentarily blinded by the midday light streaming down through the great glass roof.

Although in an alien environment they sensed familiarity. The town they had just left was being crafted out of the same material; Gilbert Scott, the architect who had designed and supervised the construction of St Pancras several decades earlier had insisted that the station and hotel be fashioned, at great expense, from Gripper's patent red bricks from Nottingham.

A last, umbilical link to the place they'd just left, before being cast off into outer space – or, rather, the Euston Road – where, gazing up at the great clock against the sky, the young travellers took note that they were running late for their connecting train and hastened their step across central London to their destination, the clock yet again doing its job, having been deliberately set two minutes fast for this very purpose.

Herbert and his mates then saw more of the world in the two days or so that it took to arrive in Turin than they had in their lives up to that point, witnessing a Europe in transition, the grandeur of London and Paris, built on a scale far larger than the Nottingham of the architect Fothergill and of his great rival Thomas Hine.

As lads abroad they dallied for a day and a night in *fin de siècle* Paris, visiting the dancehalls of the Pigalle district, goggling at the can-can, murmuring 'yes, yes' and chatting with a little bearded man who seemed at home painting pictures of the dancing ladies, although after a second glass of absinthe they had no recollection of their encounter the following day.

Staggering back to the city centre in the morning with heavy heads, they'd just had enough time to marvel at the world's tallest building, the Eiffel Tower, completed the previous year to mark the centenary of the French Revolution, before rushing off to the Gare de l'Est to catch their next train.

All the sights of these two great cities they had passed through, of the verdant French countryside as their train moved through the Champagne region and of the still snow-capped mountains as they came into view, banished from their minds very quickly any lingering thoughts of the places and people they had left behind.

The Alps presented not just an imposing physical boundary but a stage curtain, dividing their lives up to that point, into what had been from what was to come.

While Herbert and his friends had left behind their childhood dreams, they had only just embarked on adulthood.

They had resisted the pressure to stand still and felt anew the thrill of possibilities, not the dull ache of routine, sensing they were about to leave the darkened wings and to step out under the stage lights. No longer just Nottingham lads in a town of many thousands but possibly the only East Midlanders in the whole of north western Italy.

The first Frejus rail tunnel which ran nearly thirteen kilometres, twice the length of the previous longest tunnel in the world, was the first to be dug with pneumatic drills. Excavation had started in 1857, first in Italy and then from the French end. Thirteen years later French and Italian workers shook hands as the teams met halfway with the tunnels almost perfectly aligned: a triumph of engineering and progress.

A train speeding out of that tunnel offered a blinking Herbert Kilpin his first sight of the land of Italy. These carefree lads were following the worn path trod for centuries by more well-to-do compatriots... the land of the great Roman Empire, of the Renaissance of Giotto, Leonardo and Michelangelo and, more recently, of Giuseppe Garibaldi.

As he gazed at the Alpine forests and pastures flying past through the smoke in the summer sunshine, little could this Nottingham youth have known that he was going to do much more than disseminate cutting-edge technical know-how to bolster the fledgling mechanisation of the Italian textiles industry.

If he'd had the faintest idea what that was all about.

Blithely unaware, Kilpin was a stick of cultural dynamite; he was going to play a starring role in bringing a whole new means of expression, of healthy competition and joy to an entire nation.

As the train finally pulled into Porta Susa station in Turin, Herbert Kilpin had begun his awfully big adventure.

THE
YOUNG COUNTRY

The word 'Italy' is a geographical expression, a description which is useful shorthand, but has none of the political significance the efforts of the revolutionary ideologues try to put on it, and which is full of dangers for the very existence of the states which make up the peninsula.

—— *Prince von Metternich,*
Letter to Austrian Ambassador to France, April 1847

Time goes by so slowly for those who wait.
No time to hesitate.
Those who run seem to have all the fun.

—— *Madonna, Hung Up*

I

Edoardo Bosio was standing waiting for Kilpin and his friends on the platform as their train slowed into Porta Susa. With a silent companion ('Domenico, my foreman') he rushed up to the three young men to take the shiny new cases they bundled out of the carriage door and then grabbed each of the passengers in a hearty embrace before their feet had touched Italian soil.

'Gentlemen, buon arrivo and welcome to Torino! You come to work for me but you shall be my guests for as long as you remain in this wonderful city. First things first. You will be tired and hungry. Let me bring you to a special place for dinner where you can tell me all about your journey.'

As the immigrants from Nottingham were led from the station and through Piazza Statuto on their way eastwards into the heart of Turin, Bosio couldn't help acting the role of tour guide as they passed through its centre, unable to contain his pride at finally being able to show the English travellers his city after having been on the receiving end of their hospitality for so long.

'This is a centre of black magic. In Roman times this area was considered cursed because it faced west, towards the Susa valley and the setting sun. Condemned men were brought here outside the old city walls to be executed and buried. But little remains now of our Roman origins and the old city gate here was demolished long ago.'

The group passed a striking edifice to their left.

'This Monument to the Frejus Tunnel was built with dark rocks blasted out of the mountain. On the boulders lay fallen titans carved from white marble, symbolising the vanquishing of brute strength by engineering. At its summit you can see a triumphant angel holding a pen, the symbol of scientific analysis.

'Or, as some people say, it is that most beautiful of angels, Lucifer, with his free hand threatening those daring to ascend to the fount of all knowledge.

'Follow the gaze of the angel. Can you see where it leads? To that pretty flowerbed in the centre of the square. But do not be fooled, my friends, for underneath it lies the main entrance into the city's sewage system, which we Turinese consider to be one of the city's entrances directly into Hell. Perhaps you know of a story that is very well known here, in which the author is guided through the circles of Hell by the great poet Virgil...'

As the sky reddened behind them and darkness crept over the ordered city, the tired travellers were led out of the eastern end of the vast square into via Garibaldi, their straight path to the white magic centre of the city.

'You see all these straight, clean streets and grand buildings and may think this is a rational and ordered city but do not be fooled by appearances, Herbert. You are on the frontline in the cosmic battle between good and evil!'

Herbert and his companions tried to follow Bosio's meanderings but they were too tired to do so, using all their remaining energy to keep up with his quickening stride.

After ten more minutes on foot, as the first murmurings of polite discontent from the weary wanderers became audible, Bosio finally led his new employees out of the darkness of via Garibaldi into Piazza Castello, with the Royal Palace opening out to their left.

'Do you see our palace? This is where our country began. Torino was the first capital of Italy and our House of Savoy became the royalty of the new country. Victor Emmanuel II lived here until 1871 when the capital moved to Rome. The Savoys have an illustrious history. Within those walls over there the Royal Chapel contains the relic to trump all relics - the Turin Shroud - and do you see those gates, at the mid-point between the mounted statues of the mythical brothers Castor and Pollux? They mark the city's centre of white (good) magic.

'Now, look ahead at Palazzo Madama - The Lady's House. The most beautiful staircase in all of Europe has been built over the grottoes of – how do you say - alchemists? Our kings were not happy with what they had and so ordered these strange men to create the gold they hoped would make them even richer.

'You are near your journey's end for today. Domenico is taking your cases to the hotel where you will stay tonight and will bring you 'con calma' to your lodgings in the morning.

'I can't show you everything now but, if you look down that road, it leads directly to an even larger piazza and then to the river. You cross the bridge and, voilà, you reach the Church of the Holy Mother of God. Before the steps is the statue of a woman and in her raised hand is a cup and she is looking back across the city to this area and they say her gaze is focused on a point near the Royal Palace where the Holy Grail is buried, the cup Jesus Christ raised before his disciples at the Last Supper.'

Bosio looked at his guests and came to his senses, realising that he had bombarded them with stories of magic and legends of Christianity and led them on a bit of a trek across the city after they had just completed a long journey across half of Europe. It was time for them to sit down in a wonderful restaurant just off Piazza Castello to rest their aching limbs, to raise a nice glass of Dolceto wine to toast their safe arrival and to tuck into a plate of something called pasta.

'Forgive me my friends, for my enthusiasm in wanting to share with you my city and in some small way to begin to repay the hospitality you have shown me in your own city. I see you are tired and hungry and now, for today, your journey is at an end.

'Here we are. '*Il Cambio.*' This is our finest restaurant where our great leader Cavour came every day for his lunch...'

Over dinner and forgetting his vow to afford the Englishmen some rest and relaxation, Bosio launched into a history lesson, explaining that Giuseppe Garibaldi had been the brawn as well as the face of the campaign to unify the Italian peninsula, while another Giuseppe, Mazzini, had been its soul, the visionary idealist who for the most part had lived the life of the revolutionary exile in London, busying himself with good deeds within that city's Italian immigrant community, but remaining largely confined to an opera box seat in the great Italian drama; provoking, cajoling and inspiring the main players acting on the stage.

But Italy had come into being largely through the stratagems and calculated gambles devised by an overweight and bespectacled statesman who would have proved no match for the dashing figure of Garibaldi on the field of battle and instead stitched everyone up like a kipper from the comfort of his favourite caffè and restaurant in Turin, the very place where they now sat. Camillo Paolo Filippo Giulio Benso, Count of Cavour, or just *'Cavour'* to the history books: the true brains behind the unification of Italy.

Often imitated but never bettered, Cavour had died three months after taking office as the first Prime Minister of Italy, worn out at fifty years of age. Arch-manipulator and improviser, he had somewhat unintentionally fashioned a wooden puppet from disparate parts but would never get the chance to breath real life and soul into it.

And when he was gone no one would prove capable of pulling all the strings at the same time to make it truly dance. When others tried, it would all end up a bit of a lie.

The brains and the brawn had ostensibly brought the project of unification to a successful completion, although without winning hearts and souls it had remained half-baked...

By now the lads had had enough. Travel-weary, bombarded with information by Bosio and having drunk too much red wine, they stumbled out of the restaurant and remembered nothing more about that night or how they had arrived in their beds.

In the morning Domenico was waiting for them as, one by one, they shuffled into the hotel lobby, sore of foot and head, blinking in the daylight to begin their first day in Italy.

'Buongiorno e benvenuti!'

II

Turin was laid out on the west bank of the Po river, on clear days the snowy peaks of the Alps providing a majestic crowned backdrop. Above the river on its eastern side rose a high, lush hill dotted with villas and the palaces of the wealthy, looking down on the scuttling masses going about their daily work and, just to the north of the city, the silhouette of the great basilica of Superga, the last resting place of members of the House of Savoy.

From Piazza Castello in front of the Royal Palace Turin's straight roads led east, west and south, flanked by eighteen kilometres of high porticos used in bygone days by mounted royalty and cavalry officers to cross the city without getting wet.

Twice the size of Nottingham, Turin was an important centre of trade and industry of an economy that was largely devoid of natural resources and decades behind the island of growth powering the British Empire. Industry was still largely confined to small and medium-sized workshops in Piedmont, Lombardy and the Veneto to the east.

Since the late 1880s the Italian economy had slipped into a deep recession and engaged in a vicious trade war with France at a time of world depression. Only the textile sector had continued to grow, developing out of the manufacture of silk, with its access to foreign markets and capital outside of the banking system.

Bosio had brought Kilpin and others to Italy to help train his largely female workforce in a factory by the Po. At this early stage of mechanisation of textile production in Italy the Englishmen's services were at a premium and they were paid well for their work.

Barring any swear words Bosio had taught Nottingham's finest during his stay a couple of years earlier, Kilpin was without a word of Italian when he arrived and at the beginning communication with everyone other than Bosio and his two mates was a problem. Kilpin had to pick up Italian quickly to do his job properly; there was only so far he could get with rapid hand gestures, and the mimicked sounds of the gleaming new machines imported from the great British factories left his audience of young peasant girls exchanging bemused looks and shrugged shoulders.

Most of the girls here didn't even speak Italian, which he was learning from Bosio and his colleagues and, rather more slowly, from business and technical documents. The pretty signorine spoke all manner of Piedmontese dialect, with different words and accents (so Bosio said) depending on whether they came from the plains to the east of the city, from the hills to the south or down from the mountains to the west and north.

'Herbert, you must understand that the honour of these girls is most important for their families. They come from the country where they live in the same room as their cattle and their chickens and where the difference between surviving and starving depends on good weather. The city offers them a chance to improve their lot.'

The girls were even more embarrassed than he was in trying to engage in any conversation that didn't revolve around mechanisation and weaving machines. They weren't like those back home, especially on a Friday or Saturday night after a couple of drinks in Talbot's Gin Palace. Even then, Kilpin had never found it easy to speak with women.

This was a time of rapid adaptation; to another culture, a different people and their customs, to the bigger, ordered city, its climate and food.

During those first weeks in Turin in the late summer evenings after work and on Sunday mornings Kilpin spent time getting acquainted with his new home, strolling around the wedding cake elegance of Piazza San

Carlo, before stopping at one of the renowned bars under its porticos.

On the last Sunday in August the church bells were ringing, calling the faithful to mass, but Kilpin was headed for the centre to meet John Savage who was going to introduce him to some of his English friends based elsewhere in the city.

He washed with a jug of cold water (even that tasted different), put on his smartest suit and the new pair of silk socks he had just bought with his first wages from Bosio's factory, left his room in the Aurora district and walked down the street in the direction of the city.

Savage was waiting for him in the middle of Piazza San Carlo, lounging against the Bronze Horse.

'Buongiorno signor Kilpin, I trust you slept well? Allow me to buy your first coffee of the day.'

It was only just gone ten in the morning but already the sun was high in the sky as the two walked across the cobbled square to the portico lining the western side and into the shade of the Caffè San Carlo.

Savage had been in Turin for a few years and spoke Italian well. He too had come from Nottingham to work in the silk mills and had met Bosio over here. Like Kilpin he loved his football and with a couple of other expats and some Swiss engineers had formed what they believed to be the first half decent football team in the city and maybe the whole of Italy, Torino Football & Cricket Club.

Bosio had even paid for a kit, of red and black stripes,

and as they sat down at the back of the Caffè near the stairs Savage explained to Kilpin that Torino Football & Cricket Club didn't play much football and no cricket at all.

'Bosio loves his football - I think you already know that – but the only other clubs around here tend to be gymnasium teams who treat it like a bit of exercise in the fresh air, running around the field with no idea about the game.

'He knows we can't carry on like this and in the last few months we've been playing a team of well-to-do lads Edoardo met at his rowing club. They call themselves the 'Nobili' and still have a lot to learn but they're keen, although maybe a little too fixated with the notion of the 'English gentleman.'

'To your good health, sir.' Savage raised his delicate porcelain cup with a theatrical flourish and Kilpin played along, downing his own thimble full of scalding hot caffeine. The early morning espresso was a pleasant ritual in which Kilpin readily partook; not for him the frothy, milky cappuccino that the other English chaps lapped up like little kids.

The aristocratic splendour of the Caffè San Carlo with its marble flooring, array of chandeliers and salon air bedazzled the young man from Nottingham. It took time for his eyes to get used to the bright lights around him, accustomed as he was to the comforting dimness and sanded floors of the public houses back home. Catching sight of his reflection in a gilded mirror behind the bar, he still couldn't quite believe he was in this setting, rather than in the midst of the weekend hurly burly around the Market Place.

'Shall we go, young sir? We are to meet up at twelve o'clock but let's take the scenic route along the river.'

Kilpin hadn't had time for any breakfast before leaving his room but wasn't going to bother now, certainly not at the prices of the pastries and other fancy delicacies carefully arranged at the bar with the same intricacy as the mosaic designs on the floor.

Savage led him on a zigzag route down the straight streets to the banks of the Po river, into the Parco Valentino and they walked upstream. The waters reminded him a little of the Trent back home, around the same width at this early point in its long journey across the great Italian plain towards the sea.

Everything was in flow. Synchronised rowers dressed in immaculate whites powered towards them and then off into the distance back the way Kilpin had come into town. The two men followed the elegant progress of upright cyclists pedalling their contraptions down the park paths and walked past groups picnicking on the grass; workers and their families recently arrived from the surrounding countryside of Piedmont and now reconnecting with open spaces and nature, joyfully spotting the first mushrooms as they sprouted at the foot of the trees among the gilded fallen leaves.

'This is where we play the Nobili. Their leader is a

duke and I give up trying to remember all his names. He's only a lad but he's already sailed around the world in the Italian Navy and he's as fit as a fiddle, always on the go. His mate's a marquis or something. Good lads though, with not too many airs and graces and they seem really enthusiastic. I know Edoardo has been talking to them to see if we can link up in some way.'

They made their way westwards across the park, heading back into the city, to Piazza d'Armi, a vast open space south of the centre, used for military parades. The ground was very hard, the earth compacted by countless, mindless marches up and down by soldiers in smart uniforms, baked by the sun throughout the dry summer months and frozen during the cold winters.

Savage spotted his friends at the far side of the square, running around in a dust cloud following a tatty, deflated ball as it was kicked in every direction. This looked to Kilpin more like the chaos of the game played on Shrove Tuesday in Ashbourne, Derbyshire, for as long as anyone could remember, when the local lads chased a ball through the streets of the town into the outlying fields and across the river.

'Fancy joining in, Herbert?' Savage turned to him, eyebrows raised with a butter-wouldn't-melt expression on his face.

He knew what his mother or sister Lucy would have said. 'What a ridiculous suggestion. To join a melee like that, in a place like this, dressed in one's finest clothes?

Certainly not!'

But his dear mother was long gone, God rest her soul, and Lucy was more than a thousand miles away.

Herbert Kilpin could do as he pleased and he wasn't going to pass up a chance to get involved in a game of football.

III

No one was holding a position, there was no game plan, no referee.

As they approached the combat zone Savage caught the eye of one of his pals who trotted over to them in his shirtsleeves and dusty trousers, red in the face.

'Herbert, allow me to introduce George Beaton. George, Herbert has been taken on by Edoardo Bosio and has recently arrived from Nottingham. By all accounts he is some player and I suspect Bosio has brought him to Italy as much to beat the Nobili as to make his silk! Any chance we could join in?'

'My dear Johnny, no need to ask. Herbert, welcome to football, Italian-style! It's us against them. Keep your wits about you and you'll be fine.'

Kilpin pulled up his socks around his trousers, carefully placed his folded jacket on top of a pile of others and joined the game.

Despite inferior numbers the English kept the ball and dispossessed the Italians with ease. More casual spectators stepped over the irregular line traced in the dry earth with a stick to join the Italian side and soon it was ten Englishmen against at least twenty natives.

One of the opposition was particularly tenacious in his pursuit of the ball, or at least the leg that had just kicked it. Clearly untutored in the finer arts of the game he could nevertheless see that Kilpin was proficient and he ran at the newcomer with all his might. With the nonchalance of the matador Kilpin evaded the first two challenges by releasing the ball and stepping to one side but on the third occasion he wasn't quick enough and was tripped from behind as he ran with the ball and sent tumbling over the hard ground. He'd bruised his left thigh, made a mess of his Sunday best and ripped his expensive new silk socks. The assailant had already moved on to his next target, chasing the ball like a frenzied dog.

Kilpin shouted to Savage.

'Tell him to stop this nonsense now!'

Savage trotted up to the man, spoke in Italian and tried to reason with him, suggesting that he focus his commendable energy on getting the ball, not the man. The man's name was *'Claudio'*; red in the face, sodden hair stuck to his forehead, Kilpin could tell Claudio wasn't listening to Savage, his wild gaze instead following the ball as it flew and bounced around.

Kilpin hauled himself up from the ground, hands on haunches, caught his breath and waited for his prey. Beaton had the ball and Kilpin gestured for him to keep it and move towards the opposing goal.

Sure enough wide-eyed Claudio took the bait and ran in for the kill. Kilpin clipped his adversary's trailing heel as he was about to barge into Beaton. The poor man was sent tumbling through the dust, clutching the back of his foot in pain and stayed down, curled up in a ball. Beaton ran on and passed to a teammate who kicked the ball past the Italian keeper. Despite their inferior numbers, the Englishmen had scored a fifth goal and finally the Italians stopped running, holding up their hands in defeat.

'Basta! Enough.'

Kilpin felt bad about his ruined socks but even worse that he hadn't been able to reason with his opponent and moderate his admirable zeal. He glanced back to the scene of his crime but the body had disappeared. As loudly as he had announced his dogged presence, Claudio had departed the field of play with his tail between his legs.

Beaton walked up to Kilpin.

'We won't see him again. His pride will hurt more than his leg.'

'Why wouldn't he listen? Don't they want to learn how to play the game properly?' Kilpin asked Beaton, sensing for the first time that the differences between his land and this ran much deeper than what he could merely see.

'Some do, and some just want to run around and break into a sweat and have a bit of a shout. The rest of the week they're told what to do by their families or their boss. This is their chance to let off a little steam.'

'Maybe they should sign up for the army instead, Beaton...'

Another voice announced itself behind Kilpin:

'Well, well Herbie. I've seen your smart moves many times on the green grass of home but now you've shown me a little of the dark arts of your noble game!'

Kilpin turned around as Edoardo Bosio approached from the temporary touchline as the other spectators trudged away.

'Edoardo, please don't make me feel any worse than I already do. I've never descended to that level before and I don't intend to do so ever again.'

'Lighten up, he deserved it. We don't need idiots like him playing the game. How does that compare with one of your games for Notts Olympic?' Bosio asked.

'A game like that would be over in ten minutes – the Italians would all be dismissed by the referee... if there were a referee in sight.

'I can't fault the energy and enthusiasm of these fellows but the brain must command the foot and cannot abdicate all responsibility once the man enters the field of play. Who is prepared to instruct them? Without any guidance they may as well just forget about the ball, roll up their sleeves and slug it out.'

'Well that is what I understand they did in medieval Florence, they called it *'calcio'*,' Bosio replied, before changing the subject.

'But enough of all these gloomy thoughts, Herbie. Listen, unless you have other plans I'd like you to join me for lunch with my rowing crew and meet a couple of my more recent acquaintances, who I think you'll find interesting. And don't worry, you can smarten up before we eat. Mr Savage is coming along too, aren't you?

'Andiamo, Herbie?'

IV

It wasn't just Bosio's business that was by the river. He was a keen rower and member of the illustrious club, Società Canottieri Armida, founded in 1869 and based on the banks of the Po.

Bosio had learnt about the proper running of a sports club through his involvement with Armida, whose operation was anything but parochial. In the summer of 1881 the club had organized a celebratory eight-day row from Turin to Venice, garnering applause from the riverbank as the crew rowed their way across northern Italy to the sea. Venice had welcomed the weary rowers as heroes and forever since the club had bestowed the distinction of honorary membership upon all Venetian mayors.

Several years after its formation Armida had adopted its first constitution and in 1888 it had helped to establish the Italian Rowing Club, the sport's governing body that organised the first national and international regattas.

From the beginning the club's rowers understood the

importance of cementing friendship as well as crowning their successes by dining with much exuberance in a trattoria - *Disbarco* - on the other bank of the river.

Kilpin cleaned himself up at the Armida Club, lining the washbasin with a film of grit from Piazza d'Armi and changed into an elegant spare suit of Bosio's, a size or two too large for him so that the cuffs of his jacket almost brushed his knuckles, before the men crossed the river and headed for lunch.

'Now you look smart enough to join our little celebration and help seal an understanding with our enthusiastic friends. And don't worry, they speak perfect English.

'In fact...' Bosio added, his voice getting louder and not just on account of the level of noise within Disbarco as they entered and headed towards a group of young men standing by the bar, '...allow me to introduce you to Prince Luigi Amedeo Giuseppe Maria Ferdinando Francesco di Savoia.'

'Please, dear Edoardo, "Luigi" is just fine, otherwise there will be no time to talk!'

The youth who turned to Kilpin couldn't have been more than eighteen years old but he possessed all the aristocratic bearing required to carry his weighty name. Nevertheless, he was charming and *'simpatico'*; there was amusement in his eyes and a smile on his lips.

'I have heard very good things about you, Herbert – if I may be allowed to call you by your first name? I am told you have a particular understanding of the game. Both I and Alfonso,' he gestured to the smiling friend by his side, the Marquis Ferrero of Ventimiglia, 'are ardent admirers of English culture, your sense of *'fair play'* and of how your Empire has introduced scientific advancement and good governance around the world. We are a young country, still finding our feet and have so much to learn and, let me assure you, the younger generation is willing to learn.

'Especially the rules and tactics of this splendid game of football. We row, we cycle, we climb mountains but we are yet to master this team game your countrymen have given the world, putting mind and body to the test.

'Edoardo may have mentioned that we formed our own club some time ago. We have played the Torino Club and some gymnasium teams here in this city, but we are keen to grow, to embrace the spirit of the age; who knows, maybe to challenge clubs from other towns and cities...'

By now, Bosio had caught the eye of the restaurant owner who glided across the floor with glasses of champagne on his silver plate and it was time to corral Prince Luigi and focus on the matter in hand. Bosio cleared his throat and delivered the little speech he had been rehearsing.

'Gentlemen, it has been four years since I returned from England with many happy memories and a leather ball to kick around with my business acquaintances but my passion for football is only stronger and I sense it is a contagion that is spreading. Who can resist pitting one's wits against worthy opponents on the field of play?

'Allow me to raise a toast to the success of an alliance between the Nobili and Torino Football & Cricket Club...

Internazionale Football Club, a brotherhood that shall know no bounds!'

'To Internazionale!'

In the space of an afternoon Kilpin had gone from being kicked into the dust by a thug to toasting to the success of an international football club with the Italian aristocracy.

The footballers sat down to eat with members of the Armida, celebrating yet another regatta victory, and spoke of their ambitions for the new club. The Marquis of Ventimiglia was a measured young man with an eye for detail who gently reigned in his excitable friend whenever the prince soared too highly on a flight of fancy, as was happening with ever greater frequency as the afternoon progressed and more champagne was quaffed.

'We shall challenge teams from far and wide, not only in Piedmont but throughout the land, to show our people a new game that can be theirs and which will unite all - Piedmontese and Lombards, Neopolitans and Venetians - with a sporting passion that pushes them to the limits of their capabilities!'

'One step at a time, Luigi. First we must decide upon a constitution for Internazionale Football Club, who can join and how we are going to run the club that is to be a marriage of equals,' counseled the wise marquis.

'Of course Alfonso, of course. Yes, we build upon firm foundations and mutual respect. My dear Edoardo, I've been thinking about team colours and I hope you don't

mind if the Nobili were to be allowed the honour of be-
stowing our amber and black stripes upon Internazionale?
Alfonso and I will ensure that all players of our 'family'
are provided with a new shirt.'

Kilpin had been a polite observer of the animated exchanges between the founder members of this new venture,
pretending to sip the same fizzy drink he had held all afternoon. He glanced at Bosio and within the space of seconds
saw a range of emotions play across his friend's face.

First, the relaxed bonhomie of the man who has steered
his vessel safely into port and secured the agreement of
influential allies to back his grand project, before then allowing them to indulge in their idle chatter.

Next, the sudden concern and alarm at having his project commandeered by people used to getting their own
way, however politely they went about it.

Then, the equally quick recovery of poise, in recognition of the long game he was playing and the need to make
necessary concessions and compromises along the way,
even if this meant discarding the red and black stripes of
the first football club in Italy.

Kilpin decided to help his friend regain his footing
with a diversionary tactic, and began the conversation for
the first time.

'Perhaps Internazionale could lead the way in Italy by
emulating the latest advances in the game being played in
England? You may all have heard that the first goal nets
were used recently (in Liverpool, I believe) to avoid wast-

ing time returning the ball to the field once a goal has been scored. I hear this has been a most welcome development back home.'

Prince Luigi's face lit up even more.

'My dear Herbert, what an excellent idea! We must lead the way and bring all along with us. Although we are many miles from the sea my naval colleagues should be able to pull some strings – if you will forgive my little joke- and source some fishing nets from Genoa to save ourselves effort in retrieving the ball after we have scored!'

Kilpin's little ploy had worked. Only he had noticed Bosio's disappointment with the presumption of the young aristocrat who was now quite taken with the thought of using brightly coloured nets to allow games to continue at dusk (wait until he told Luigi about the possibility of floodlit games), while his marquis friend continued thinking about rules and regulations.

He had only just met these people - he, the son of a butcher, dressed in an oversized, borrowed suit covering his battered body - but was holding his own with aristocrats.

Even if, thinking about it, the ancestors of these refined young men would also have cut off a few heads and shed lots of blood to establish the family lineage.

The ease with which he could interact with people from all levels of society was an ability honed during the years he had helped out in his father's shop back in Nottingham, dealing with a clientele from both sides of the tram track: on the west side the more well-to-do living in their fine new houses built on the Sand Field around the Arboretum and, on the east side, the poorer labourers cooped up in gloomy terraced housing behind the shopfronts on the Clay Field, quietly entering the shop on a frosty December's morning to hand over the last of the coins for the Christmas Goose, ordered way back in the summer.

'So, cari amici, once again let me propose a 'brindisi' (I hear you say 'toast', but is not that how you eat your bread in the morning?) to the future success of Internazionale Football Club.

'Cin, cin!'

***

However, despite all the initial exuberance, Prince Luigi and many of his aristocratic entourage - excepting the steadfast Marquis - quickly moved onto the next fashionable pastime. For them football was just the latest 'thing' from England.

Other adventures beckoned for the young Prince. Before meeting Bosio and Kilpin in Turin, at only sixteen years of age he had already travelled the world with the Italian Navy and in the months immediately following the formation of Internazionale Luigi was seen less on the football pitch and more often climbing the mountain peaks visible on clear days in the distance. Then in 1893 he was back off around the world on a battleship, first to suppress an uprising in the recently established colony of

Somaliland in eastern Africa.

In his first letters back to his big sister Kilpin had made sure to mention his new friends in high places with their grand-sounding titles, not because he was impressed but because he knew she would be fascinated by the exoticism and that it would transport her to an imagined world of ballrooms and rides in the country, as she coped with the drudgery around her.

But there was no pretending that this was a meeting of equals: while Kilpin, Savage and Bosio might mingle with their aristocratic acquaintances in Caffè San Carlo as well as on the football field, they knew that still their path was barred to that most exclusive of clubs, the Whist Society in Piazza San Carlo, founded by Count Cavour in 1841 and reserved for the social elite.

V

Eventually Kilpin settled into a life of work during the week and playing football on Sundays, or more accurately, having a kickabout in the park with work colleagues or against lads from the gymnasia clubs.

It suited Kilpin to live in Turin. He didn't think he would stay more than a year or two when he arrived but ended up hanging around for six. Although he earned decent money to train workers in the mills and factories he wasn't there just for that or he would have already returned home to Nottingham with his accumulated savings. He didn't marry during his stay, sensing that Piedmontese society was closed to him as an Englishman, especially for one without wealth or prospects and, in any case, there was no time for any courting at weekends.

Without family of his own in this new city Kilpin spent time snacking in bars or eating out in taverns and in the homes of colleagues and friends. Besides being a city of magic and of royalty, it had been evident from the beginning that Turin was a city of very fine food.

At first sight its straight, wide streets and clean, uncluttered squares offered no clues to the barely contained gluttony within. But Turin, as Bosio advised him when they ate lunch in the trattoria in the shadow of his factory, was a fake slim person, nonchalantly holding in her stomach until admirers had passed by.

Kilpin had been given lessons in culinary history by Bosio, despite not asking for any. He was told that much delightful food had first hit the palate in Turin, often given a royal seal of approval before being taken up enthusiastically by the common people.

Although Turin may have only briefly served as the capital of Italy it had long been the capital of chocolate as prospectors arrived from all across Europe - even from Switzerland - to learn the art of transforming the modest cocoa bean into dark, edible gold.

Guido, the owner of the trattoria, had his own little theory that the people of Turin proudly called themselves bugia nen *('never move')* because they saw no point in going anywhere with all the food on offer close to hand, or maybe just because they couldn't move out of their chairs after having fallen into temptation.

A particular local favourite was *bicerin*: a combination of chocolate, coffee and cream, mixed on the spot and served in a small glass - a bicchierino - with a metal handle. A morning ritual for the masses, for doctors, lawyers and princes, Bosio explained that the price of bicerin had been kept at a relatively modest fifteen cents for the whole of the second half of the nineteenth century and that there was a choice of fourteen types of biscuit to dunk into the hot, sweet brew, from the garibaldin and the parisien for the more cosmopolitan, to the friar's dick and the nun's boobs for the less sophisticated.

'Herbie, the sacred and the profane also gave rise to *'zabaglione'*. In the 1500s after travelling across half of Europe a friar called Pascal de Baylon turned up at the church of St Thomas to hear confessions. He was also an expert cook and ended up giving sound advice to the pious women of Torino who lamented the lack of virility in their menfolk.

'So, to reinvigorate flagging spirits he recommended a magic formula of 1+2+2+1: one egg yolk, two teaspoons of sugar, two eggshells of marsala wine and one of water.

'Can you believe it, a priest who boosted the love lives of the Turinese? Friar Pascal ended up a Saint: san Bajon… zabaione…zabaglione.'

Kilpin had no sweet tooth and held back as the other

expats succumbed, unable to help themselves. But the butcher's boy from Nottingham still couldn't resist a steaming plate of bollito misto - a mix of boiled meats, different pieces of cow, veal's head, pig's trotters - or fritto misto, a lucky dip of a dish comprising up to a dozen or so deep-fried items: liver, sausage, brain, marrow, and even pieces of apple or other sweet bits, which he placed with a grimace on Savage's plate.

Nor did Kilpin pass up the chance to try the local aperitivi, in particular Cinzano. One Sunday evening after a game Bosio could see that Kilpin was fed up with the standard of play, that it hadn't moved on since the day of his first dust-up in Piazza d'Armi and he tried to lighten his friend's mood.

'Herbert, amico mio, cheer up and enjoy life! The world is changing fast. It's so much smaller. This game of yours was meant for my people, to allow us to express our artistry. Sooner or later it'll catch on, you will see. But you must be patient. Rome was not built in a day, as you English say!

'We don't like much change but when we feel a passion for something then it takes root in our whole being. We take something and we make it better.

'Take this vermouth. A drink that's been kicking around for centuries since the time of the ancient Greeks. Thanks to the bright idea of a young lad called Carpano many years ago, now we're selling it to the rest of the world. He came from north of here, near Biella, and he had the idea of blending our fantastic wines with the herbs of the mountains.

'So he went off back home and the local friars gave him their ancient recipes, he experimented, changed a few things and his vermouth was a big success. The King made it the aperitivo of the royal court.

'And how do we produce this fantastic drink?

'First, you take your base, a nice light white wine and then you add up to thirty herbs, such as rhubarb, coriander, rosemary and cinnamon. There are many, many variations.

'Then you add sugar, to taste, and finally the caramel colouring.

'But do you know what is the real secret, the magic ingredients?

'Time and patience!

'You must wait. The vermouth must do nothing, just rest, for up to eight months. Only then is it bottled.

'But what, you find this vermouth too sweet? Try this one instead: Punt e Mes.

'With Punt e Mes you have one 'point' of sweetness and half a point of bitterness (that's the quinine).

'Ah, I see that's more to your liking, Herbert, much more bitter, yes?'

He had truly found himself in the land of the lotus eaters, reluctant to shift out of his chair after yet another heavy meal, earning enough money for his expertise with machines of the industrial age and even cosseted from any inclement weather by mile upon mile of covered walkways to get him from trattoria to bar and then to bed.

VI

In the spring of 1893 Kilpin received a letter from Lucy with news of their family. She had never understood football but knew what it meant to her brother and dutifully informed him towards the end of her message that Notts County had been relegated from the First to the Second Division for the first time.

I know your teams were Olympic and St Andrew's but I thought you might want to know that County finished bottom this year and that alas they will be playing teams like Woolwich Arsenal and Manchester City. I hope you're not too upset.

Around the same time the following year Lucy had cause to be more upbeat, after updating him on the latest local gossip, in which he had no interest whatsoever.

...You will recall last year I told you that County had been removed from the first division and because you did not reply I feared you had received this news badly.
I hope to lighten your spirits by informing you that County have won the Football Association Challenge Cup after defeating the Wanderers of Bolton with four goals (and only one in reply) in Liverpool. I am told more than thirty seven thousand people were in

attendance. Do you play in front of such large crowds in Italy?

We all went into town to see the cup when the players returned from Liverpool. As we neared the bottom of Mansfield Road a couple of men couldn't contain their excitement and were dancing around and kissing people as they passed. Joseph learnt by heart one of the songs they kept singing and he keeps repeating it around the house, just to annoy father. I thought you might like to know the words:

Great excitement there has been in good old Nottingham,

The people cheered and seemed as if they didn't care a fig,

Spectators they were jubilant and glanced around in glee,

When in the Final for the Cup, Notts gained the victory.

I can't remember a scene like it. The streets were full of people all the way to the station and we heard a brass band playing. We were told it took the coach and four carrying the players and cup nearly an hour to get from the station to the Lion Hotel in Clumber Street, where we waited. There were speeches and toasts and the players came out onto the balcony to show the trophy to the crowd.

Afterwards the cup went on display in the shop of Mr Pickerill the tobacconist in Arkwright Street. Apparently he is one of the club's biggest supporters and the rumour is that, much to the dismay of Mrs Pickerill, he took the cup to bed with him at night.

Lucy

***

Months and then years passed and Lucy still wrote, when she found the time, in the hope that her brother would come back to Nottingham to visit his family. His youngest sisters were growing up fast and Edward the patriarch was noticeably ageing as he continued to work in his shop, approaching his seventieth birthday.

Kilpin's responses back to Lucy were brief and intermittent; a telegram here, a Christmas card there. He never revealed much, only that most of his free time was spent kicking a ball. His sister saw no other way to try to engage him, and while she had only sad news to convey she thought it might provoke a response when she wrote yet again, in the early summer of 1896:

Dear Herbert

All is well with us. However, we have heard some sad news from elsewhere which I thought you would find of interest. You will recall the cup triumph of County two years ago. The hero of the day was Logan the Scotsman who scored three times. More recently he has been playing for Loughborough Athletic and Football Club and some weeks ago his team travelled to Manchester, to play a game against a new club, called Newton Heath, I believe. Loughborough mislaid their kit and had to play in their everyday shirts because their opponents could not offer them spare shirts. It rained during the game and the players had to wear their wet clothes on the journey home. Logan caught a chill which unfortunately developed into pneumonia and he recently died. He was only twenty-five, a few months younger than you, and he has been buried in a pauper's grave less than two years after scoring three times in the Challenge Cup Final.

How sad this seemed to me, Herbert, when poor Mr Logan was the cause of so much rejoicing in our town not so long ago. The good seem to die young and I keep thinking about little Arthur and Sarah who never had a chance to grow to adulthood.

I am sorry if my words are heavy and bring you dismay. I would lighten your mood if I knew how.

Please keep all of us in your thoughts and write when you can.

God bless.

Lucy.

What did Herbert Kilpin think of all this? Wasn't poor Jimmy Logan's fate a timely reminder of the fleeting nature of fame?

Kilpin didn't care about fame.

All he wanted was a proper game of football.

HARD TIMES

It was the best of times, it was the worst of times.

—— *Charles Dickens, A Tale of Two Cities*

I

Still relatively young and unattached, in 1897 Kilpin moved to Milan.

He was stepping onto a bigger stage, to seek out opportunities in a city that had assumed the mantle of workshop of Italy: Milan was the young country's beating heart, sucking in people from the surrounding countryside and further afield to work in its factories.

Bosio had told Kilpin to be patient but surely not as patient as the worshippers of Milan. Work had proceeded slowly on the city's great cathedral, its Duomo, for more than five centuries after the ground had been broken in 1386 on the most central site in Roman Mediolanum. By the time of Kilpin's arrival in Milan towards the end of the nineteenth century the Duomo was more or less complete: the third largest church in the world or, to put it in Herbert Kilpin's terms, within its walls you could comfortably fit the biggest football pitch ever.

Every Sunday morning, to the sound of peeling bells, the pious people of Milan made their way down streets from all directions into Piazza Duomo, attracted to the fantastical stalagmitic exterior of the church, with its forest of pinnacles, spires and riotous assembly of marble statuary, passing through its great carved doors into a cavernous, sparse interior, to participate in the restrained and ordered rites of the holy mass.

On most evenings of the week many of the same people could be found silently filing into a nondescript building a few hundred yards away. They entered a separate world, adorned with gold leaf, red velvet and glittering chandeliers, to take their seats as the lights went down to be bombarded, night after night, with a sung extravaganza of tales of tragedy, of great love and heroism. The Milanese took their opera very seriously and after a fire destroyed the Royal Ducal Theatre in 1776 the rebuilt opera house - *La Scala* - soon became the pre-eminent meeting place for the noble and wealthy of Milan, doubling up as a casino with gamblers and all manner of traders.

The third great landmark of central Milan linked the other two: the Galleria Vittorio Emanuele, a covered double arcade comprising two glass-vaulted galleries forming a cross and intersecting in an octagon.

Giuseppe Mengoni had built the Galleria between 1865 and 1877 in homage to the first King of the new, united Italy.

Now that the city was indisputably the country's main industrial centre Mengoni had wanted to use steel and glass to make a big, bold statement that Milan was at the cutting edge of technology and innovation: a construction to rival the Crystal Palace in London and the bridges of Isambard Kingdom Brunel.

The mosaic floor of the central octagon displayed the coat of the House of Savoy and, around it, the symbols of the four capitals of Italy: the red cross of St Ambrose of Milan, capital of Napoleon's short-lived Kingdom of Italy; the bull of Turin; the white lily of Florence and the suckling wolf of Rome.

All told, a grand monument to unity and the self-confidence of a progressive new state.

But how awful that two days before the grand inauguration on New Year's Day in 1878 and having toiled for much of his adult life on this labour of love, Mengoni slipped and fell to his death from the top of the Galleria into the snow in front of Bar Zucca, while making final inspections of his masterpiece before its unveiling.

And even more tragic, that the King in whose honour the Galleria had been named passed away just over a week later.

Not an auspicious beginning for a monument dedicated to the glory of the new country.

II

But here is Herbert Kilpin nineteen years later, standing at the bar in Zucca, finding his feet in this new city, swapping the Cinzano of Turin for a Campari and finding it very much to his liking.

Until he asks the waistcoated barista what exactly gives the drink its bright pink tinge.

'Signore, only one person in the world is entrusted with the entire formula of this wonderful aperitivo but I can tell you that the red colour comes from crushed insects. Un bel colore, no?'

With commendable composure Kilpin smiles, grabs a couple of olives from the bar to cleanse his mouth and, after counting to ten, slowly takes his leave, walking back into Piazza Duomo, his half-finished drink standing on the bar.

Getting his bearings in Milan, Kilpin had recently taken up a position with one of the textile businesses in the Navigli canal district.

Yet another step up in terms of size, this city and its people impressed Kilpin with their sense of purpose. This looked like a place where you could get things done.

But he wasn't casting himself adrift from his circle of friends and acquaintances in Turin and had deliberately taken lodgings in via Settala, no more than ten minutes' walk from the railway station, so that he could get back as quickly as possible to Turin at the weekends to keep playing for Internazionale, although he had to be selective and couldn't return every weekend, especially while bedding into life here in Milan.

This move just seemed a little badly timed right now, with football picking up in Turin. It had certainly been slow going for a number of years. After the merger with the Nobles it had taken another three years for a second proper team to emerge, F.B.C. Torinese, but at least they had provided some decent opposition. Gradually, more players turned up at Piazza d'Armi on Sunday mornings and now there were even moves afoot to set up a national competition.

In 1893 a group of English ex pats had established the Genoa Cricket and Athletic Club at the British Consulate. In the grandest tradition of Empire the rules provided that only subjects of Her Majesty the Queen could become members. Games of football were played as well as cricket, often when ships docked and sailors came onto dry land.

This was of course completely different to the football played inland in Turin by Internazionale, by British, Italians and others, side by side. But things changed after a ship sailed into port some time in 1896. It brought to Italian shores a young Englishman, James Richardson Spensley, who came to work as a doctor for the British sailors passing through Genoa.

Rangy, with a twinkle in his eye and a smoking pipe on his smiling lips, Spensley brought a different mindset to the exclusive expats' club. At its annual general meeting on 10 April 1897 he promoted the admission of Italians as members.

That year Genoa also had their first proper ground at Ponte Carrega, on the banks of the Bisagno torrent, a couple of miles inland from the port: a sign that football had now finally disembarked in the city and wasn't remaining aloof from the Genoese.

Soon Spensley and his colleagues learnt of the extent of footballing activity on the other side of the Maritime Alps in Turin and established contact with Bosio, the Marquis

Ferrero and others. Telegrams and letters were exchanged and an exploratory meeting took place as Spensley and Bosio sized each other up and gauged the possibilities for organising competitive games. In late 1897 plans were made for a first match to take place on the Feast of the Epiphany, Thursday 6th January 1898 at Ponte Carrega between Genoa and Internazionale.

At the last minute Ghigliotti of Genoa swapped jerseys and was loaned out to Internazionale for the duration of the game when Weber fell ill and couldn't turn out for the visitors. The cost for entrance to the spectacle and a seat was two lire and the match attracted a crowd of one hundred and fifty four curious souls, including a couple of boys who had travelled all the way from Turin on the train.

Internazionale won with the only goal of the game, scored by Kilpin's old friend John Savage who had introduced him to football, Italian style, seven years earlier.

Kilpin hadn't played that day, unable to get away from Milan, but a return tournament was arranged for 6th March at the Umberto I Velodrome in Turin.

Everyone took this all very seriously. In great secrecy the Genoa team left the coast the day before the game and headed for a small town outside Turin where the club had booked an entire hotel for the travelling party. The best laid plans often go awry and the team got off the train at the wrong stop and had to spend the night in a restaurant, with the drawer of the shortest straw sleeping upright in a chair. Adding insult to injury Genoa still had to pay the full price for the rooms they'd booked in the hotel in the other town.

Yet despite the botched preparation, lack of sleep and empty pockets Spensley still led his side to victory against Internazionale, with a strike from Schaffauser.

Further discussions about the Federation took place that weekend and the Italian Football Federation was established in Turin with four founding members: Genoa, F.B.C. Torinese, Internazionale and the Turin Gymnastic Association. On 26th March the Gazzetta dello Sport newspaper announced that the first national football championship would take place in Turin on the second Sunday in May, just before the Italian General Exposition. Up for grabs would be gold and silver medals, as well as the Challenge Cup for the winning team donated by the Duke of the Abruzzi, dear Luigi, the adventurous aristocrat.

Kilpin remained in touch with his teammates in Turin and readied himself for the challenge, training by himself in the Public Gardens near his home. One warm spring evening he came back, having worked up a sweat, to a letter from his sister.

13th April 1898

Dearest Herbert

Now your town is a city! Queen Victoria has bestowed

the honour in the year of her Diamond Jubilee, although nothing much has changed.

I thought you would want to know that earlier this month Forest won the Football Association Challenge Cup, 3-1 against Derby (of all teams) at the Crystal Palace in London. Once again the Market Place and surrounding streets were full of celebrating crowds, just like a few years ago when County triumphed, but this time the colour was red. I thought back to that day all those years ago, when you came home with a huge grin on your face in your red shirt after winning a cup at the Forest.

While pleased that the Reds had won the cup Kilpin had more pressing concerns. He could not fail to take note of the discontent down south as he continued his training for the first official Italian football championship around the streets and open spaces of Milan.

The price of wheat had rocketed following a disastrous harvest the previous year and a wave of violence and disorder surged up the country and hit Milan the following month.

Men born in 1873 were called up for military service as Italy prepared to reprise its colonial misadventures in Africa. In recent decades successive governments had strained to strut their stuff on the world stage by conquering tracts of desert lands in Africa but despite its army's superior arms and numbers Italy found itself on the end of a series of humiliating defeats.

In nearby Pavia the son of a radical politician was killed during a clash with police and on the morning of Friday 6th May three employees handing out leaflets demanding more rights for workers were arrested outside the Pirelli rubber factory in Milan, close to the train station. Although they was released later that day, someone else was led away to the police barracks on nearby via Napo Torriani for having thrown stones at the forces of law and order. Police fired on people looking for their arrested companion, leading to one death and five other casualties.

Moderate socialist leaders tried in vain to calm demonstrators as the disorder continued in the city the following morning, led by students and workers protesting against the high cost of living and demanding social justice.

Then the authorities lost their nerve and called in the army.

On the Saturday afternoon a state of siege was declared in Milan with full powers given to General Fiorenzo Bava Beccaris to quell the disorder. Bava Beccaris set up his battle camp in Piazza Duomo, a big black spider at the centre of the web of streets radiating from the cathedral, with the plan to push outwards in all directions to crush the revolt.

The *protest of the stomach* was disorganised but fierce. Bava Beccaris gathered his forces for the coming storm and called in an Alpine Regiment from its summer training camp. Troops occupied the towers and the historic gates of the city, then the suburbs and the railway stations and finally the factories and refineries.

Bava Beccaris arrested the editor of *Il Secolo* newspaper and stopped it rolling off the presses. His troops dismantled the barricades piled up at Porta Garibaldi and Porta Ticinese, using cannon at zero elevation.

Somehow, early on the Saturday morning Herbert Kilpin got out of Milan before all hell broke loose. He left his apartment soon after seven in the morning. Walking the streets was unsettling. Normally at this hour when he rose to travel to Turin for games the sleepy calm was punctured by the creak of doors and the roll of shutters as shopkeepers opened up, whistling as they put their wares on display, stopping to hail acquaintances across the street, while their children ran around the public gardens and little squares, making the most of their hours of leisure, corralled from balcony windows by keen-eyed mothers and older sisters.

This morning was too quiet. Routine was out of the window and no one was sure what was supposed to happen next. The shopkeepers were too scared of looters to step out of their doors and the women had imprisoned their children: only the pleading of little voices deep within the shuttered palazzi reassured Kilpin that he wasn't the only person alive in Milan that morning as he made his way quickly through the streets towards the railway station.

Standing on the platform waiting for his train the

twenty-seven year old Kilpin was a lonely sight, at his feet a bag packed full of nothing more threatening than a nicely ironed yellow and black striped shirt of Internazionale Football Club of Turin and a pair of shiny boots.

He may have been risking life and limb to get to the station that morning but once there he had done the right thing.

He was off to join old friends and new acquaintances for the Italian Federation's first football championship – all to take place on one day, Sunday 8th May 1898 – in an oasis of calm in Turin, ninety miles to the west.

Soon after his train left the Army was given the order to close the station and seal the city, and Kilpin had avoided the carnage that was to follow later that day.

III

By now preparation was almost complete in the Parco Valentino for the General Exposition. Turin might have lost its status as capital of Italy but the city was determined to show how it was building on its past to create a brighter future based on science and technology. The newspapers had gone overboard with their rhetoric, reporting how an enchanted city had sprung up in the park at the touch of a magician's wand, in which beat Italy's heart and from which rose a powerful yet gentle hymn celebrating and encouraging industry and labour, enlivened by liberty and science.

To Kilpin it just looked like a grander and more upmarket version of Nottingham's Goose Fair, including a full size replica of the façade of the *Ca d'Oro* - the House of Gold - on the bank of Venice's Canal Grande, containing a pavilion of Venetian glassware. (He reminded himself to get out to Venice whenever he could and write to Lucy all about it.)

While Spensley's men were about to check into a hotel after their train journey from the coast, Kilpin made straight for Savage's flat: his old friend had stuck with what he knew and remained in Turin when Kilpin had opted to move to pastures new.

That evening the two of them settled for a quiet meal and Kilpin even refused a glass of wine.

'Herbie, what's Milan done to you? You're looking mean and lean. Don't tell me you're too busy running around with all the rest of those serious Milanese earning a fortune to spare any time to indulge yourself a little?'

'Al contrario, amico mio, I intend to let loose tomorrow evening but before then we have a job to do and a cup to win. We've waited a long time for this moment so let's do justice to it. You remember the chaos of my first experience of Italian football. Here's hoping we've all moved on from that...'

Herbert Kilpin was about to find out at nine o'clock the following morning at the Umberto I Velodrome, when the referee blew his whistle and in front of a crowd of fifty people he found himself playing in the first game in the history of the Italian football championship, a local affair between Internazionale and F.B.C. Torinese.

Internazionale prevailed with a goal from Savage and were joined in the final just after midday by Genoa Cricket and Athletic Club who had beaten Turin Gymnastic Association by two goals to one.

A light lunch and refreshments followed, courtesy of Diltey's the baker's before, at three o'clock in the afternoon and in front of an expectant crowd of one hundred and twenty seven onlookers generating gate receipts in the grand sum of a hundred and ninety seven lire, the colourful striped final began: Genoa, in their white and red prepared to face the yellow and black of Internazionale.

The following week the *Gazzetta dello Sport* reported on a game that had turned into a bit of an epic:

After the morning's knock-out games Genoa and Internazionale contended the title. The game was lively and fiercely contested. After two hours the teams were tied on a goal apiece and so they played another twenty minutes. Even though Genoa were down to ten men through injury they managed to score another goal and to win the Italian Championship Cup. The honour of scoring the winning goal fell to Leaver.

Genoa's effort with fewer men was even more notable, considering that the Velodrome's pitch inside the cycle track was twice the size of their home ground at Ponte Carrega.

In years to come, Kilpin would look back with some satisfaction at how far football had come during his playing career on the pitches around the towns and cities of northern Italy.

But at the time he had just lost the biggest game of his life on what had been his home patch and if there was one thing Herbert Kilpin really didn't like, that was losing a game of football. He had received a medal but it was silver, not gold.

Fixing a faint smile on his face which ended up more of a grimace, he joined members of all four teams and their entourage as they headed back to The Velodrome Racer's caffè for the celebratory banquet, to which each had contributed five lire.

All the players sat together at a big table – most of the lads from the three Turinese teams were very familiar with each another from years of playing football together in the parks and open spaces of the city – to talk animatedly about the day's events, shamelessly exaggerating exploits of only hours earlier and planning the following year's tournament, to be hosted in Genoa by this year's winners, as the glasses clinked and plates of hot food were hurriedly brought out of the kitchen by the harassed owner and waiters, to more than forty hungry adults.

Some women watched the game but the overpowering smell of tobacco smoke, sweat and lingering dirt saw off any wives or fiancées long before the Genoese visitors were given their winners' medals and the silver trophy was presented by the still youthful Duke in person, taking time out from planning an Arctic expedition for the following year, perfumed handkerchief discretely in hand.

All hail Genoa Cricket and Athletic Club, from contenders to football champions of Italy in less than a day.

IV

The day after the night before and after bidding farewell to a sleepy Savage, Kilpin gingerly made his laboured way to Porta Nuova train station, lugging his dirty, smelly kit through familiar streets.

He had just played over three hours of competitive football in one day and his limbs felt it.

Hung over, hoarse of voice, with stubbled chin and bad breath and longing for a bath he clambered aboard the next train to Milan and slumped in the corner of an empty carriage and dozed off well before the train had left the station.

As it passed the paddy fields around Vercelli Kilpin was woken by the sun burning through the morning mist, its rays bouncing off the watery underworld of inverted farmhouses and row upon row of poplar trees, reflecting the hues of the big sky.

Momentarily disorientated by the vast expanse of water, water just about everywhere, with not a drop to drink for his parched throat – was this still Italy, or had he overslept so badly that he'd missed his stop and the train was now passing through China? – slowly Kilpin gathered his wandering thoughts.

Except that no amount of laboured musings could prepare him for the reality that awaited because he didn't return home to Milan on any ordinary Monday morning.

Because that day was Monday, 9th May 1898 and Kilpin came back to a smoking war zone.

In the following days he learnt that the troops of General Bava Beccaris had used cannon to breach the walls of a monastery outside Porta Monforte on the basis of intelligence that a group of rioters was taking refuge within. The state's finest soldiers rushed through a dust cloud into the ruined building, clambering over shattered timber and masonry, bayonets at the ready for close combat, but stopped in their tracks to behold the extent of the threat the forces of law and order were facing: a group of cowering beggars who had come to receive a bowl of soup from the friars.

The military authorities were clearly affected by the hysteria that had overcome the ruling elite and which prompted the good ladies of Milan to bring cakes and Marsala wine onto the streets to nourish the valiant gunners as they quelled the remaining dissent and restored a semblance of order to the revolting city.

Kilpin had been oblivious to the mayhem engulfing Milan while he had been away playing football in Turin, but he wasn't stupid. Briskly he made his way back to via Settala, past the broken barricades, rubble and looted shops, quickening his step to the sound of nearby gunshot. He dug out the keys to his palazzo, climbed the stairwell, unlocked the door to his apartment, closed it quickly behind him, dropped his bag on the floor and threw himself onto his bed.

The government's official count was eighty dead and four hundred and fifty wounded. Everyone knew the real numbers were far higher. Two soldiers had died: one had accidentally shot himself and the other had been shot on the spot for refusing to open fire on the crowds.

In the following days the government closed down over a hundred newspapers and made thousands of arrests. King Umberto added insult to injury by decorating Bava Beccaris with the Cross of Great Officers of the Savoy Military Order to reward the service the General had given to the country's institutions and civilisation and as a sign of the King's affection and gratitude.

The jarring contrast between Umberto's honeyed words and the brutal repression for which they gave thanks didn't go unnoticed, either in Italy or on faraway shores where news of the death toll in the streets of Milan dismayed the immigrant Italian communities.

With his brief, effusive words Umberto Ranieri Carlo Emanuele Giovanni Maria Ferdinando Eugenio of Savoy, or *'Umberto the Good'* as he had been known before that weekend, had effectively written his own death warrant and the clock had begun to tick for the second King of Italy.

Kilpin returned to work on the Tuesday morning, grateful that everyone was so preoccupied with the events of recent days that he didn't have to answer any searching questions as his tired mind and aching body continued to recover.

'So Herbert, what do you make of it all?'

'I don't really know. I've been playing football with my pals in Turin. And how was your weekend?'

His work colleagues exchanged puzzled glances, before reasoning that maybe the English were more accustomed to street warfare than they were here in Italy.

This quiet man was an odd fish. Since arriving in Milan the previous year he had done his work conscientiously enough, spoke Italian well and had gained everyone's respect. But he didn't engage in small talk and none of his work colleagues saw him in the local bars around the canals after work had ended. He was straight off back into town, with no family to go home to, even though he was understood to be in his late twenties.

Some people started to wonder precisely what Kilpin was getting up to in his spare time, even whether he had sympathies with those misfit anarchists who had been carrying out terrorist outrages across Europe for much of the last six or seven years

There hadn't been any major conflict involving the great European nations since the Franco - Prussian War back in 1870 and the last few decades had been a period of great optimism for many, of growing opportunity and prosperity, fuelled by scientific and technological advancements. But across the continent life remained very grim for a lot of poor people who were being left behind.

The repression that followed the Milan uprising didn't last and most of the main subversive groups were assimilated into the political mainstream.

Most, but not all, because the anarchists remained on the fringes, opposed to engagement in a system they saw as fundamentally unjust and the enemy of the people and they sought the maximum impact from the most extreme form of protest, *'propaganda by the deed'*: the assassination of high profile political and royal figures around Europe.

Four years previously, when he had still been based in Turin, even Kilpin had read about Sante Geronimo Caserio, an impoverished baker's apprentice from a village just outside Milan, a quiet and religious lad before his head had been turned by anarchists and in whose name he had already served months in prison for handing out leaflets inciting rebellion.

On his release from jail Caserio had found work with a Swiss baker but soon quarrelled and lost his job. With his back pay he had bought a dagger sheathed in a scabbard of black and red striped velvet and made his way to Lyon where on 24th June 1894 he attacked the French President Sadi Carnot riding through the streets in a carriage, stabbing him to death.

At his trial the young Italian explained that he had killed the President in revenge for the execution of anarchists who had recently bombed the French parliament and a Parisian railway station. Sentenced to death Caserio had remained defiant to the end, yelling out 'Long live anarchy' as the guillotine fell on his neck.

But like the mythical hydra, as one head was severed, another one appeared elsewhere.

One Saturday morning in the summer of 1898, four months after the Milan uprising, Elisabeth, Empress of Austria, left her Geneva hotel with a lady-in-waiting to stroll the short distance to the steamship on the lake that was to take them to Montreux.

As Elisabeth and her companion were walking along the lake's promenade, with the steamship just ahead of them, a young Italian anarchist called Luigi Lucheni stumbled into the Empress.

She collapsed and as Lucheni made off the hotel concierge ran to assist the Empress, supporting her as she stood up to stagger the final yards to the boat, when again she collapsed and lost consciousness.

The assassin had stabbed Elisabeth in the heart with a sharpened four-inch file. She had boarded the ship unaware of the severity of her condition and asked her companion what had happened. The strong pressure from her corset had staunched the bleeding but once the garment was removed the royal blood gushed out.

Lucheni wanted to kill the Duke of Orléans, who had been in Geneva but was gone by the time the Italian arrived. Failing to find him, Lucheni had turned on Elisabeth instead, afterwards explaining that he just wanted to kill a royal, it didn't matter which one, as long as it got in the papers.

Less than three weeks after the death of the Empress, on 29th September 1898 the Italian government sent out invitations for a conference to be held in Rome to organise the fight against anarchism. The International Conference of Rome for the Social Defence Against Anarchists was held from 24th November to 21st December 1898 and was so shrouded in secrecy that some questioned whether the conference had been held at all. Attended by fifty-four delegates from twenty-one countries, the conference agreed on a definition of anarchism, being any act having as its aim the destruction, through violent means, of all social organisation.

On matters of practical policing a protocol included provisions to encourage participating governments to have police keep watch over anarchists, to establish in every participating country a specialised surveillance agency to achieve this goal and to organise a system of information exchange among these national agencies.

In the period of suppression of anarchist elements still active in Italian society following the Milan uprising in late 1898 the Italian police were given an anonymous tip-off to trail a mustachioed foreigner around the city. Initial surveillance of the man's behaviour gave rise to concern.

After working by day in a factory near the canals, why did the man then return in the evenings to the city centre, not to the bosom of a family, but to pound the streets and open spaces to engage in deep conversation with the students of the high schools and with other foreigners on the Trotter Field near the train station?

Were these outdoor locations chosen deliberately to minimise the chances of carefully prepared plans being overhead by curious souls?

Suspicion mounted until, after following the object of his surveillance to the offices of various respected men of business, the police officer assigned to the task afforded himself a little smile and a steady sigh of relief: no anarchist worth his dynamite would ingratiate himself with such established pillars of society.

And when towards the end of the day the man returned to the Trotter Field, took off his jacket, laid it carefully on the muddy ground and then - no spring chicken, mind - proceeded to run around chasing a ball of leather like a young boy, well by then the surveillance officer knew it was time to clock off and return home to the *risotto alla Milanese* his wife was preparing for her family that evening.

This man was surely no threat to the established order. An anarchist? Never!

At worst, an eccentric fool.

THE RED AND THE BLACK

5

He was so stirred by his admiration for the great virtues of Danton,
Mirabeau, Carnot, men who knew how to avoid defeat...
...but she soon found out that he had but one attitude of mind:
the utilitarian, an admiration for the useful.

—— *Stendhal, The Red and the Black*

I

Herbert Kilpin was not a happy man.

'Are you blind, sir?' he shouted at the hapless man sitting uncomfortably on his chair by the goal line, the goal judge, who had just confirmed to the referee that the ball had indeed crossed the line and so Genoa had scored their second goal against Internazionale in the second Italian championship final.

Kilpin wasn't finished.

'Do you play to different rules here in Genoa? That was no goal...'

Edoardo Bosio was trudging back towards the halfway line. He was looking straight ahead, back towards the Genoa goal as he passed the carping Kilpin, but slapped his teammate's back, maybe a little too hard, before adding:

'Time to move on, Herbie. We are losing by two goals, even without the help of that little goal judge. Save your energy and let's get back in the game.'

Kilpin flashed a wild glance back at Bosio, then at the terrorised official who by now was asking himself why he had bothered to put himself on the line in this way, in preference to spending a lovely spring Sunday afternoon walking with his wife down the via Roma and having a nice coffee at Caffè Mangini.

Kilpin rejoined the fray but with only ten minutes left to play he knew that Internazionale were down and out and that for the second successive year he and his team were going to come off second best. He had been playing football in this cursed country for nearly eight years, mainly against muscular youths from gym teams who had no idea how to play the game.

And now this bearded little goody two-shoes doctor Spensley from London who couldn't even keep goal properly had come sailing into Italy to lead a team carrying all before them.

At the post-match banquet both teams ate and drank together in friendship after the exertions of the final.

Kilpin faced Edoardo Pasteur at the table and watched the young man closely throughout the meal. Son of a Swiss surgeon, related to the great scientist of the same name, Pasteur had completed his studies abroad. A supreme amateur sportsman: tennis champion, accomplished rower, mountaineer, yachtsman and now, turning his hand to football, double champion without even trying. Twenty-one years young, with his whole life still ahead of him. A good-looking lad too.

Forcing himself to jest and sing along with everyone else, over dessert and fuelled by glass upon glass of the local Vermentino wine, finally Kilpin snapped. Leaning across the table to Pasteur he looked his rival in the eye and yelled, more in promise than boast, so as to be heard above the din of laughter and singing and the clinking of glasses and china plates:

'That's the last time you're going to win! I'm going to form a team in Milan to beat you!'

The noise stopped. It was just like the time a couple of summers previously when Kilpin had taken a trip to the coast, not so far from here. He'd approached an olive grove high above the deep blue sea and below the midday sun. The noise of the crickets chirruping away at a mighty volume had stopped in an instant as he had entered the welcome shade of the grove.

Pasteur stared back at Kilpin, expressionless, while everyone else was looking at Pasteur.

Then, with the poise and timing of a great man of the stage (consummate actor as well as sportsman) a beaming smile broke across Pasteur's face. He leapt to his feet, raised his half-full glass of wine above his head and gazing theatrically at all those assembled and then back to Kilpin's puzzled face, he responded.

'To Mr Herbert Kilpin and the future success of Milano Foot-Ball Club!'

Pasteur's teammates stood and in unison repeated the toast. At Bosio's sign, the Internazionale players followed suit and Kilpin was left sitting alone at the table, more than twenty pairs of eyes bearing down on him.

Well, there was nothing for it now; he'd made the promise. Time to deliver.

Still sitting, he looked up, slowly raised his glass and, after the briefest of pauses to milk the last of the silence, responded to the toast with a wink and a 'Cin, cin, chappies,' giving the sign for the crickets to carry on chirruping.

Early the following morning Kilpin left his teammates

with a casual goodbye as they returned to Turin from one train station and he headed back to Milan from another.

'Ciao, Herbie, see you in two weeks.'

'That you will my friend, as always...'

But Kilpin's weariness from travelling incessantly between Milan, Turin and Genoa at weekends and living out of a bag, coupled with his bold statement the previous evening in front of twenty or so witnesses who would hold him to his word, all pointed to this next game being a last hurrah with his teammates.

He had plenty of time to ponder and plan on the way back home.

Returning to Milan from Genoa the signs of spring and rebirth were there in the thin coastal strip protected by its own microclimate; vines cultivated on the impossibly steep terraces already bearing grapes and dots of bright yellow appearing on the gnarled lemon trees scattered all around the mosaic landscape, the waxy, pock-marked fruit almost close enough to touch in little gardens hemmed in next to the train track.

As the engine climbed higher into the Ligurian Alps, Kilpin pushed open the window to his carriage to let in the cold mountain air to blow away his hangover...and sat back and gently dozed ...until the train entered the first of many tunnels hewn out of the mountain rock and the carriage and his lungs were filled with a black cloud of smoke left with nowhere else to go.

II

Two weeks later, at 4pm on Sunday 30th April 1899 in a game billed as a *'Grande Match Internazionale di Foot-Ball'*, a Swiss team took on an invitation Italian side at the Umberto I Velodrome in Turin, where the first Championship had been held just under a year earlier.

Once again Kilpin hopped onto a train from Milan to take his place in the ranks of the Italian side, promising his employers lots of overtime for their indulgence in allowing him again to delay his return to work.

He knew the Swiss were keen footballers. He'd heard how they'd picked up the game from young English industrialists and engineers who had studied in polytechnics in the major towns and cities in the Alps; in Geneva, Zurich and Lausanne. Bosio himself came from a Swiss family, even though he'd been born and raised in Turin.

This would be no walk in the park and Kilpin's fears were realized as the Swiss won 2-1 despite facing a team of the pick of the Italian clubs, players who on any other Sunday would be lining up against one another.

Before the match Kilpin had sat at the centre of the gathering for the official team photograph, clutching the match ball. The first team of Italian *'all stars'*:

Beaton *(Torino)*, Dobbie *(Torino)*, De Galleani *(Genova)*; Pasteur *(Genova)*, Spensley *(Genova)*, Bosio *(Torino)*, Agar *(Genova)*, Savage *(Torino)*, Kilpin *(Milano)*, Weber *(Torino)*, Leaver *(Genova)*.

This time the Genoese were on his side but soon Kilpin would line up not just against the old foe but also to face those who had been his teammates in Turin for most of that decade.

The city names after those of the players denoted their provenance, not their football teams. There was no 'Milano' football team in April 1899 but here was Kilpin's official announcement to the world that he had severed his links with Turin and was ploughing his own furrow.

Since moving to Milan he had played occasionally with the local gymnasium team Mediolanum, in the grounds of the medieval Sforza Castle. A throw back to those first days in Turin six years earlier when he had joined in the kickabout on Piazza d'Armi.

Unhappy with the initial difficulties he encountered in forming his own team in Milan and desperate to keep playing at a decent level, he had kept returning westwards at weekends to play with Internazionale, but enough was enough.

Along with Savage, his other friends - Beaton, Dobbie and Weber - had all stayed in Turin. Kilpin was the only one who either skipped work on Monday or caught the last train back to Milan, arriving back in the early hours of a Monday morning before heading straight to work for another week in the factory.

He'd taken quickly to life in Italy on his arrival but still gravitated to other expats in Turin and Milan, to share their company and to vent his frustrations over a drink.

Samuel Richard Davies was a sounding board for him. Three years Kilpin's senior, Davies hailed from Manchester, the world's first industrial city. The recent opening of the Ship Canal had turned the city into an inland port from which cotton goods were exported to markets around the globe.

A skilled worker like Kilpin, Davies had been recruited by Milanese entrepreneurs as fledgling Italian industry aimed, somewhat late in the day, to catch up with the rest of western Europe. Born in the heavily industrialised Ardwick district in east Manchester, Davies immersed himself in the new game of football from an early age as it took off in his city and had played a few games for a local club founded by the daughter of a vicar trying to curb gang violence and to steer young men away from alcoholism.

Over drinks in the American Bar one evening in the spring of 1899, Davies told Kilpin what his friend already knew.

'Herbie, why bother traipsing all the way back to Turin every weekend? Set up a proper team here and find yourself a nice girl and settle down.'

'What do you think I've been trying to do since I came here?'

'Well, you're not going about it in the right way. You're telling me you can't find eleven lads in this great big city to whip into shape and to give a proper game to all those doctors and poseurs in Genoa or to your mates in Turin?'

Davies narrowed his eyes as he took a long drag on his

cigarette, tilted his head back and blew the smoke slowly and very deliberately through his nose towards the high ceiling, before continuing with his train of thought.

'Alfred Edwards is your man. He's the fixer in this place. We had to speak with someone in customs to get our silk out to France and he sorted it within hours, after we'd banged our heads against a brick wall with those useless government officials. He's a cricketer and probably knows next to nothing about football but I'll bet you a hundred lire that he'd be interested in the sniff of a chance of rubbing shoulders with your wealthy factory-owning mates. He's the Vice-Consul. Go and see him – what have you got to lose?'

Davies saw this suggestion register with Kilpin and quickly added a recommendation to his suggestion:

'And when you do, make damn sure you give me a game too. And don't even think of sticking me in goal.'

Davies stubbed out his cigarette, picked up his hat and slapped Kilpin on the back as he made to leave the establishment, pointing to Kilpin's empty glass on the bar.

'Oh, and I'd cut back on the hard stuff if you're half serious about all this: it's enough to have one football in your sights, not two…Arrivederci, my friend.'

It hadn't been an easy decision to move to Milan but Kilpin had wanted the chance to earn more money and to avoid the prospect of returning home to Nottingham years older and with no prospects other than to charm the single ladies around the Market Place with soft words in

Italian. He'd do anything to avoid the '*I-told-you-so*' look on his father's tired face. And anyway, they'd offered him good money to come here.

He wasn't getting any younger and had to focus his energies. It was now or never for him to form his own club in this great city. Davies was right, there was plenty of potential talent to draw from: foreign workers, especially the Swiss and English; keen high school students and the most adaptable players from Mediolanum.

So in the same way Kilpin had broken away from his previous life in Nottingham when it would have been easier to have carried on with his old routine, he took the decision to make things happen. Throughout the summer of 1899 he built up momentum, working continually at creating a constituency of support for a proper Milanese club for which he'd laid the ground since arriving in the city in 1897 but hadn't been able to develop while adapting to his new surroundings and the demands of his work during the week, before catching the train to Turin (or Genoa) to play football on Sundays.

There was no point hanging around the Sforza Castle anymore, other than to sound out the better players from Mediolanum, to ask them the loaded question: did they want to play football for real, against teams from other cities in an organised league, or would they prefer to remain where they were, running up and down and sticking out their chests? Their choice.

He'd already spent time after work and at weekends

with other expats at the Trotter Field close to the train station, watching the horse races or kicking a ball around with lads from the local technical high school during the long, warm evenings.

Through the sons of the local textile owners Dubino, Valerio and Cederno, he'd met Piero and Alberto Pirelli, sons of the owner of the big rubber factory around the corner on via Ponte Seveso, where all the trouble with the workers had flared up the previous May when he'd been playing in the championship in Turin. Like the aristocrats in Turin years earlier, these young men had been keen about the new venture, but their interest in setting up the first proper team in Milan to compete with clubs from other cities seemed more durable than that of dear Luigi and his flighty crew.

Carefully penned letters led to conversations and meetings. Cooped up all day at work he was out of the door on the whistle, grabbing his hat as he said his hasty goodbyes. Munching a prosciutto-filled panino as he moved from one dark tavern to the next, over the course of rainy evenings in the autumn of 1899 Kilpin gradually set about getting what he needed. He was a man on a mission, working his own piece of intricate lace.

So he went to Birreria Spaten, to chat with the owner's son Guerriero Colombo, propping up the bar and already piling on the pounds as he downed his papa's tankards of beer, before hastening around the corner to the American Bar to speak again with Davies and with other Englishmen abroad, men like David Allison, a couple of years younger than Kilpin, but an experienced footballer all the same.

But Alfred Ormonde Edwards, British Vice-Consul in Milan, was the key.

III

Kilpin's focus was on getting Edwards to back the whole enterprise. He had written Edwards a brief letter and left it at the Consulate, asking the Vice-Consul in the politest of terms if he would bestow upon Kilpin and his associates the honour of becoming the first President of the Milan Foot-Ball Club, a new Anglo-Italian venture that had ambitious plans to bring sporting glory to this great city.

Edwards had quickly glanced at the note before lifting it with two fingers and asking his secretary to take it away and respond in the usual way to time-wasters.

Dear Mr Kiplin

I was humbled by your most generous invitation to become President of the Milano Foot-Ball Club but with the deepest regret I must inform you that at this time I am unable to assume any further positions, even ceremonial, as I strive in my small way to seek to promote the interests of Her Majesty's Government

and its citizens in this Kingdom of Italy.

I wish you and your colleagues every success with your new venture.

Yours sincerely
Alfred Ormonde Edwards

In playing his initial hand Kilpin had expected nothing more and indeed quite a bit less. The fish hadn't bitten the bait so it was time to raise the stakes.

He wrote back to Edwards to thank the Vice-Consul for his kind words, to acknowledge the demands upon his precious time, to assure him that he and his associates (including the Pirelli brothers and signori Dubino, Valerio and Cederno) were steadfast in their resolve to make a success of their plans.

Oh, and that upon further consideration the founding committee had decided to introduce the wonderful English export of cricket to Milan and, on behalf of the committee, Kilpin wanted to ask the Vice-Consul whether he would do Kilpin and his colleagues the honour of assuming the role of President of the Milan Foot-Ball and Cricket Club (while apologising for his impertinence in writing again).

Edwards read this second letter more carefully than he had the first. In fact he re-read it before asking his secretary to find out some information about Mr Kilpin and on learning that he was a relative newcomer to Milan, that he wasn't a man of substance but was clearly someone who knew quite a few who were, he sent a much more matter-of-fact response back to Kilpin.

Dear Mr Kilpin

Thank you for your letter dated 18 September 1899. Please arrange an appointment with my secretary Signora Peirone to discuss your proposal at these offices.

Yours sincerely
Alfred Ormonde Edward

The meeting took place at the Vice-Consul's office overlooking the Sempione Park one late afternoon in October 1899. Kilpin was ushered into Edwards' room, its walls lined with bookcases and photographs of landmarks and of encounters with various people, all no doubt well known or well connected.

Edwards sat back in a grand chair that was clearly having to work hard to support his bulky frame. Davies had been right about Edwards: he was a man of considerable weight in all senses of the word.

It was getting dark outside and a chandelier lit only the centre of the room, leaving the Vice-Consul in the shadows. His most noticeable feature was a bushy, grey moustache.

So this is the big fish then? More like a big walrus.

'So Mr Kilpin, what can I do for you?'

Charming. No, 'Would you like a drink and can we take your coat?' Well, he may be a diplomat but he's come straight out of the blocks with me. Fair enough, here we go.

'Good afternoon, Mr Edwards. Thank you for taking the time to see me. As I said in my letters my associates and I would like you to become the President of our new club.'

'I must say, Mr Kilpin, that I'm very flattered by your most kind offer and I commend you for intending to form a club to play our great games of cricket and football, but I am wondering why I have been singled out for this honour.

'I understand you have been in Italy for a good number of years, if only in Milan for the last two - you have a position of employment in the textile industry, down by the Navigli, isn't that so? May I ask how you will manage to find the significant time and funds I imagine will be necessary to get this venture off the ground? While I am charged by Her Majesty's Government with the duty of supporting the interests of its citizens here in Italy, I was given this honour because I am first and foremost a man of business, with some standing in the local community. I look at all proposals with a discerning eye and with a wish to maintain and enhance my reputation, so that in turn I may continue to discharge my official duties to the best of my ability.'

'Thank you for your candour, Mr Edwards. I assure you that I do not come here cap in hand to seek your financial backing, only your patronage.

'As I explained, we are fortunate to have the full support of Piero and Alberto Pirelli who have been able to convince their father to provide the (modest) startup capital to pay for use of a field for games at the Trotter Field, near the railway station, to subsidise the cost of travel to away games and for other sundry expenses.

'Of course the club will be financed on an ongoing basis primarily from the subscriptions of members. We are fortunate already to have over forty founding members.

'We know a very good cobbler who can provide the leather and craft for football boots and, as you might expect from our substantial connections within the textile trade, arrangements for our kit are already in hand. We have settled on a design.

'We are finalising the club's constitution and expect to formalise everything before the end of the year. We have booked a room at the Hotel du Nord et des Anglais for a reception to launch the Milan Foot-Ball and Cricket Club.

'I played football in Turin for seven years and was a losing finalist in the first championship last year in Turin and again in the second championship in Genoa this May. I have no wish for my only experience of the Italian football championship to be as a loser. Milan is twice the size of Turin, it is the engine of this country, where ambitious people come to realise their dreams, a place of winners.

'And I intend to win.

'So, Mr Edwards, I know you are a very busy man and

I don't wish to take up any more of your time. Does the Presidency of the Milan Foot-Ball and Cricket Club appeal to you?'

Edwards continued to look at Kilpin in silence, betraying no emotion, his only movement the slow stirring of his spoon in a cup of coffee on the side table next to his chair. With a delicacy of movement surprising in such a big man he lifted the spoon out of the cup, gently turned it over to allow any remaining fluid to drip back into the cup and without a sound placed it on the saucer, all without taking his eyes off Kilpin.

'Are you a batsman or a bowler. Mr Kilpin?'

'Neither, Mr Edwards. I stick to what I'm good at and football is my game. My colleague Mr Nathan Berra is taking care of the cricket side. I understand he is a very good batsman.'

A smile flickered across Edwards' face.

'Very good, Mr Kilpin, very good. Clearly you are a builder and are laying your foundations well. I wish you every success – and I would be honoured to accept the position of President and, in due course, to meet all your esteemed colleagues.

'May I offer you a drink to toast to the success of the Milan Foot-Ball and Cricket Club?'

'Sir, my colleagues will be delighted to hear this news and while it is very kind of you I must decline your offer on this occasion as I still have many matters of detail to attend to in readiness for our grand launch and I hope you

will excuse me if I bid you farewell for now
that together we raise our glasses to future succe
Hotel du Nord.

'Invitations to the launch are being prepared as w
speak and you shall be the first to receive one.'

Kilpin had left nothing to chance.

A beautiful piece of lace didn't come out of nowhere,
but from a relentlessly applied methodical process and
much labour.

IV

The record books say the club was founded on Saturday
16th December 1899 but that doesn't mean they are right.
When would be the best time to celebrate the beginning of
this great new enterprise? They say the darkest hour is the
one before dawn. Milan Foot-Ball and Cricket Club was
actually founded on Wednesday 13th December 1899 on
the longest night of the year (according to the unreformed
Julian calendar), on the feast of Santa Lucia, 'Saint Lucy',
whose name derives from *lux, lucis*, the Latin word for
'light'.

And wouldn't people be in particularly high spirits
during the season of goodwill when indeed the spirits
would be flowing most freely?

The exclusive venue was the Hotel du Nord et des
Anglais, one of the grandest hotels in Milan, five minutes'

A fitting setting for the launch

an Anglo-Italian collaboration. lomat, chief executive, artistic leader, all rolled into one.

HERBERT KILPIN, IMPRESARIO

A meeting room on the ground floor near the lobby was booked. At Kilpin's direction the gaslights were turned down low, the slim flames casting long shadows over these conspiratorial devils as they entered the room, the light catching moving profiles, in chiaroscuro fashion: a modern Caravaggio canvas in the artist's own city, composed by the butcher's son from Nottingham.

All the key stakeholders were gathered together in one place for the first time.

The enthusiastic young industrialists, the Pirelli brothers, as well as Dubino, Valerio and Cederno, the sons of textile entrepreneurs; decent young Italian players like the Angeloni brothers, Daniele and Francesco; Kilpin's English mates, including Samuel Davies, the rough diamond from Manchester and David Allison the much-travelled cosmopolitan; Italian students from the Technical Institute Carlo Cattaneo, just down the road in via Santa Marta.

And of course the spider at the centre of the Milanese

social web, signor Alfred Edwards, diplomat, shrewd man of affairs and the official seal of approval for this new venture.

There was no aristocracy within the ranks of the founding members, as there had been with Internazionale in Turin towards the beginning of the decade and there were no workers from the factories, but nevertheless the mix of businessmen, students, English expats and Italian professionals was a motley crew.

HERBERT KILPIN, DIPLOMAT

People needed to take responsibility if this was going to work and names had been proposed in advance of the meeting for the various official positions within the new club:

President: Alfred Edwards

Vice President: Edward Nathan Berra

Secretary: Samuel Richard Davies

Captain *(football)*: David Allison

Captain *(cricket)*: Edward Nathan Berra

Directors: Barnett; Henry Mildmay Saint-John; Pietro *(Piero)* Pirelli.

And lurking in the background like some dark prince, Giovanni Camperio, a young engineering graduate, was closely watching proceedings with a faint smile on his lips, pleased by the progress being made before his eyes.

The captaincy of the football team was deliberately given to Allison even though Kilpin was by some distance the most recognised and experienced footballer. Kilpin was not in it for the prestige but to make things happen. He was going to be the main man and while Allison could flip a coin at the beginning of each game everyone knew who was in charge.

Kilpin had no official position within the club. He didn't need one because he was pulling all the strings and the important thing was to secure buy-in from others. Edwards was given the Presidency in exchange for his Milanese book of contacts and to land the big fish/walrus Kilpin had been perfectly happy for the club to play cricket, but Nathan Berra could look after the chaps in white flannels and if it didn't work out then provided this didn't affect the football side of things it wouldn't be a disaster. It was clear from the beginning that this club was first and foremost about football. It was to be the Milan Foot-Ball and Cricket Club: his friends from Genoa Cricket and Football Club (as it was now known) ought to take note and get their priorities right.

He'd spent weeks preparing his speech, making sure to thank all the people who had made this all possible - and even those who hadn't done a great deal, to store up credit for the months and years to come.

HERBERT KILPIN, CHIEF EXECUTIVE

He spoke in very passable Italian, having now lived in the country for eight years and to overcome his nervousness at the prospect of speaking to such a formal gathering, at first Kilpin kept to the script, following his notes to the letter, starting with the boring but necessary detail.

He explained to his audience how the Trotter had been hired for the club's use, all about Milan's plans for recruitment and for creating a 'B' team, imminent enrolment in the coming championship and initial discussions with Mediolanum for a friendly match.

HERBERT KILPIN, ART DIRECTOR

He had thought of everything. His guests were impressed, excited by the prospect of involvement in an enterprise of modernity at the dawn of a new century.

Still he continued, exhorting the Milanese to ensure that their great, growing city had representatives at the next championship, competing with teams from the lesser cities of Turin and Genoa.

Then Kilpin put down his notes, picked up a bag from the table before him and took out a new striped shirt which he held up to the assembled gathering, under low lights in the midst of swirling cigar and cigarette smoke, in Milan's own little version of the Inferno.

'Our colours will be red, because we will be the devils and black, signifying the terror we will strike into the hearts of our opponents.'

HERBERT KILPIN, TALISMAN AND CHEERLEADER

'Here we are, Milan, the team of this great city! The flaming colours of red and black will be our symbol. Italians, Englishmen, but not confined to those nationalities, together we will bring a sense of mission to this new venture and we will go down in history, in every nation, on account of the power and beauty of the way in which we will play the game.'

Kilpin carried on speaking, off the cuff, warming to his theme, before raising his glass of champagne and proposing a toast to the gathering.

He returned to his seat to receive a standing ovation, handing his untouched champagne to Samuel Davies on the way, muttering to him under his breath:

'Down this and you can stand me a glass of Black & White whisky at the Toscana Bar next week...'

V

By happy coincidence the badge of the new club was the red cross on a white background, the ensign of the patron saint of Milan, St Ambrose, as well as the flag of St George. Herbert Kilpin was planting his own standard on Italian soil and rallying his troops, with considerably more success than King Charles I of England had done at Nottingham Castle over two hundred and fifty years earlier.

That week Kilpin had read in the newspaper of the British Army's three devastating and bloody losses within the space of three weeks in southern Africa, defeats that were forcing wide open the complacent eyes of Her Majesty's Government and of its troops who, up to that point, had assumed the Second Boer War would be won very easily. His countrymen had underestimated the opposition and had been woefully unprepared but Herbert Kilpin would not make the same mistakes.

The Gazzetta dello Sport commemorated this historic moment in its pages on Monday 18th December 1899 in the section *'Sports - Football'*:

Finally! After so many fruitless attempts, finally the Milanese sporting community will have its own football club. For now, even though we can't talk in terms of any advantage, we can however confirm that the number of members has reached around fifty and that applications for membership are numerous. The aim of this new sports club is the most noble one of forming a Milanese squad to compete for the Italian Cup next Spring. To that end the presidency has al-

ready secured for team training the vast Trotter Field. The new club wishes to inform that whoever would like to learn how to play football need only turn up at the Trotter on scheduled days and they will find trainers and teammates.

The club's headquarters were to be at the Fiaschetteria Toscana in via Berchet, a Kilpinian compromise: a stone's throw from Birreria Spaten-Colombo, the Italians' haunt on via Ugo Foscolo, both bars near Galleria Vittorio Emanuele, and a little further away from the American Bar where the English gathered, on corso Vittorio Emanuele.

So the players went for a beer on the evening of Saturday 16th December; celebratory drinks after the club's formation at Hotel du Nord et des Anglais, to seal the Devils' pact. This was the players taking their ties and jackets off.

The birth of the club was celebrated with abundant alcohol on one night but Kilpin had been laying the foundations in Milan for the best part of two years, even before vowing to Pasteur after the second championship in Genoa that he would return in triumph with his own team.

Taking his leave after many hearty slaps on the back with best wishes for Christmas Kilpin stumbled off into the dark streets, under a vast sky of bright stars, oblivious to the bitter cold of the clear December night, his innards warmed by half a bottle of Black & White.

At moments like these Kilpin became philosophical,

freed from daily cares to wonder whether our lives only make sense and have any order with hindsight, when we look hard for meaning and structure.

As he had aged and seen more of the world he feared that everything really happened by chance and that there was no grand design. He was jealous of the belief of those around him that God knew what he was doing and, ultimately, would see us right if we behaved ourselves.

But might there be a master plan after all? Herbert Kilpin, serial creator of three football teams in three different cities, every eight years: the Garibaldi Reds in Nottingham in 1883, Internazionale of Turin in 1891 and now, in 1899, Milan Foot-Ball and Cricket Club.

Puffing on his umpteenth cigarette, plumes of smoke and breath trailing in his wake, Herbert Kilpin had a million and one things running through his head: kit, registration of the squad, trials and training schedules...

Realising that he was running out of time - he was going to be thirty years old the following month - Kilpin was waging his own private little battle, quickening the pace while his body was beginning to slow down, as Italian football finally got off the ground.

Carpe diem, 'do or die.'

That night the walk back to his apartment in via Settala north of the city centre took slightly longer than it should have done.

As he staggered in the direction of home he suddenly checked, did a military about-turn and started in the opposite direction towards the Galleria Vittorio Emanuele.

The streets were deserted. Just a few hundred yards away Arturo Toscanini was conducting the inaugural performances of Wagner's *Siegfried* at La Scala, but not a note could be heard outside the plain façade to give any hint of the opulence lurking within.

Feeling very small as he entered the vast, empty arcade, Kilpin's footsteps echoed as he walked past its shuttered shops and restaurants and approached the mosaic floor at its centre. At his feet lay the symbols of the three capitals of a united Italy and of Milan.

Passing the lily of Florence and the wolf of Rome, he stopped at the bull of Turin.

Then, with the deliberation and thoroughness of the very drunk, he began grinding the right heel of his boot into the worn testicles of the bull, slowly and repeatedly.

One of the first things he'd been told on arriving in Milan a couple of years earlier was that this was a tradition to bring good luck.

He stopped, carefully surveyed his handiwork and, with a satisfied look, headed off back the way he had come, to home and to bed.

VI

The first game of Milan Foot-Ball and Cricket Club took place at three o'clock in the afternoon on Sunday 11th

March 1900, less than three months after its inaugural meeting at the Hotel du Nord et des Anglais.

In keeping with the anglicised name, the Milan team was largely Anglo-Italian: four Englishmen, five Italians, one Swiss and a Welshman in the line-up. It sounded like the beginning of a joke but their first opponents Mediolanum weren't laughing. The gym team was well known to Kilpin. Since arriving in Milan occasionally he'd joined in a game with them, leisurely kicking a ball around the vast courtyard of the Sforza Castle.

This was not only the first Milanese derby in history but a symbolic break with the '*football*' hitherto played following the ponderous rules of the gymnasium: this game was played in accordance with the rules adopted by the Italian Football Federation only two years earlier.

The young athletes of Mediolanum were left in no doubt that the real game had reached the historic gates of Milan, as a bunch of wizened Englishmen (and their Welsh cousin) combined with their Italian charges to frighten the living daylights out of them, screaming at their opponents on the few occasions when they managed to get the ball, constantly harrying and harassing until the job was done with a 2-0 victory, courtesy of goals scored by Allison and Kilpin.

The founder had pledged that the Red and Blacks would instill terror in their opponents and here he was practising what he preached, as well as recruiting a couple of the more promising Mediolanum youths to the ranks of the *Diavoli* to teach them the dark arts of the game.

For their second *'friendly'* the next Sunday Kilpin had lined up very different opponents, F.B.C. Torinese, with lots of familiar faces: Beaton, Dobbie, Nasi the footballing aristocrat, Weber and, of course, Edoardo Bosio, his great friend and former sponsor, the very reason Kilpin was here in Italy.

Same Milan team as the previous weekend, but a very different result. Kilpin's old *'pupil'* led the rout, as F.B.C. Torinese ran out 4-0 winners.

Dear old Edoardo had somewhat pooped this party, but no matter. He was thanked for bringing his boys to Milan and Kilpin looked forward to renewing battle the following month: Milan were to play Torinese in the first round of that year's championship.

To get hammered once was unfortunate, to lose heavily twice within the space of four weeks, to the same team, was beginning to give cause for concern and Milan's debut in the third Italian football championship on 14th April 1900 was something of a learning experience.

Edoardo Bosio may have arrived in Nottingham twelve or thirteen years earlier, wet behind the ears his mamma had so lovingly scrubbed before sending him off to the cold north where they ate like barbarians, eager to learn all about football from Kilpin and his mates on the pitches around Nottingham. But to give him his dues, he had learnt well.

At thirty-six years of age the erstwhile apprentice put

on a masterclass, scoring a hat-trick against the Devils who suddenly didn't look so devilish. Bosio scored goals in the fifteenth, eighteenth and seventieth minutes. This was not a lucky win right at the end of the game but a clinical, systematic dispatching of pretenders by old hands.

Here was the reality check. During his flight of oratory back in December at the posh hotel down the road Kilpin had got carried away, promising the earth to his acolytes. But here he was tasting it, flat on his face, after slipping in the cold mud, really breathing in the smell of failure.

So there would be no glorious debut in the championship, no immediate opportunity for vindication against Pasteur's Genoa who the following weekend went on to beat Torinese and take the title for the third year in a row.

Again, Kilpin would have to exercise patience. Progress had to be achieved in incremental steps. *'A goccia a goccia si scava la roccia'* - *'drop by drop you wear down the rock'*. Or maybe even, *'drop by drop you begin to forget your cares,'* as the velvety whisky took away the nasty taste of the mud.

At this point did Kilpin have doubts about whether he had done the right thing, starting from scratch rather than putting up with the inconvenience of travelling to Turin every week?

He needn't have worried.

On 27th May 1900 Milan played the final of a new competition, the King's Medal, at the Civic Arena on the other side of the Sempione Park to the Sforza Castle. Built in 1806 and officially opened by Napoleon Bonaparte during his period of occupation of the area around Milan, originally the arena had been used for military displays and, like the Colosseum in Rome, could even be artificially flooded to stage mock naval battles.

The King's Medal had been donated in honour of King Umberto, a lover of sport and uncle to Luigi, Duke of the Abruzzi, Kilpin's old acquaintance.

Milan's opponents Juventus had also debuted in the championship that season, founded back in 1897 by students in Turin at the Liceo Massimo D'Azeglio in the area just south of the city centre where football had taken root in the early 1890s, close to Piazza d'Armi, the scene of Kilpin's first Italian kickabout. School teams of the era commonly chose Latin names and the Turinese students eventually plumped for the snappy title of *'Youth'*, after thinking long and hard about Fatigando Delectamur - *'In toil we delight'*.

While almost all the Juventus players were Italian, there was a familiar face in the ranks of the team lining up in pink against Milan: John Savage, Kilpin's first guide on his arrival in Turin, almost nine years earlier. Savage had been in Italy longer than Kilpin and had remained in Turin, scoring the first goal in the first official game in Italian football history on 6th January 1898. After Internazionale had folded Savage hadn't followed Bosio and others to F.B.C. Torinese but had instead joined Juventus.

So here were the old friends from way back, competing for a prize put up by the King of Italy in the grand setting of the Civic Arena. Milan won 2-0 with goals from Giovanni Camperio and David Allison to get their hands on that all-important first trophy for the Red and Blacks, six months after the club had come into being down the road at the Hotel du Nord et des Anglais.

All in all, a good first season for Milan Foot-Ball and Cricket Club, even if the public had not immediately taken to the spectacle. The local newspaper of the thrice-crowned champions, *Il Caffaro* of Genoa, still had to explain the game to the public in the most basic terms.

The object is to bring the ball, 30cms in diameter and pneumatically inflated, into the opponent's half and to pass it between two goalposts.

Respectable Sunday strollers enjoying their hard-earned leisure time were perplexed and some not a little vexed to see a large group of grown men march onto an open grassy clearing, partially disrobe to leave their outer garments in a great mound before proceeding to chase a leather ball around the field amidst much noise and confusion.

What was the point of all this? There was no real display of agility or discipline. What did the players get out of it? It all seemed most indecorous, unedifying and without purpose. The majority of people simply didn't have the time to spare for such frivolity. Many Italians had been leaving the country in increasing numbers to find a better life, to make enough money to send back to their family and to scrimp and save with the intention of eventually returning home to buy a plot of land and live modestly into old age. Some crossed the Alps and went to France and the coalfields of Belgium or crossed the Channel and settled in England or Scotland. More headed for the Americas.

Gaetano Bresci was one such emigrant. A skilled textile worker and militant anarchist from northern Tuscany, in 1895 he had organised a strike, for which he had been sent, with fifty other protestors, to police confinement on the island of Lampedusa, off Sicily.

An extremely well-dressed anarchist, spending his money on fine clothes to impress the women, earning a nickname in his village, *'The Peacock'*, at the beginning of 1898 Bresci emigrated to the United States along with many other Italian textile workers, to Paterson, New Jersey.

That May news had reached the eastern seaboard of the massacre of civilians by the army during the Milan uprising. Along with his comrades and many others in Italy and abroad Bresci had been sickened by the praise King Umberto had lavished upon General Beva Beccaris for restoring order and, inspired by the anarchist bloodline, he resolved to avenge the slaughtered protesters.

And so, in the aftermath of the uprising, while appearing to settle down to family life with his partner and their infant child and continuing to work in the textile factories of New Jersey, Bresci abandoned photography as a hobby to concentrate on target practice.

Towards the beginning of 1900 he announced to his wife that he had to make a trip back to Italy to share his father's estate with his brothers.

Some months later Bresci bid farewell to his family and left New York for Europe, arriving in Genoa on 5th June where he picked up a suitcase containing five hundred lire. Two days later The Peacock was back home in his Tuscan village holding court at his brother's house, telling old friends of his life in America, paying for meals and drinks and showing off his fine clothes.

From his village he went to Bologna to see his sister and then one day in July he received a telegram telling him to go to Milan, where he arrived on 24th July, to take up lodgings with a family in via San Pietro all'Orto, behind the Duomo.

Wednesday 25th July 1900 was a balmy evening. It was the hour of the evening promenade, the passeggiata, on the streets of central Milan. Kilpin had finished work for the day and was on his way into the centre to meet his teammates for drinks at the Fiaschetteria Toscana, to plan the second campaign for the Milan Foot-Ball and Cricket Club.

He turned the corner of via Agnello, into via San Raffaele, a couple of minutes' walk away from the bar, absorbed in his thoughts and bumped into his better dressed, perfumed double, making his own way back to lodgings from the direction of La Scala, having seen the local sights, in particular the charming young ladies of Milan.

The other man dropped the ice cream he had been eating.

'Excuse me, I'm so sorry, allow me to pay for that,' Kilpin offered, annoyed at how distracted he had been, digging into his pocket for a coin.

'I wouldn't even let you think of it, signore! I was too busy admiring all the sights, colpa mia, I wasn't looking where I was going,' replied the dandy in good humour.

'Very well, a good evening to you then, sir.'

'Addio, signore, addio.'

A fleeting meeting, between two men of strikingly similar appearance but with very different fixations. One, thirsty for a quick whisky and set on a quest to assemble the best football team in the land (to finally end the domination of those blasted Genoese). The other, a man readying himself to assassinate royalty, to strike a blow for the underdog against an establishment that had trained its cannons on its own people for daring to protest against the high price of bread.

Born within ten weeks of one another, both immigrant textile workers, although Kilpin had arrived in Italy in search of adventure, while Bresci had left following incarceration for his political beliefs and actions. Kilpin took so little interest in politics he had been playing football in Turin during the Milan uprising.

And so they went their separate ways, while the ice cream melted quickly on the pavement.

VII

The following Monday evening Kilpin was in a very subdued Fiaschetteria Toscana. Guerriero Colombo was reading aloud from a newspaper to the group sat at the back of the tavern.

The previous day King Umberto had been guest of honour at a gymnastics competition in Monza ten miles north of Milan. At just after nine in the evening the clubs had lined up to greet the King's arrival in an open top carriage from the nearby Royal Palace. It had been a sweltering day with temperatures reaching thirty-six degrees in the shade.

The King had listened politely to a brief speech by Professor Draghiccio, director of the Gymnastics Competition, who spoke of the great achievements of the participants, before watching the choreographed exercises of the gym clubs, applauding and nodding his head in approval throughout.

Umberto had handed out medals until after ten o'clock in the evening when the royal carriage was brought beneath the stage and, flanked by his generals, the King walked off the stage, shaking hands as he went before stepping into the carriage. He rose again, his hat raised in his left hand in greeting.

The crowd thronged around the carriage as it moved off at a snail's pace, the Monza police struggling to open a path through the adoring masses. The royal party had moved about ten metres, with the king standing on his feet, hat raised in greeting towards his subjects, when amid the cheers and general applause there were three loud bangs.

The first bullet hit the King in his chest under his left arm, still raised in a salute. Its force twisted his body to face the crowd full on as the second shot went straight to his heart. Then he took a third bullet in his left shoulder.

Umberto was dead within ten minutes. The assassin, Gaetano Bresci, had been grabbed by the crowd at the scene, taken first to the local army barrack and then to the police station where he was interrogated and freely confessed that he had returned to Italy to avenge those slain on the order of General Bava Beccaris, 'the Butcher of Milan' and to address the offence caused by the King's decoration of the orchestrator of the slaughter.

The only thing the police found in Bresci's pockets was a piece of paper bearing the name of a lady in via San Pietro all'Orto in Milan. During the course of that day Bresci had spent all his remaining lire. He had entered the same ice cream parlour, the Caffè Vapore, on five separate occasions and each time he had eaten the same vanilla ice cream...

'Guerri, let me have a look at that please.' Kilpin grabbed the newspaper without waiting for Colombo's response and glanced at the photograph of Bresci.

Colombo noticed Kilpin's reaction.

'Herbie, what's up? You look like you've seen a ghost!'

Kilpin looked up, but it took a moment for the question to register.

'It's nothing…I'm tired. I'm off home… see you all at training tomorrow.'

He stood up, said his goodbyes and walked out into the late evening sunshine as the church bells tolled around the city in mourning.

His teammates exchanged puzzled looks. Gianni Camperio couldn't resist a dig.

'He's an odd one. You would have thought the King of England had been murdered!'

Someone piped back:

'He may be odd, but he's our very own mad man and I'll put up with his eccentricities all day long if he keeps on bringing us success.'

THE
GLORY

I believe even to this day that when someone gets it in their head to achieve something they will succeed with their plan, despite all the difficulties.

—— *Giacomo Casanova,*
Story of my flight from the Piombi Prison

I

Sixty-three years on the throne, the figurehead of an Empire that spanned the world and upon which the sun never set, Queen Victoria breathed her last at home on the Isle of Wight on Tuesday 22nd January 1901, attended at her deathbed by her son, the future King and by her eldest grandson, the German Emperor, Kaiser Wilhelm II.

At the end of that week and deep in thought making plans for Milan's second season Kilpin had finished work and was walking up via Manzoni, heading for a pub on via Daniele Manin for a meeting. A couple of weeks previously Milan had played Mediolanum in the semi-final of The Christmas Tree Trophy and beaten them 11-0. Amidst all the carnage Kilpin had seen something in a lad called Catullo, still intent on trying to organise his defence even though his teammates had already given up the ghost and were thinking only of a consolatory drink waiting for them in the pub. Kilpin had seen in Catullo's eyes the defiance he so prized.

It was cold and dark but as he passed the big hotel on the other side of the road Kilpin sensed something else was...missing. He had just left the noise and crowds of the centre but was still well within the city walls, carriages were making their way up and down via Manzoni as usual and, huddled in overcoats and buried in hats, people were moving in his direction out of the city back to their evening meals and their loved ones, or passing him into the city for a night at the opera or maybe looking for love.

What was different tonight, as the wind blew into his ears and straw floated around the street?

It was the near silence, punctuated only by the occasional squeaking of carriage wheels. People weren't talking, just walking in a measured and calm way, the odd child admonished by a parent for shouting out.

And even though the horse-drawn carriages went past as usual, there was no sound of horse, just the sight of clouds of hot air spurting from straining nostrils. Kilpin looked across the street and saw the cobbles were covered with straw, deadening the sound of the beasts' hooves.

Kilpin went up to a man standing on the corner of via Bigli.

'Che c'e? What's going on here?'

'Well, you must be the only one in Milan who doesn't know.'

Pointing across the street to the hotel the static spectator elaborated, 'Up there, somewhere, the Maestro is about to leave us.'

'Who's the Maestro and where's he going?'

Who was this guy and where had he been, he sounded like a foreigner, even though his Italian was good.

'Verdi, Giuseppe Verdi, the composer, you know?' For emphasis he started humming the *Chorus of the Hebrew Slaves* until recognition finally dawned on Kilpin's face, and he carried on his way to his appointment.

The day before Victoria's death, Verdi had suffered a stroke while staying at the Grand Hotel et de Milan.

The authorities spread straw over via Manzoni and the surrounding thoroughfares so that the hooves of passing horses and the noise of the carriages they pulled didn't disturb the repose of the gravely ill Maestro.

Profoundly shaken by the assassination of the King of Italy the previous summer, the great patriot of Italy grew weaker each day until that Sunday he too bid farewell to earthly cares.

A King, Queen and now a Master were all dead, but life went on and the new year started well for Milan with their retention of the King's Medal that March. In the first round the local whipping boys Mediolanum were routinely overcome, but this time made a better fist of it and only lost 5-0.

That day saw a new player in the ranks of the Rossoneri. Catullo Gadda had been the leader of Mediolanum but by now had had enough of routine thrashings at the hands of Kilpin's Milan. Feeling unable to celebrate a victory against his friends and former teammates, at the final whistle he still felt the thrill of a first clean sheet and that real progress had been made.

The next Sunday Milan faced the pink kitted students of Juventus in the semi-final and beat them 3-0 to set up a final against Genoa the following week. The encounter ended 1-1 in Milan but deadlock ensued over where and when the rematch should take place. The issue couldn't be resolved and much to Genoa's annoyance Milan were adjudicated victors, as the holders of the Medal, without another ball being kicked.

A week later Kilpin returned home to receive a letter in his sister's hand which he read and re-read, before continuing to stare at the words on the page, sitting motionless on a chair, as the night drew in and his small room grew darker, until he could no longer see the page.

Dearest Herbert

It is so hard for me to have to tell you in this way that dear father has passed away. He died on 7th April. The death certificate says 'strangulated hernia' and I cannot lie and tell you that his parting was free from pain. But at least I was with him until the end.

I ask God why an elderly man who toiled honestly all his life cannot be allowed to leave this world with just a little comfort and dignity. We are all numb and things are forever different. Father's funeral will take place on 15th April but I know this letter will not reach you in time.

Herbert, you have been away so long and it feels like you too have left us. Your silences are ever longer. I have never asked you before but please come home to see your family and to provide us with some comfort.

Lucy

So he would never again see the old man, nor receive any parental recognition for making his own way far from his family, learning another language and all the while managing to carry on playing football. Edward had indeed toiled hard for his family. Why could he never accept that having left his village as a young man to earn his living, so too his son had decided to chance his arm far from everything he knew? Herbert might be the black sheep, but he was proud he hadn't followed anyone; all the others had huddled together, grazing on the local patch.

What was the point of returning to Nottingham after the funeral had taken place? He had changed too much since leaving. He would honour his father in his own way.

In the championship semi-final on 28th April Milan again faced John Savage's Juventus but this time the game was harder fought, with the Turin team keen to use home advantage to reach the final at only the second attempt. Twice Juventus took the lead but twice young Negretti struck to level the scores for Milan.

Kilpin played the game in midfield alongside Lies and Angeloni, looking to orchestrate its flow but towards the end of an epic struggle he charged up the field to score the winner.

Milan had prevailed by three goals to two, setting up a final against the champions of Genoa. The old dog had done it.

A close shave? A slice of luck? Luck didn't come into it.

Did Savage really think that luck had anything to do

with Kilpin running thirty yards onto the ball that had stuck in the mud before taking it towards the Juventus goal and booting it under their goalkeeper ten minutes before the end of the game, with the match tied at 2-2 and his lungs fit to burst? No, he knew Kilpin better than that.

After two final defeats to Genoa and after taking the best part of two years to assemble a new team from scratch, in a new city, it wasn't luck that came to mind, but another four-letter word, beginning with 'F.'

Fate.

II

Kilpin made absolutely sure all his team got onto the first train bound for Genoa on the morning of Saturday, 4th May, the day before the championship final, knowing how arduous the trip across the mountains would be – all at their own expense. He was looking to give his players every chance of performing to their very best the following day.

While President Edwards and the other Milan officials would travel to the coast on the Sunday morning in the comfort of first class, Kilpin shepherded his charges from the platform at the station into the third class compartment of the standing train, giving a theatrical kick up the backside to mummy's boy Guerriero Colombo who was dawdling towards the back of the group, yawning and rubbing his eyes.

Milan had to go to the home of the three-times champions of Italy, the only champions to date.

Kilpin had already lost two of those finals with Internazionale of Turin.

Genoa were still nursing a very recent grievance over the failure to arrange a rematch of the King's Medal Final, which had cost them the chance to snatch it from Milan's grasp.

The players had a five-hour train journey ahead of them.

Train doors slammed shut in quick succession, the station master blew his whistle and Milan Foot-Ball and Cricket Club were finally away, in a haze of smoke, southward to Genoa.

The lads chatted and joked, playing cards and gazing out of the window. Settling down for a long journey, Kilpin lit a cigarette before observing those in his carriage and listening to the laughter down the corridor

He recalled his solitary return to Milan two years earlier, after Internazionale's second final defeat to Genoa, rapt in thought about his plans to form a new team, sat by the window of a dark carriage on a train straining up the Maritime Alps on that May day.

Now, with the morning sun lighting the peaks of the same mountains he was on his way back to the sea to face the old adversary, this time with his very own team, to contend for the highest honour.

In his mind's eye he trained the spotlight on each of his

players, a proud leader introducing his team for the final, from the tip of the pyramid to its base: 1-2-3-5 (with a substitute).

HOODE

SUTER   GADDA

ANGELONI   KILPIN   LIES

RECALCATI   NEGRETTI   DAVIES   ALLISON   COLOMBO

[NEVILLE]

Hoberlin Hoode. Short for a goalkeeper but height was not the most important attribute for a footballer of the pioneering age. Tough with bushy handlebar moustaches, bristling at the prospect of imminent danger; a primitive early warning system indispensible in the Wild West of early Italian football when the five-men base of the attacking pyramid bore down on the two-men resistance at the tip of the defending one. Mayhem often ensued, especially from corner kicks when everyone would cram into the opposing box, blissfully untroubled by tactical positioning or zonal marking.

Then we had the defence, Hans Heinrich Suter and Catullo Gadda.

Suter. Tall and dapper, an elegant player hailing from Zurich who had played for Grasshoppers and at Easter-time in 1899 for the Swiss against Kilpin and the rest of the Italian representative team. An assured presence at the back.

Suter's defensive partner was Catullo Gadda. Also tall, wiry and combative, and most unused to winning any games and so very keen to pick up a medal or two while he could.

In the middle of the pyramid, he, Kilpin, the beating heart focussed on bringing this team to life.

Then alongside him in the centre of the park, Lies and Angeloni, all three together forming a strong Anglo-Swiss-Italian axis.

Kurt Lies. Young-looking, tall and powerful, Swiss like Suter, he'd already told Kilpin this would be his only season in the red and black of Milan and he was set on leaving with a winner's medal.

Daniele Angeloni. A highly respected and skilled Italian midfielder and one of the club's founders, along with his brother Francesco. One of the first recruits from Mediolanum as Kilpin had pounded the streets of Milan, in the summer and autumn of 1899.

Agostino Recalcati. Nicknamed *'topolino'*, the little mouse. Like Gadda recruited from Mediolanum and a valued addition but seeming to pine for his pals at the gym club.

Ettore Negretti. A teenage sensation who couldn't stop

scoring.

Samuel Davies. Another of the club's founders, having egged on Kilpin to set up Milan and here was his reward, a shot at glory.

David Allison. An Englishman born on the French Riviera. Centre forward and evader of the offside trap par excellence.

Guerriero Colombo. A decent player and true competitor, involved from the beginning. Nice little moustaches too, often wetted by beer froth.

Penvhyn Llwellyn Neville. The Welsh Dragon from Swansea. Founder member and adaptable team player, just the man to come off the bench when needed.

The Dirty Dozen.

Herbert Kilpin and his band of merry men were going into battle with the mythical *'grifone.'* The champion had watched the qualifying games from the sidelines, patiently polishing its talons, waiting to see who would reach this year's final and stand between it, *Genoa - La Superba, the Proud* - and a fourth consecutive championship victory.

But Hoberlin Hoode hadn't come along just for the ride. Neither had Suter or Gadda, Lies, Angeloni, Recalcati, Davies, Negretti, Allison or even Colombo (although he was still very sleepy from the early start and the long journey from Milan).

This was because they all had faith in Kilpin and Herbert Kilpin had a plan.

He'd played against many of the Genoa players for the

best part of four years and alongside some of them in the match against the Swiss side in Turin two years earlier. As well as appreciating Genoa's strengths he was aware of his opponents' weaknesses and how to exploit them.

He knew, for example, that Milan had to put Spensley under pressure, because although he was a lovely man and a great organiser he wasn't a very good goalkeeper, so Milan had to try to shoot on sight every time and to let him know they were there at corners, to yell...to tug at his beard. Whatever it took.

That if Milan stopped playmaker and all-round clever clogs Edoardo Pasteur from getting the ball and running the game then they stood a chance of winning it.

And that if Milan scored an early goal that would really put the wind up the expectant home crowd, who would turn up expecting their usual victory.

In those very early years there was no regulation of the playing surface. Each pitch was quirky, unique, uneven, best known to the team that played on it every other week. This gave home teams a noticeable advantage even before a ball was kicked.

At Ponte Carrega, in the hills on which the outer city perched above the sea, Genoa played on a pitch much smaller than Milan's. While some observers were calling Kilpin presumptuous he knew he was just being thorough and well prepared when he'd insisted that Milan practise at the Trotter on an area smaller than their usual pitch - even before the semi-final with Juventus.

While Milan might have only squeezed through to the final, here they were now, battle-hardened, knowing they would have to keep things very tight and rely upon the undoubtedly superior conditioning they had achieved after playing two tough games on larger fields, while the reigning champions had loitered about without a challenge.

And Kilpin had a hunger which Genoa just wouldn't believe. He remembered how little he'd enjoyed the food at the banquet after the final those two long years ago. If Pasteur had forgotten Kilpin's promise to create a team to beat Genoa, Kilpin had dwelt on it virtually every day since, especially as he'd restlessly paced around Milan working out how to fulfil his oath lest it fade to a stale boast.

So, finally, in front of a sizeable crowd on a beautiful spring afternoon Herbert Kilpin stood facing the Genoa players, men he knew better than the teammates dressed in red and black who surrounded him. Referee Ghiglione from Turin blew his whistle and to a great hurrah from the spectators the game began.

Genoa were never in it. Although they weren't at full strength the spine of their treble championship-winning team remained: the Pasteur brothers, Ghigliotti, Dapples and Spensley did everything possible to keep at bay the brilliance of their opponents, but the Milanese maintained a clear supremacy over the Genoese to secure the most complete of victories, outpassing, outrunning and out-thinking their hosts on a pitch that looked a picture. The home crowd tried its best to urge on its team, but in vain.

Negretti scored twice, *a doppietta*. And the other name on the scoresheet was Mr Herbert Kilpin.

The whistle blew and the gentlefolk of Ponte Carrega on their afternoon stroll after Sunday lunch wondered what on earth was happening on the other side of the high brick wall surrounding the sports field, as a couple of boater hats were hurled from unseen hands into the clear blue sky, amidst cheers and shouts.

The football party made a brilliant return into the city, amidst the bustle of carriages, bicycles and cars and the day concluded with a succulent lunch at the Concordia restaurant, offered by the Genoese to their Milanese guests and which ended at a late hour, amid interminable hip hurrahs.

Mission accomplished.

III

While Davies and Allison snored loudly in their beds behind him as he sat at the window of their inn, Kilpin was content in the fug of his triumphant drunkenness, staring out to the dark sea, at the lights twinkling around the coastline. He puffed on a fat cigar and with his free hand caressed a squat silver chalice: the Fawcus Cup, the brand new cup of the champions.

The Spensley Cup was gone forever, gifted to the now former champions of this city of sailors and traders and explorers, glittering all around him in the dead of the night.

In its place Kilpin held in his hands the holy grail he had pursued for nearly a decade. Kindly purchased by Mr Daniel G Fawcus, formerly of North Shields, England, past player and current President of Genoa Cricket and Football Club, put up for grabs for the first time the previous day and promptly taken by Messrs H Kilpin & Co without needing to be asked twice, thank you very much.

For a good hour Kilpin surveyed his domain, following the tiny lights of the fishing boats making their way back to port with their catch. For that short time in the dead of night Herbert Kilpin was at peace with himself.

All his travelling, his hours of persuading, organising and directing, his willingness to exercise patience as well as his ageing body before finally making his move when the time was just right, all these had now borne fruit.

Then his mind started to wander. To the next campaign, to thoughts of how to go about replacing Hoode in goal, Gadda, Recalcati and Allison who had all decided this was to be their last game for the club. Who to promote from the second team? Could Lies or Suter persuade a couple of their Swiss mates to come over from Zurich and make their home in Milan? He could ask Piero Pirelli if there were any decent desk jobs at his dad's factory. Then there was the need to think about moving from the Trotter Field, the land now needed to develop the city's new train station. Raising the money for a new kit, for both the A and B teams, was a big issue too. The red and black shirts were fading badly after a two-year cycle of mud baths during games and laundry starch afterwards. Edwards had just changed the subject when Kilpin raised the question of new shirts straight after the semi-final victory. Miserly bastard, despite all his money - or was that why he had so much? - Edwards still preferred cricket but now Kilpin had handed the old walrus on a plate the prestige he would no doubt use to impress all his fancy business connections. Time to speak again with good old Piero or his brother; they would come up with the lire needed and didn't need telling that walking out onto the field of play in worn and faded kits would be no way for the champions of Milan to defend the Fawcus Cup in 1902. Absolutely not…

Suddenly Kilpin had a headache and noticed he was very tired and that his body ached. He stubbed out his cigar butt, picked up the cool silver of the cup, pressing it against his forehead for a few, soothing moments - although it did whiff of whisky, better rinse it out in the morning before giving to Edwards for safekeeping - before carefully placing it back on the table near Davies' bed. He closed the window and crept to his bed for a couple of hours of oblivion before facing the hangover that was surely coming his way.

IV

Back in Milan, as anticipated, President Edwards was busy telling everyone who would listen about Milan's success. He arranged for a team photograph in the Sempione Park the following weekend. Everyone was ordered to turn up freshly scrubbed and combed, changing in the bushes into their freshly laundered kit, before assembling in a carefully orchestrated portrait of power.

Burly Edwards sits on a chair in the centre, choosing to wear a light-coloured suit surrounded by his players in red and black, his left arm resting nonchalantly on a small cloth-covered table, almost touching the silver trophy placed at its centre.

Sat to the left of Edwards, a stern-looking man with a sharp nose in a dark suit and straw boater hat, set off by seriously waxed moustaches defying the laws of physics: Giovanni Carlo Camperio. A man of elegance and poise.

Next to him we find Daniele Angeloni, founding member of the Milan Foot-Ball and Cricket Club and secretary-designate for the coming season and, completing the row of power, Herbert Kilpin, sat to the right of Edwards.

All the other players stand or sit on the grass.

Somehow even Nathan Berra, the first captain of the cricket section of the club, manages to make it into the photograph: what a little glory hunter he is, seeing that his cricketers are struggling to find a match to play, let alone win a championship.

The faces are looking at points all over the place out of the frame of the photograph, none seeming overjoyed and instead seriously focused on posterity's demand for formality.

The football champions of Italy.

EVERYTHING IN ITS RIGHT PLACE

There are two colours in my head.
What is that you tried to say?

—— *Thom Yorke*

I

Kilpin sat near the centre circle caked in mud, sleet falling on his head and sprinkling his wet hair with white crystals. There was very little red stripe visible on his soiled shirt.

Play had moved on towards the Milan goal. Kilpin had been dispossessed and the referee was telling him to stop moping around.

'Forza, Herbie, get up and on with it, you old dog...'

Kilpin smiled, relaxed about the casual insult coming from his dear friend and old mucker Albert Weber.

'Don't worry about me, dear Albie. I'm just embarrassed that the league champions and holders of the King's Medal are hosting a match on this swamp.'

It had rained for days and the Trotter Field wasn't fit for pigs to wallow in, let alone for a semi-final of the King's Medal against Genoa on 16th February 1902.

The sleet and biting wind compounded the misery of the twenty-two men staggering around the field, referee Weber, one hardy journalist from *Il Sportivo* newspaper and the two hundred or so masochists who continued to linger along the touchline.

Kilpin wasn't happy but he wasn't going to keep on moaning, because Milan were winning 2-0. His team had started the game with an intensity of play that had hardly relented, continuing to push Genoa back into their own half,

After twenty minutes Antonio Dubini had raced down the right wing, taking the ball almost to the goal line before delivering a perfect cross that bounced off the outside thigh of a Genoa defender past a bewildered goalkeeper and into his own goal. Giulio Cederno was having a marvellous game in defence, leading the attack from the back. Kilpin instructed his teammates to keep the ball in the air as much as possible to avoid it sinking into the quagmire. Milan ended up scooping passes through the Genoa midfield to release Edward Wade who ran on to a final pass to bury the ball past the hapless keeper.

Weber blew his whistle for half-time and called over Kilpin and the Genoa captain, the heroic Edoardo Pasteur, to inform them he'd taken the executive decision to limit the break to two minutes so the players could keep moving to avoid mass hyperthermia. Kilpin told Cederna to tell the boys to jog on the spot and ready themselves for the second half while he ran over to Giovanni Camperio, the only man who was managing to stay dapper in the tempest, despite his drooping moustaches.

'Gianni, you can see for yourself but I ask you, how can we continue to play on this swamp? We're the champions of Italy, for God's sake. We play our part and it's down to you and Edwards to give us a decent pitch. When are you going to sort it out?'

Camperio didn't appreciate being spoken to in such a blunt manner in front of others, even if this was the founder and club captain giving him a piece of his mind.

But he, Giovanni Camperio, betrayed no emotion, knowing that his composure would wind up Kilpin even more.

'My dear Herbert, calmati, heaven knows what you would be saying if we were losing. I'm working on it. The council is about to decide on plans for the new railway station and we're looking at a few sites. For now, why don't you just finish the job and get us into the final, there's a good chap?'

Kilpin glared at Camperio but kept his mouth shut, realising he was being goaded. He turned and ran back to his team and to Weber, waiting to blow his whistle to herald the beginning of the second half, to allow the Red and Blacks to finish the job, which they indeed did, running out 4-1 winners, the highlight of this half being the worst penalty miss seen by anyone present. Ermolli in the Milan goal stood on the spot watching the ball bobble over the sticky mud before it stopped short at his feet.

Kilpin held a team debrief in the pub the following evening. Milan had won well, against a very good team, but still that wasn't good enough because Kilpin sensed that his team had been coasting. Everyone was in a relaxed mood, chatting over their beers. He stood and looked at them, raising a newspaper in the air.

'Ragazzi, have you all read the report in *Il Sportivo*?'

A few nodded; most shook their heads.

'So, why did we beat Genoa in that bog?'

'Because we were fitter and faster than them and we never stopped running.'

'That's right, Sam, and the reason you are fit is because I push you every week in training and I tell you to eat properly and to get enough sleep. And we're champions because we wanted it so badly last year. But boys, we don't slacken off, do you hear? Because as soon as we do, we're dead.'

At this point Guerriero Colombo made the mistake of leaning over to Ettore Negretti to carry on their private conversation but was silenced by the anger in the cold voice trained on him.

'And what do you say, Guerriero, have you heard enough?'

Colombo's face flushed in the glare of all the others now turned to his.

Herbert was great but he was a real ball-breaker and he didn't hold back when he had something to say. He, Guerriero Colombo, being told off like a naughty schoolboy in his dad's own bar. Thank God Mamma wasn't around tonight to hear this.

'I entirely agree, Herbert. I scored the last goal at the end; what more can I do?'

'True, Guerriero, very true. But how many more goals might you score if you had that extra few yards on the last defender? I'm guessing you haven't read the match report?'

Those who had seen the report exchanged knowing glances and a quick smile.

'Because if you had, you wouldn't be answering me back. 'Mr G.G' - whoever he is - went out of his way to mention your substantial paunch. That's hardly going to put the fear of God into Torinese on Sunday, is it? Why don't you take a little more care about what you eat, spend a little less time in here and join me for a run in the park some time?'

Now he had everyone's attention, and rammed home his message.

'Boys, the hardest thing when you're on top is to stay there and that's the challenge I lay down to all of you now. Come on, one more game to retain the King's Medal, to make it three in a row and keep the damned thing for good. And of all teams, Torinese. Many of you weren't there two years ago but I don't fancy another thrashing by Bosio's men and it shouldn't happen, but we all need to stay focused. Do I make myself understood? Can I count on you?'

'Yes, capitano!' they all shouted together.

Wagner murmured under his breath to the crestfallen Colombo. 'Don't take it personally, Gerri, he's desperate to get one over Bosio. They go back a long way, just make sure you keep running and try a few sit-ups to flatten that stomach. Or just hold your breath.'

The message got through and Kilpin secured his precious revenge against Torinese the following Sunday with a 7-0 victory.

At the final whistle a smiling Bosio walked over to Kilpin.

'Herbie, what did we do to deserve that? You were a team possessed today, why couldn't you stop at three, like we did a while back, if I recall correctly...' he said, winking, making sure Kilpin wasn't going to forget this result was only an evening of the scores.

'You know me, Edi. Once I start I need to finish a job. It's taken us long enough to get this far with the team and I don't intend to stop, even if these boys need a kick up the backside from time to time,' looking around at his teammates slapping each other on the back, laughing and joking.

'Well, I fear for your next opponents, Herbie. I don't want to be bringing our boys back here any time soon.'

'That's the trouble Edi. Fear is good, fear keeps us all on our toes. What might we miss out on if we don't have it? We need to fear more and relax a little less - on the football pitch at least.

'But come, my dear friend, let me offer you some of my finest Black & White to forget your disappointment...'

II

He knew his instinct had been right. Despite trouncing Torinese, the champions had reverted back to coasting as they waited to see who would face them in that year's championship final. Not surprisingly Genoa, winners of three of the first four titles, emerged from the pack to secure their place in the final, to be played on Sunday 13th April 1902, in Milan.

Or was it?

'What exactly are you saying Gianni?' Kilpin asked, with a hint of menace in his voice.

'I'm trying to explain, dear Herbert, that I've listened diligently to your entreaties and ensured that the final will be played on a fine playing surface, fit for Champions...' retorted Camperio with a skilful parry.

'But half a day away in Genoa, at the home of the challengers, rather than here? We have the right to host the game, we won it at their place last year.'

'You know the Trotter is unplayable, it's worse than it was when we played them in February.'

'Only because you keep renting it out during the week. What was it last week, Buffalo Bill's Travelling Circus? How much did Genoa pay you, Gianni?'

'They've given us a significant amount and we need every lira to make the move work next year; we're signing the lease on Acquabella next week. Herbert, someone needs to deal with the numbers while you lead the lads on the field.'

'Don't lecture me about the nuts and bolts Gianni. You of all people know what I had to do to make it all happen. How can you sacrifice home advantage for thirty pieces of silver?'

'What are you scared of Herbert? We're champions, we've thrashed Genoa and Torinese in the last few weeks and we can do it again, home or away.'

'You've messed up there, Gianni, mark my words.'

And mark them, Gianni Camperio did indeed. It hadn't felt right to Kilpin from the moment they had stepped back aboard the train bound for the Ligurian coast on the Saturday morning before the final. There was no cockiness, that would never happen when they played against Genoa who would always command respect, but the atmosphere was too relaxed. The lads were playing cards or snoozing or just gazing out of the window as the train ascended, first through the hills and then into the mountains.

Again Kilpin urged them to victory, warning that Genoa would be smarting after the recent defeat in the sleet and mud at the Trotter Field but also still nursing their deeper wounds after being vanquished at their own ground the previous Easter, when Milan had left the coast with the cup.

The boys had seemed to take it all in, even Guerriero this time, nodding in agreement and they had all trained well enough, but it had all still seemed a little flat.

Kilpin's instinct was proven right on the Ponte Carrega pitch on another beautiful spring day by the sea when, in front of a large home crowd and despite losing the toss and having to play the first half into the wind blowing in from the sea, Genoa were at their best from the off and wrested the trophy back from Milan, winning 2-0.

So, Milan had climbed to the top of the mountain only to be dragged off it into the sea by Genoa, claiming their fourth victory in five years.

There was no point labouring any lesson on the quiet train back to Milan in the dark that Sunday night. Everyone was aware they hadn't performed and that there wouldn't be another chance to put it right for another year but Kilpin knew that it would take a lot longer. This side had reached its peak. More than half of the team of champions from the previous season had gone. Kilpin was now thirty-two years old, a decade or more older than most of the players who were turning out to play every Sunday in the towns and cities of northern Italy. He was working harder than ever to stay fit, running around Milan most evenings after work, even during the long summer evenings in the off-season, when everyone else was having a drink by the canal or engaged in the passeggiata in Piazza Duomo or walking around the Publics Gardens, watching a solitary figure jogging past the ornamental lake.

Nevertheless, Kilpin could sense Father Time creeping up on him: when he walked to work in the mornings the stiffness of his limbs would now last well into the week following each Sunday's exertions. During games he caught the occasional glance between teammates when he couldn't connect with a well placed pass and the ball was intercepted by an opponent.

Next season there would be no choice: he would have to adapt, drop back and dictate the play from defence.

To top everything, now even Edwards was butting in. He'd been pretty hands off so far but Kilpin was sure Camperio had been whispering in his ear, telling him that the times were changing, that now the club was established it was time to turn it from an amusement for ex pats into a side fully integrated into Milanese life, with Italian players.

At least Camperio delivered on his promise of a new ground. In the spring of 1903 Milan Foot-Ball and Cricket Club vacated the Trotter Field to allow the site to be cleared in readiness for construction of the grand new railway station. The club moved east to the Acquabella ground adjoining the Milan-Venice railroad. The pitch was smaller but it was all theirs, not to be shared with the horses of Milan, or with Buffalo Bill's Travelling Circus.

And an old friend, and increasingly problematic new foe, visited Kilpin's Milan at Acquabella for the qualifying round of the league championship on Sunday 22nd March 1903.

'Mr Savage, how the devil are you?' Kilpin smiled, walking up to John Savage.

'Splendid Herbert, all the better for seeing you.'

'What is this I hear about your new strip? I was very fond of your fetching pink shirts, especially when we continued to thrash you.'

'That's the point Herbie. Juventus is youth and cannot stand still, we need to keep growing.'

Kilpin broke into a sly smile. 'Black and white stripes? Very nice. Now where have I seen those before? Get them free of charge, did you?'

'Believe it or not, I was under orders to get the Forest

strip. You know the obsession the bloody Turinese have with Garibaldi and his red shirts. But winning the FA Cup the other year and going on a long unbeaten run last year has made the Forest shirts a little too popular. You can't get them for neither love nor a lot of money. Either that, or my supplier just messed up. So we've had to make do with good old County's colours. A little ironic, don't you think, our oldest professional club bequeathing its shirt to the team of 'Youth'?

'The boys weren't too pleased when I turned up with twenty of these shirts but they soon shut up - you've heard no doubt that we keep on winning? Amazing what a little change can do for morale!'

Savage wasn't wrong. Sensing that Milan were in transition as Kilpin stepped onto the field to lead a team of fresh-faced Milanese, Savage and his charges went for the kill, after inviting Milan to attack them. The kids in red and black were keen to make a good impression in front of their families and friends at their new home but got badly exposed twice on the counterattack by the White and Blacks and were unceremoniously booted out of the league championship after the first game.

But there were still plenty of other fish to fry. Football was now expanding its reach throughout Italy, beyond the old hub of Genoa, Milan and Turin where it had taken root, and there were other victories to be gained.

That season Kilpin finally visited the place he had heard so much about: Venice, *La Serenissima*. the island city that had become an Empire. For the first time the team took the train east beyond Lombardy, rather than west towards Turin or south to Genoa, passing through Verona, Vicenza and Padova, before crossing the long bridge spanning the lagoon late one Saturday afternoon in spring. The players spotted an irregular reddish silhouette on the horizon until it loomed larger and the detail of heavy bell towers and terracotta roofs floating on the water revealed itself as the train slowed into the station.

Kilpin was transfixed by the beauty of the city and ecstatic after Milan trounced Vicenza 5-0 to win the St Mark of Venice Cup. He was a man of few words, except when the mood took him and on the way home to Milan on the Sunday evening it certainly did. He ripped some blank pages from the dog-eared journal in which he normally jotted down his thoughts and plans and began one of the few letters he wrote his sister.

Dear Lucy

I wanted to tell you that this weekend I have visited Venice, Venezia, the Most Serene One. Do you remember dear old Brownleaf telling us at school about the beautiful city and mighty empire that began with a few huts built on muddy patches rising out of a lagoon. We thought it was a fairy tale but the reality far surpasses his description!

You approach by train, over an endless bridge across the water as the city comes into view and arrive at the train station, Santa Lucia - Saint Lucy! I was told there was a church on the site dedicated to your name saint, which they had to knock down to make way for the railway.

You get off the train and it looks like any old station, until you make your way out, but not onto a busy tram-filled street but facing silent water lined with the most fantastic palaces.

We took a boat down the Grand Canal, past hundreds of these beautiful buildings, one next to the other, only broken up by the occasional piazza. Hundreds of churches in such a small area. We glided under the Rialto Bridge and then to the far side of Saint Mark's Square.

Would you believe that last year without warning the bell tower of the Basilica just collapsed one morning? No one was killed except the caretaker's cat! They have already started to rebuild the tower, just as it was, where it was.

Then we carried on past the main island towards the Lido where we played our game against Vicenza, on a field like any other. We could have been back on the Forest, except when the sea breeze carried the sound of the church bells ringing at midday! I feel I am only really beginning to explore this captivating land, twelve years after arriving!

Your loving brother, Herbert

Lucy had never received a letter from Herbert quite like this. Previously he had limited himself to a couple of lines, the minimum to assure everyone back home that he was fine and hoping that his greetings found all in good health, et cetera. But it was the tone of this letter she found very strange.

Her brother had always been matter-of-fact, brusque even, but here he was writing like a poet, delighting in his surroundings, with a lightness of heart she had never associated with Herbert the football obsessive.

She wondered what had happened to him and would only find out months later.

Maria Beatrice Capua was what had happened to Herbert Kilpin. A name that was about as illustrious as it got for an Italian woman: Maria, the mother of God; Beatrice the love of Dante's life; and Capua, with a nod towards the fair daughter of Capuleti and the object of Romeo's desire, Juliet of Verona.

After living nearly fifteen years in a foreign land where he had learnt the language and gone native, love had finally come knocking on Herbert Kilpin's door.

She came from Lodi, twenty-five miles south east of Milan and, despite the beauty of her name, neither she nor her life were glamorous. She was the small town girl who had come to the big city to earn her way and send a little money back to her large family back home. She worked as a waitress by day and supplemented her meagre pay in the evenings as a seamstress, darning the worn garments of her neighbours in the Navigli neighbourhood.

One day a man came into the latest trattoria where she had found work. He sat by the window and gazed out at the street life until she came over to take his order.

'Bean soup and then some chicken please,' the man said politely, smiling at her.

She couldn't place his accent, maybe he came from the north, from Como perhaps.

She took his order to the kitchen and then served another customer. By the time she brought a steaming bowl of zuppa di fagioli to his table five minutes later he had sheets of papers spread over it, with scrawled designs on some, lists on others and a half-written letter in front him.

He rapidly gathered the papers and made room for his food and she thanked him:

'Grazie, signore. That looks complicated,' she said with interest.

He looked up, still lost in his own world, before understanding what the waitress was talking about.

'Well sometimes that's what my team think until I explain how simple it really should be.'

The woman looked puzzled, so he carried on with his explanation.

'It's the plan for our next game. I run a football team over town, in Acquabella.'

'I've seen some men kicking balls in parks and didn't know what they were trying to do.'

Maria paused, unsure whether to proceed, but curiosity got the better of her, so she continued.

'But...what is the point?'

Kilpin looked affronted, but at the same time stumped by such a simple question, challenging him to justify the purpose of the activity that consumed his every waking moment.

'The point...is to kick the ball past the man who stands in front of the goal, to prevent your opponents from scoring against you and to end up with a higher score.'

'Why?'

His soup was getting cold, but Kilpin was more perturbed that this lady didn't get it and that he couldn't answer her questions.

'Because... it is good to work as a team to challenge another team and to score more goals than them.' This didn't sound great and Maria wasn't convinced.

She could see he seemed a little lost so out of politeness she changed the subject and asked him what he was writing.

'It's a list of our games for the rest of the season: there could be others, depending on whether we progress in the cup competitions...'

'Oh... I see.'

Yes, he could see that he hadn't managed to convert another non-believer to his cause.

They looked at each other awkwardly, then she lowered her eyes, apologised for having detained him with her questions and left his table to serve the group of workmen who had just entered the trattoria to take seats near the door.

Kilpin looked at his scribbled papers, then over to her slim figure and then towards the cooling bowl of thick, greyish soup in front of him. He looked back up and caught her eye. She smiled back at him, a genuine smile, even if there was still puzzlement on her face.

He'd not won any minds but maybe, just maybe, there was the chance of a heart...

III

The year of 1905 started on a high. Maria Beatrice Capua was to make an honest man of Herbert Kilpin.

Kilpin was nearly thirty-five years of age; Maria thirty-three. Both had enough experience of life to know that romance was a luxury reserved for the young and carefree, whose adult lives were ahead of them and whose heads were filled with dreams that might still come true. This couple were in the midst of messy life and old enough to settle for what they could get.

So, finally, domestic bliss had arrived for Herbert Kilpin.

Or maybe not.

Some of the younger footballers were dissipating their energies chasing young ladies and having a ball when not running around after one. But Kilpin was not even with his bride the morning after their wedding night, on Sunday 8th January 1905. He was on a train bound for Genoa, to play a game of football against Grasshoppers of Zurich.

The previous evening a telegram had arrived at the newly-weds' apartment. Maria had been watching her groom's face with an expectant look as he opened the telegram, assuming it conveyed good wishes for their marriage that morning, a small affair at the civil registry office witnessed by a couple of her friends.

Instead Kilpin announced in a matter-of-fact way that he had been invited to play with an Italian representative team against the Swiss in Genoa the following afternoon. Then he looked straight at Maria with an absent expression, asking himself rather than her what time train he could catch from Centrale station to arrive at the coast by midday at the latest.

At some point Maria had heard from someone, probably from one of her close friends, or maybe from a travelling salesman in one of the trattorie in which she had worked, about a particular sense of humour beloved of the English and she was very much hoping Herbert had chosen this moment to display this national trait.

She was still looking at her groom with the expectant look on her face, but hadn't caught his eye and he had already turned towards their bedroom, to fetch a bag for his kit.

That joke wasn't funny any more.

'Herbert, per l'amor di Dio, for God's sake, please tell me you're not actually going to accept?'

He stopped and turned to face her, with a surprised look.

'Of course, I don't have work or a game tomorrow, so why not?'

The poor girl felt sickness in her stomach as she realised he truly wasn't having fun at her expense.

'Because we married today and you want to spend your time with me rather than with your friends kicking a ball around a field... one hundred miles away?'

It had started as a direct response to his stupid question, but as the words came out and she saw that he thought her initial question the stupid one, it petered out into a weak, pleading question to which she already knew the answer.

He frowned. 'We've already spoken about this. I told you before I asked you to marry me that if you wouldn't let me carry on playing football then I wouldn't commit, and you accepted...'

'Yes, but...' she gave up and turned away as he returned to his bag-packing, tears streaming down her face and trying not to think of the words of her father a few months ago when she had returned alone to Lodi to announce her engagement to her family (while Kilpin was away in Turin playing a game) and he had told her that her family would not attend her marriage to this protestant man.

'These foreigners, they're not like us, they don't have the same values, our respect for family life. He hasn't even asked me for your hand in marriage!

'This man, he's older than you and he's been in this country for how long, fifteen years? And it's taken this long for him to commit to you - how many skeletons are in his closet?'

Alas, Maria knew there was very little for Herbert to hide and that the problem had been in plain sight from the beginning.

She already knew Kilpin would be faithful to her in every conventional sense. There would be no other women and her father could rest easy on that count.

But that didn't make it any easier for her to accept that there would always be football in this marriage.

None of this troubled Kilpin. He was gone by the time the church bells called Maria to the Feast of the Epiphany first thing in the morning while it was still dark outside and she lay alone, awake, in their cold bed.

By the time she had left mass at midday and had accepted her friends' offer to eat lunch at their house, while they exchanged alarmed looks as Maria quietly sobbed into her crumpled handkerchief, Kilpin was standing in the weak midwinter sunshine by the edge of the Ponte Carrega pitch in Genoa, one foot resting on the top of a motionless ball, hands on his sides, deep in thought, set apart from his joking teammates.

During the game he dived to reach a cross and for his trouble took a kick full in the face. The Swiss boot smashed his nose and the blood gushed out. Play stopped for five minutes as a couple of spectators ran onto the pitch to offer Kilpin their crisp embroidered handkerchiefs to staunch and soak up the blood. Five lovely pieces of linen had been ruined by the time the referee decided it was time for Kilpin to leave the pitch and for the game to restart.

The referee was a man Kilpin had not met before who clearly had no idea, so the groom had to spell it out for him.

'I'm ready to carry on, now that the blood has clotted.'

'You've lost more than a litre. I'm a doctor and you're not fit to carry on running around. You need to sit down and watch the rest of the game.'

'Thank you for your advice and concern, sir. I don't want to disappoint my teammates or these gentlemen who have travelled a long way to play this game. Let's continue.'

The referee was about to respond but caught the look in Kilpin's eye behind the bright red rag held to his face and thought better of it and the game continued, with Kilpin.

IV

Late that night Maria opened the door to a stranger with a mangled face. Frightened, she quickly made to close the door until he called her name.

'Maria, what are you doing? Let me in!'

Maria Kilpin screamed.

'Herbert, what's happened? Are you suffering?'

'I'm absolutely fine! If only you knew how light my head feels!'

She put her arms lovingly around his back and guided him into their bathroom to clean up his bruised face and apply ointment. She wondered whether this was to be her life from now on, as she led him through to the kitchen and poured him a glass of Black & White.

Yet despite his cavalier attitude towards domestic bliss, the contentment of early married life temporarily took the edge off Herbert Kilpin. The following month Milan were dumped out of that year's championship at the qualifying stage. Having drawn 3-3 at home to Unione Sportivo Milanese, on 19th February Milan lost the away fixture 7-6.

It was only three years since Milan had ruled the roost, defeating the champions of Genoa in their own backyard but alongside Kilpin only Angeloni and Colombo now remained from that all-conquering team.

Kilpin had been true to his word five years earlier when he'd vowed to Edoardo Pasteur that he would assemble a team to rival Genoa. But now Milan were looking increasingly like a flash in the pan, a star that had risen in the firmament before falling straight back down to earth.

For someone who hated losing as much as Kilpin it was galling to have assembled a winning side piece by piece, but then to watch most of his teammates retire or leave and the students of Juventus get ever stronger and for them, not Milan, to mount the only serious challenge to Genoa. And even worse to watch on as Genoa claimed their sixth title in seven years.

GOLDEN YEARS

I'll stick with you baby for a thousand years
Nothing's gonna touch you in these golden years.

—— *David Bowie*

I

Herbert Kilpin was nothing if not pragmatic and, after much practice, very patient. He resolved to make the best of circumstances and the limited resources currently at his disposal and began to build again, looking for easier pickings in friendlies and tournaments against gymnasia teams to develop the skills and confidence of his fresh-faced team of mostly homegrown talent.

On the final day of the 1905 championship, which Juventus were to win for the first time, Milan won its first Dapples Ball match, beating Andrea Doria in Genoa by a single goal.

Henri Arthur Dapples had been one of the first foot-ballers of Genoa and a member of the winning side in the inaugural championship of May 1898. Born in Genoa the son of a Swiss banker, he had won five championships with his hometown club before retiring at the grand old age of thirty-two and resolving to give something back to the game that had given him so much.

His largesse came in the form of a replica football made out of silver - the Dapples Ball - which became the ultimate challenge trophy for northern Italian sides, even more prestigious than the national championship.

The idea was simple. Genoa laid down the gauntlet and it was up to all comers to challenge for the right to win the Ball, while acknowledging that such a valuable trophy put up by good banking stock would always remain the legal property of the Grifone.

Whoever won the match kept the trophy and the next challenger was the team quickest to consign a letter by hand or by telegram to the holders after the final whistle had blown. The challengers had to win the game to wrest the prize from the holders and a draw didn't even give the right to a rematch.

Teams soon worked out how to maximise their chances of being at the front of the queue, sending a telegram to both teams still playing the latest game, timed to arrive just after it was reckoned the match would end.

The rules of the tournament attracted lawyers like ants to sugar. Players who stood up in court for their day job tested the boundaries: on one occasion a challenge had been declared out loud on the field of play as soon as the game ended, in the presence of two witnesses and a notary.

The summer of 1905 was the last time cricket was played by Milan Foot-Ball and Cricket Club. It had never really taken off; Italians were bemused by the lack of pace of a game that could take forever without ending in a victory and where most of the players stood or sat around most of the time. So it remained just an expats' diversion, unlike the brand of football imported by the English and Swiss, which appealed to the expressive Latin temperament.

Having ditched the cricket, Kilpin sensed the following season of 1905-06 would be a defining one. His old teammate Daniele Angeloni was to take over as coach, Kilpin would remain captain and he and chubby Guerriero

Colombo were the only survivors from the 1901 championship-winning team. There had been signs of improvement,
flashes of something, as the young Swiss players had begun
to gel towards the end of the previous season.

The club moved to Porta Monforte, not far from Acquabella, and for the first time had its own proper ground,
complete with wooden stand holding six hundred spectators and a ticket office.

Kilpin was looking to make a statement to kick-start the
season and he was rubbing his hands when the time came
to play Casteggio FC in the Negrotto Cup in October.

Samuel Davies was put in goal but wasn't happy.

'They are crap, Herbie, I won't have a save to make,
why do we need to have a goalkeeper at all?'

'Because we must show them some respect, Sam. You
haven't played for years and I can't let you waltz back into
the side and put you up front. Do as you're told and we'll
see how we get on.'

Davies had kept on grumbling but saw Kilpin wouldn't
reconsider so let it lie...until the day of the game when,
just before the players took to the field, Davies was still
dressed in his suit and wearing a boater hat.

Kilpin had already walked past, focused on the match
ahead, but sensing that something was not quite right he
turned around to face Davies.

'What are you doing Sam? We're about to start.'

'I know, but I'm not expecting to be overworked today
Herbie.' Davies replied nonchalantly. He turned away and

walked to the changing room, came back with a chair and headed towards his goal, sat down, lit a cigarette and crossed his legs.

'What the devil is he playing at?'

Guerriero Colombo was the first to respond. 'Don't worry Herbert, at least his chair is facing the right way.'

Kilpin was fuming, not least at the disrespect Davies was showing the players of Casteggio who were first puzzled and then angry as play began and did their best to break down the defence marshalled by Kilpin to have a shot at Davies sat on his chair, smoking a succession of cigarettes.

Kilpin thought about letting them through but pride got the better of him and he ensured all the action took place at the other end as the goals went in, one after another, until the score reached 19-0.

By now his anger had subsided. Finally he turned to Davies, staring into space, with cigarette butts strewn around his chair.

'Go on then Sam, sod off up front for the last ten minutes.'

Davies stood up, had a little stretch and trotted off up the field, leaving his goal unguarded and within a couple of minutes he had scored Milan's twentieth goal.

II

The championship evolved quickly from the one-day affair with which it had begun on a sunny Sunday morning in Turin back in 1898. Now there was a regional qualifying round in January 1906 that saw Milan prevail in the Lombardy section, to face the winners from Liguria and Piedmont - Genoa and Juventus respectively - in a mini-league with home and away legs played in the spring.

After the games Milan were tied with Juventus on five points each and a play-off was arranged with home advantage to Juventus at the Velodrome in Turin because the White and Blacks had scored more goals in the championship games, although this was on the understanding that if the game didn't resolve matters then a further match would take place on neutral ground.

A cagey game at the Velodrome finished goalless. Then the Football Federation incensed Juventus by ordering a second decider to be played at the ground of Unione Sportivo Milanese, just across town from Milan's ground.

Juventus explained their objection in a letter to the President of the Italian Football Federation.

The management of FC Juventus absolutely refuses to accept the choice of Unione Sportivo's ground as a neutral one because a neutral ground has to be not only the ground of another team but to have all the other characteristics of neutrality, which means pre-

senting the same advantages and disadvantages to both sides. The ground of Unione Sportivo Milanese does not have these characteristics for the following reasons:

1. It is not fair that FC Juventus would have to make a tiring trip from Turin to Milan to play the game.

2. The Milan Cricket players are used to playing on the Unione Sportivo Milanese pitch.

3. It's not fair for Milan Cricket to enjoy the support of the Milanese public.

For these reasons the management of FC Juventus confirms that if the decision of the President is not revoked then FC Juventus will withdraw from this year's Italian football championship.

Despite the persuasive logic and no doubt keen to assert its authority, the Federation remained unmoved and Milan had won the championship, without having to kick another ball.

It was a second title but the players felt cheated: Milan hadn't been given the opportunity to earn their victory.

Nevertheless success was success, even when handed to the club on a plate and was something to build on, and build it certainly did.

III

While 1906 had been a good year in which Milan had re-established itself as a successful team, the first five months of 1907 saw the culmination of everything Kilpin had worked towards since arriving in Italy seventeen years earlier.

He wasn't getting any younger and was now playing with lads who could have been his children. In what might have seemed a counterintuitive move, he decided to play up front instead of in defence so that his anticipation of play and sense of positioning compensated for his lack of pace and his quicker teammates could feed him the ball in those areas of the pitch where he could do serious damage to opponents.

Milan began the season winning four successive Dapples Ball matches by a cumulative score of 15-2.

The format of the championship now involved regional qualifying rounds in Lombardy, Piedmont and Liguria and in the regional qualifiers for that year's championship Milan were pitted against Unione Sportiva Milanese, Juventus against Torino and Genoa against Andrea Doria.

All first leg ties were played on 13th January, with Milan securing an emphatic 6-0 home victory at Porta Monforte, Kilpin scoring twice in his new position in attack.

On waking of the morning of the return fixture, Sunday 10th February 1907, the first thing Herbert Kilpin noticed was the silence. Padding over to open the wooden shutters of his bedroom window he let in a white world that had cancelled out outlines, snow covering the tree branches in front of his apartment block like icing sugar on the panettone Maria had bought for Christmas only weeks earlier.

No football in Milan that day then. What could he do to avoid attending mass with Maria?

While Torino and Andrea Doria prevailed over their more prominent city neighbours in milder climes to qualify for the final round of games between the regional winners and went on to grind out a goalless draw in the first game of the final group on 10th February, Milan were left waiting until early March to play out the formality of their return leg against U.S. Milanese, winning it courtesy of another Kilpin goal early in the game.

Milan were unable to defeat Torino either home or away, drawing both games, a considerable achievement for the club from Turin, formed only months earlier and facing up to the reigning champions.

In between the two ties against Torino Milan let loose against Andrea Doria at home, scoring five goals without reply, the fifth coming in the eighty-sixth minute courtesy of Herbert Kilpin, still running around a heavy football pitch at his age, after all those years, at that time in a game.

A week after Easter Kilpin returned to the familiar surroundings of Ponte Carrega in Genoa where nearly six years earlier his team had stormed the citadel of the reigning champions and taken the Fawcus Cup back to

Milan. Now they were contesting its replacement, the Spensley Cup, donated by none other than Doctor Goody Two-Shoes himself, James Richardson Spensley but this time they were to face Andrea Doria, not Genoa.

Kilpin was the last man standing from the 1901 championship-winning side. A few members of that team had gone on to play for other teams but most had given up running around a field chasing after a leather ball, while some had taken up administrative and managerial posts in the game.

Kilpin carried on because he didn't know how to stop running. In the humid summer months between football seasons in the weeks leading up to the first games he ran and trained by himself, in the streets between the train station and the city centre, in the Public Gardens near his home and up and down the stairs in his apartment building, to the irritation of the block's residents, wondering what possible reason there could be for this mad Englishman with a red face and no sense of decorum to soak himself in his own sweat and seem to be inviting a heart attack.

He pushed himself, whipping his ageing body into shape between September and May, refraining from indulging in the rich foods for which he had acquired a taste back in Turin in the 1890s when he had let himself go, not driven by any sporting challenge, without a goal.

People thought he was crazy but here he was, well into his thirties, continuing to hold his own against men almost half his age. His teammates weren't laughing when, towards the end of a game as they stooped for breath, arms on knees with bowed head, Kilpin barked instructions and cajoled them to rejoin the game.

What was the matter with him, why was he so bothered about a stupid game, with a glazed look in his eye? Didn't he have a life?

Yes he did, and it was largely played out on a football pitch.

If Milan had lost the game against Andrea Doria in Genoa then Torino could have clinched the Spensley Trophy the following weekend against the Genoese.

But they didn't. After an hour of deadlock first Alessandro Trerè and then Johann Ferdinand Mädler scored to leave Torino with a mountain to climb in the last game of the season, needing to beat Andrea Doria by more than eight goals to secure the title.

It didn't happen because Andrea Doria didn't turn up (literally) and Torino were given a forfeit victory but only by a modest two-goal margin. Milan had secured their third Italian championship victory and their second in a row.

Kilpin was thirty-seven years old, back in attack and had scored a hatful that season, four in the championship alone. Once again a winner and that spring his side kept on winning, retaining the Dapples Ball by beating Torino.

For good measure Milan also won the Lombardy Cup again and this time were allowed to keep it before rounding off the season in style by beating Andrea Doria at the

Gymnastic Federation Championship in Venice on 10th May 1907.

The proudly patriotic organisers of the gymnasium championship were nonplussed that a cosmopolitan team of Italians, Swiss, a German and this old Englishman was taking on and defeating all comers and thwarting the pride of Italian youth. When would Kilpin hang up his boots? He seemed to be hanging around forever, like a bad smell. Looks of concern were exchanged between the council members of the Gymnastic Federation as the trophy and medals were handed out to the Milan players in Venice with slow, slow handclaps.

Maybe someone was out to get Milan: having proudly hung goal-nets at their new ground at the beginning of the previous season, the press reported on the curious incident of their theft.

IV

Milan began the 1907-08 season on an upbeat note, with a resounding 6-0 victory in the Dapples Ball against Ausonia on 3rd November.

The following Sunday, 10th November, Ausonia's entourage was getting ready to send another telegram to line up a third successive match, with the team losing 2-0 and looking to keep the defeat to a respectable margin, when the ball burst and, for want of a replacement ball the players could kick (the Dapples Silver Ball obviously not being suitable for this purpose), the match was abandoned.

A prophetic sign, as something else was about to burst.

People are always looking for an excuse or for someone to blame when times are tough. There was an economic crisis in 1907 and some Italians looked to close ranks.

Nationalism was a powerful current of thought and feeling in much of Europe from the turn of the century, but in Italy the increasingly beleaguered position of the state allowed it to enjoy unusually wide resonance and appeal. The movement had emerged at the turn of the century as a reaction against socialism and the perceived weakness of Italy's ruling classes. The Nationalists had a much sharper sense of what they disliked than what they liked. They loathed the corruption of politicians in the capital and were critical of what they believed to be the provincialism and complacency of much of Italian life.

Kilpin's career was drawing to a close at this unhappy time when the Italian press was calling for a championship reserved for Italians. This was the anthithesis of the Milan founding spirit - *Italians, Englishmen, but not confined to those nationalities, together we will bring a sense of mission to this new venture* - and resistance was found in typically English humour.

On 15th November 1907 on the occasion of a Lombardy Cup match the Gazzetta dello Sport published what looked to be an almost exclusively English line-up to replace the cosmopolitan squad that had so recently retained the championship title. From where had Kilpin enlisted so many compatriots - and so quickly?

Hieronimus Root.

Guido Fashion.

Alfred Bosshard.

Charles Whites.

Mark Hall.

Peter Wool.

Herbert Kilpin.

The players hadn't changed, just their names. The team had pulled a linguistic stunt, anglicising the names of the Italian players, in the same way the club had been baptised with the English name of its city.

'Root' was Radice, 'Fashion' Moda, 'Whites' Bianchi, 'Hall' Sala e 'Peter Wool' good old Pietro Lana. Of the Italians only Trerè's name remained untranslated into 'Three Kings'. The Italian players were standing shoulder to shoulder with their founder, telling the world that they were all English.

Alas, Giovanni Carlo Camperio II didn't see the funny side. He had invested a great deal of his time and energy in Milan Foot-Ball and Cricket Club from the very beginning, as a founder member, player and now as manager. He was also widening his sphere of influence within the Italian Federation and gaining prominence at a national level. He knew as well as anyone how much Milan owed to the foreigners who had played such a large part in the club's formation but it was time for Italian football, like

Italy, to come of age. The gym clubs within the Federation were particularly keen to restrict the championship to Italian players and Camperio could see the sense in this. Encouraging the development of home talent would only quicken the game's development in the Fatherland.

Camperio spoke with Edwards. This little stunt was not behaviour befitting the reigning champions and Kilpin was to be told with the necessary tact and deference due to the old dog that it must not be repeated.

V

Herbert Kilpin was not well on Sunday 8th December 1907, the day Milan were to defend the Dapples Ball against Unione Sportivo Milanese.

Leading up to the game Milan had retained the trophy on fourteen consecutive occasions in a winning streak that went back more than two years.

In two games in January and March that year Milan had defeated U.S. Milanese by an aggregate score of 7-0 to coast through the qualifying stage of the championship, which they would go on to secure.

Without Kilpin keeping them all on their toes the Milan players thought all they had to do was to turn up.

They lost 1-3.

After the game nobody wanted to go and tell Kilpin the result. Someone suggested drawing straws until finally one of the seasoned players who knew Kilpin well volunteered to break the bad news to him.

Later that evening Maria Kilpin heard footsteps in the stairwell approaching her apartment. Then they stopped and there was a pause before a firm, rather hurried rap sounded on the door. Maria turned the handle and pulled it towards her.

'Signora Kilpin? I am Johann Mädler.'

Maria responded with a polite smile. She knew why Mädler was here and ushered him into her home, beckoning him to follow her through the compact, ordered living space, before she stopped at the slightly ajar bedroom door and whispered:

'Herbert, sei sveglio? Are you awake? Mr Mädler is here.'

Silence and then, a few seconds later, a low voice escaped from the crack in the door.

'Send him in.'

Motioned forward by Maria who quietly retired to the corner of the living room where she had left her darning, Mädler gently pushed the door further open and peered in, the gaslight in the living room illuminating the far wall and shutter and the edge of a double bed, the rest of the space still shrouded in darkness.

'Entra, Hans. Come in, don't just stand there.'

Mädler walked lightly across the room, to a chair that appeared out of the dark by the side of Kilpin's bed and sat down.

'How are you Herbert? You look shattered.'

'I'll live. Did we win?'

'No, we lost, 3-1.'

'Did someone get the telegram sent off in time?'

'Of course, it was sent less than five minutes after the game.'

'Thank God for that.'

'We sent the kid De Vecchi who ran to the telegraph office, knocking down an old man on the way and beating one of the lads from Ausonia who was sniffing around all afternoon. He's a quick boy.'

'He's still a cheeky little devil and needs to show more respect.'

'Don't you want to know how it all went? We were a little unlucky, especially when…'

'It's gone, finito, Hans. Forget it. Unione Sportivo have old Henri Dapples and the important thing is to grab him back next Sunday, no?'

Silence for a few seconds. Mädler tried not to stare too closely at Kilpin's sweaty face, at the wet hair stuck to his forehead.

'Did anyone take any knocks during the game?'

'Not really, Imhoff was kicked a bit and kept moaning but that's usual.'

'He's a big baby. Tell Camperio I'll be back next Sunday.'

'Really, Herbert?' Mädler was a little taken aback. 'Are you sure? I hope you don't mind my saying this, but you look as though you could do with some rest.'

Shooting a dark look across the bed at Mädler, Kilpin took an age to raise himself onto his left elbow, reaching across with his right hand to a glass on the small cabinet next to his bed, in the darkest corner of the room. He swallowed the liquid noisily in one gulp and, as slowly as he'd propped himself up, he lowered his back down onto the mattress.

'No problem, I'll be there. Just let Giannino know.'

'Va bene, okay, But please keep warm Herbert and take care of yourself.'

Kilpin smiled slyly at Mädler's bemused face, reading him like a book.

'In case you were wondering, it's only water...'

Mädler feigned puzzlement then rose awkwardly from the chair.

'I'll be off then.'

'Maria,' Kilpin called. 'Hans is going.'

Maria's slight silhouetted form silently reappeared at the open doorway. Mädler nodded towards Kilpin's direction with a parting smile and with a 'ciao' turned away and walked out into the light, carefully closing the bedroom door behind him and following Mrs Kilpin back through the flat towards the front door.

'Goodbye Mr Mädler. It was nice to meet you.'

'Likewise, Signora Kilpin. Please make sure Herbert gets his rest and doesn't start rushing around too soon.'

'Oh, I'm sure you know how carefully Herbert will listen to everyone's advice!'

Mädler smiled uncertainly, a bit taken aback that such a demure, self-effacing woman could pull off sarcastic humour with such ease, put on his hat, tipping it towards Maria, bade her an 'ArriverderLa Signora' and was halfway down the echoing stairwell by the time Maria had gently shut the door behind him.

In the darkness, Kilpin stared up at the ceiling and listened to the click of Mädler's footsteps fading down the street.

'Maria! Heat me some of your lovely soup please and I'll get up.'

He lay motionless for minutes, listening to his wife stirring in the kitchen and to the beat of the old clock in the living room. When Maria prised open the door five minutes later to announce that supper was ready her husband was fast asleep.

VI

Kilpin would never have passed anything resembling a fitness test the following Sunday but all the same he appeared on the field of play in the unfamiliar surroundings of via Comasina heading out of the city centre, to dampen the enthusiasm of the excited supporters of Unione Sportivo Milanese who had turned up in numbers to cheer on their team against the champions of Italy.

He'd be damned if he would let this bedraggled assortment of exiles from Mediolanum - the leftovers he hadn't bothered to cherry pick for his team years ago - finish off a spectacular year for Milan on a low.

Kilpin was not really well enough to stand up, let alone play football on a field in Milan ten days before Christmas, but his hectoring presence was enough to galvanise his team into scoring three goals, conceding just one at the other end, to grab back the Dapples Ball at the first attempt, allowing U.S. Milanese a grand total of just one week in possession of the trophy in the six years during which teams from northern Italy were to compete for the prize

Having tasted success Unione Sportivo Milanese naturally wanted a little more. Half expecting Milan would come at them like a wounded beast that day, they'd made thorough contingency plans to ensure they would beat both Ausonia and Torino to the telegraph office - if not Milan on the pitch - to earn the chance to knock the Red and Blacks off their perch again just in time for Christmas.

And so for the third week in a row the teams lined up against one another, this time on Milan's home turf, at Porta Monforte.

Now sufficiently recovered to walk around the field of play, but not to do much more, Kilpin hung back in defence for the entire game, spending the last thirty minutes using all his remaining energy to shout at his teammates, instilling terror at the prospect of slipping up and losing the slender advantage they were holding, until the referee finally blew his whistle. With home advantage Milan had edged past U.S. Milanese, 2-1.

Squatting on his haunches amidst the *hip hip hurrahs*, staring down at the cold mud and waiting for his heartbeat to slow down and for the icy air to stop cutting his throat, Kilpin reflected on a well-fought 1907 campaign. Champions of Italy for a second successive year and now winners of the Dapples Ball for the fifteenth time.

Surely time to have a word with old Henri Dapples to persuade him to part company with his nice silver ball on a permanent basis.

And time to call it a day.

Kilpin looked up to see Umberto Meazza walking towards him, smiling. A nice, bright lad, ex-Mediolanum, lawyer and wine merchant.

'Well played avvocato. You've run us close again,' Kilpin complimented the young man.

Willingly accepting Meazza's outstretched hand Kilpin hoisted himself to his feet as nonchalantly as he could, his joints stiffening by the minute, and offered his opponent a qualified consolation prize.

'Dear Umberto, allow us, in recognition of a valiant opponent, to offer your splendid team a round of Christmas drinks at Fiaschetteria Toscana - in return for one small favour.'

Ever the cautious lawyer and with raised eyebrow Meazza awaited the pre-condition.

'Could you find me a nice bottle of Barolo before

Wednesday? My wife is going to buy a lovely piece of lamb for our Christmas dinner. But don't go mad - nothing too fancy...'

Kilpin left the field of play, warm within, almost frost-bitten without. Never complacent, he could still afford himself a few moments of quiet satisfaction and reflection as the players gathered their clothes and together made their way west, in the general direction of the Duomo, twilight falling on the procession of young men and Mr Herbert Kilpin, aged thirty-seven years and eleven months.

But despite Kilpin's efforts above and beyond the call of duty, Milan were about to lose the grip on Italian football he had spent most of the last eight years painstakingly securing.

Trouble was brewing on the horizon and a team better than anything Genoa had ever fielded was about to announce its arrival on the big stage.

THE
DARK WOOD

In the middle of the journey of our life I came to myself within a
dark wood where the straight way was lost.

—— *Dante Alighieri, The Divine Comedy (Hell)*

All that is necessary for evil to succeed is that good men do nothing.

—— *Edmund Burke*

I

He had felt for some time that certain people were acting a little differently towards him.

Not everyone and not all the time. At work, the greeting of the occasional customer visiting to inspect or collect his goods was awkward, where before it had been jovial and unrestrained. When he entered the boardroom and the directors were discussing how to deal with the latest strikes of the workers protesting about their pay in these hard times, there was still affection and recognition but glances were exchanged and papers shuffled to fill the momentary silence before Kilpin left the room and the murmuring picked up again.

The lads were always the lads though. Still laughing, joking and grumbling, although Hans Mädler and his Swiss compatriots were getting agitated by the shenanigans going on within the corridors of power at the Italian Football Federation.

The National Gymnastics Federation had never accepted Genoa's title of first football champions of Italy. Essentially it had been a *'foreign'* team, galvanized by the Englishman James Richardson Spensley. Now Milan, with their own English leader and group of Swiss players were threatening to dominate the game as Genoa had until five years ago.

Initially Giovanni Camperio had resisted, for purely selfish reasons. Milan were in line for three successive championships, but ever the pragmatist he could see which way the wind was blowing. Italy's economy was in trouble, the workers were revolting and the magic solution for the country was clearly greater moral energy and devotion to the Fatherland, unity within Italy's borders and suspicion towards those on the outside.

'What the fuck have they done and how can they do it?' was Hans Imhoff's double question.

'Hans, I'm impressed by your command of Italian, encompassing such colourful language. They've done it because they can.'

Kilpin was angry too but he wasn't going to let anyone know it, because this was something that needed cool heads to resolve.

The Italian Football Federation had finally caved into pressure from the gymnasia clubs and decided that the coming 1908 championship season would be reserved for Italian players.

The Italian contingent piped up, led by Gerolamo Radice.

'We need to hit them where it hurts, undermine their credibility. We're the champions of Italy and we're not going to take part this year.'

Kilpin felt pride but again didn't betray his emotions.

'That's very noble Gerolamo, but the team won't have this chance again to win three titles in a row. Seize it now. I'll sit out the campaign and shout at you all from the sidelines.'

The Swiss were amazed. Hans Imhoff continued to speak for them.

'Herbie, you can't seriously mean that. We weren't around but we know how this all began, how no one was excluded...'

Kilpin was pleased Imhoff wasn't taking this lying down. Why should he?

Sandro Trerè spoke up.

'No, Hans is right, we're not going to play. I hear Torino and Genoa have already told the Federation where to stick their championship and Juventus are about to do the same.'

Andrea Meschia probed. He wanted to know what the President thought.

'What does Edwards say?'

'Well he'll never be happy about losing out on any glory but he needs to know Milan is Milan, not Milano, and that we're all in this together: no matter how many Italian backsides he licks, his tongue will always have an English accent.'

Kilpin had watched and listened. 'Our dear President Alfred isn't the problem.'

Everyone knew to whom he was indirectly referring. Gianni Camperio was in his element. Once upon a time brotherly love and internationalism had been all well and good, but they weren't going to help the communists and the factory workers get a bigger slice of a diminishing pie. The English and Swiss had played their part and started the ball rolling, but now it was time for Italians to make the game of football or, rather, *'calcio'*, their own.

Camperio had challenged the arguments of the Federation for as long as he could: like Edwards he was attracted to silver and didn't want to give up the chance of a straight treble without a fight. But resistance was going to be futile and he realised fast that Milan would have to adapt.

Nevertheless he kept up the pretence of resistance long enough to force the hand of the Federation and to secure a symbolic concession, when he accepted their summons and turned up at their offices one day with a long face.

'Gianni, we want to make clear that we don't condone Milano refusing to take part in this year's championship but we acknowledge you are not going to win for a third successive season and as a gesture of gratitude and recognition for the club's achievements in recent years we propose to award Milano the Spensley Cup on a permanent basis.'

At this point one of the committee members leaned over to his neighbour.

'Even though we helped them out with the first one, forcing Juventus to contest the replay here in Milan...'

Camperio did his very best to look dissatisfied and short-changed but he was smiling inside.

Alas, his work didn't manage to cheer up his colleagues when word reached them.

'Fuck, fuck, fuck. Prostitutes and whores,' was Hans Imhoff's considered view.

'Hans, your command of the Italian language improves by the day, although I think you'll find you've repeated yourself in your rather accurate description of our esteemed administrators. Soon you'll have gone completely native and no one will realise that you are, in fact, Swiss.'

'Herbie, this has gone beyond a joke and you know it. What has Camperio done? We sit out the championship but he goes above everyone and accepts the trophy. The lads in Turin have been asking us what's going on. How can we seriously carry on at this club when he kicks us in the balls like this?'

'We all know this year's cup will be meaningless. How do you think I feel, starting this club from nothing, living in the shadows of Genoa for so long, winning it all, losing it and then building again, only for these bureaucrats to knock us off the top.

'My dream was to win it three times in a row, so we could get our name on a cup, just like Spensley, but that's not going to happen, so we move on...'

'Yes, Herbie, it looks like we do have to move on...' Lana said sadly.

After all the planning, cajoling, travelling, running, tackling, all that whisky, Kilpin wouldn't get the chance to lead Milan to a glorious hat-trick of consecutive championships. He'd managed everything within his power but had been thwarted by matters beyond his control, by the decisions of suits playing games at the Federation's headquarters.

Politics had reared its head but what really hurt Kilpin was the way it was tearing his beloved club apart. The club ratified Camperio's acceptance of the Federation's permanent award of the Spensley Cup as a consolation for depriving the club of any chance of winning it on the field of play.

But for Milan's large Swiss contingent this was unforgiveable complicity in a decision that was just wrong. Foreigners playing alongside Italians had underpinned the club's success. These dissidents would remain true to the founding spirit of Milan Foot-Ball and Cricket Club that had been truly internationalist, even if the club's management had let the flame die.

A breakaway club was founded on 9th March 1908 at the Clock restaurant near the opera house, a stone's throw from Milan's first base at Fiaschetteria Toscana, as Football Club Internazionale Milano, (forty four members) with the declaration that they would call themselves '*International*' because they were brothers of the world. The group gathered at the restaurant that Monday evening included Bossard and Lana, who had stood with Kilpin in solidarity the previous year when the entire Milan line-up had appeared in English in the Gazzetta dello Sport.

The Gazzetta now announced the arrival of Internazionale.

It's the name of a new club founded a couple of days ago in Milan, the result of a deplorable schism that a number of trouble-makers have created at the heart of the Milan Club, and comprising mainly footballers and lots of supporters.

The greatest intentions are at the heart of this new club that promises good things. The main aim of the new club is to allow foreigners resident in Milan to play football and to enthuse the youngsters of the city to play and to whom the club reaches out.

For our part we wish the new club a long and prosperous life and most importantly, harmony, in the certain belief that its founders will ensure that all the good intentions shown come to fruition.

Kilpin looked on with the sadness of the ageing patriarch, his family falling apart before his eyes. He couldn't undo what had been done and Gianni Camperio had a lot to answer for.

Camperio had been there right from the start with Kilpin, a founding father, subscribing to the inclusive ethos of the new club of this bustling, cosmopolitan city. He'd scored one of Milan's goals in its first final when the team had won the King's Medal in May 1900 and a year later had lined up with the team for its victorious photograph showing off the Fawcus Cup.

But he had posed in the group picture in his suit and boater, not in the team's kit. Keener on playing the game of power behind closed doors, his ambition was channelled into the machinations of committee meetings and boardrooms.

Giovanni Carlo Camperio II was a true 'player' all right.

II

Thirty-eight years old and worn down by all the battles off the pitch, Kilpin helped his team to retain the Dapples Ball with a 1-1 draw against Libertas Milano on 29th March 1908 before facing the Swiss of Narcisse Sport of Montreux at the Porta Monforte ground on Palm Sunday, two weeks later.

Both teams had gone for it from the start. Milan had been weakened by the exodus of players to Internazionale the previous month but the diehards still couldn't let down their founder, captain, coach and talisman as he prepared to depart the stage and, for the love of Herbert, they scraped home with a 4-3 victory.

Then the team prepared for an Easter weekend international tournament at the Civic Arena, organised by the Gazzetta dello Sport and featuring four Italian sides - Vercelli and three local teams, Ausonia, Libertas and Milan - who would do battle with French and Swiss opposition.

In the early evening on Good Friday Kilpin was lounging on a chair in the bar finishing a cigarette and staring into space, his glass emptied of all trace of Black & White as he readied himself to get up and walk home to spend some time with Maria before he disappeared for the entire weekend.

Guido Moda, twenty-two years of age and some sixteen years younger than Kilpin, looked every bit the master's apprentice. He was quietly reading the Gazzetta and suddenly smiled and spoke.

'Look at this Herbie, the Gazzetta's gone to town with the tournament!'

Moda placed his open newspaper in front of Kilpin who, under the heading 'Come on the colours of Italy!' spotted a montage featuring cut-out images of captain Canelle of Club Français of Paris and of Milan FC's very own Mr Herbert Kilpin, placed either side of an oversized leather ball on which was pasted the all-consuming question, *'Paris or Milan?'*

The writer of the piece acknowledged that the Italian sides could have chosen easier opposition than the former champions of France and the runners-up in Switzerland, but praised the champions of Lombardy and Piedmont for pitting themselves against such worthy opponents, noting that, finally, foreigners could leave Italy to return to their homeland and say *'Italian football exists and that it is enthusiastic, brave and inspires trepidation...'*

Without a trace of irony the Gazzetta writer entrusted the honour of the nation's sporting colours to the Italian sides, in this time of Resurrection, and in particular to the great Milan side led by the Englishman, Mr Herbert Kilpin.

'Can't live with you, Herbie, can't live without you...'

La Stampa reported on the game played that Sunday afternoon, in terrible weather, on a good pitch, before a decent crowd. The game started evenly with both sides getting the measure of each other as the ball was booted from one end of the pitch back to the other until Milan struck first, through Alessandro Trerè, and held the lead until after the break when Club Français scored twice in quick succession and began to impose themselves, gradually getting used to the pitch at the Arena and overcoming the handicap of heads and limbs heavy from a long overnight journey from the French capital.

Milan scored a second through Bianchi to achieve parity for a time until the Parisians finally prevailed, the winner struck by captain Canelle towards the end of the game. The writer noticed that justice has been done as, in normal conditions and with the benefit of a good night's sleep, the French team's superiority would have been clearly in evidence.

Old Boys of Basel were next up the following day. Milan edged the opening exchanges, with the Italians quicker, more daring and even more impetuous, but then conceded a soft goal from Winter. Milan's young goalkeeper Attilio Trerè had contrived to let a speculative shot drift into his net despite remaining unchallenged for the ball.

Basel kept their lead until half-time. Kilpin rallied his troops during the break, told Attilio to forget his error and to renew his focus. Milan came out of the blocks in the second half, going on all-out attack and equalizing with a Pedroni strike before Hopf stepped up to take a penalty, keeping his nerve to smash the ball past Schmassman into the visitors' goal.

Glory for Italy against the Boys from Basel, delivered

by Basel's very own Carl Hopf.

The photographer from Domenica Sportiva had captured a moment in time for all time during the game. For him this was just another assignment when he would rather have been at home with his young family, making the most of a precious day of leisure, waiting for his wife to serve the roast lamb, rather than standing around the playing fields of the city watching grown men chasing a ball across the grass. His sport was cycling and given a choice he would have been in the mountains that day, recording the climbs of true athletes battling themselves and the elements. He'd heard that plans were afoot to emulate the success of the French Tour in Italy by staging its own Giro and he wanted to be part of that. The only way was to keep going, giving his editors what they wanted, making known what he really wanted to do and hope that one day soon he would get his lucky break.

The ball was out of shot. Was this deliberate: a subtle act of protest by the subversive photographer, dismissing this pointless game? If so, the slight only heightened the power of his work. While unseen, it is clear where the ball is, offstage, about to be floated into the Basel penalty area from the Milan right wing, with the Basel goalkeeper and ten outfield players frozen in time, all eyes fixed on the object of their desire, stood in the theatre of the Arena, seated spectators visible on the terraces, seemingly very far away.

Four players nearest the photographer are caught the

moment before they leap in the air to contest the ball. Six others are caught in no man's land on the far side of the Basel penalty area.

In between the two groups, all alone, stands Herbert Kilpin, his left arm nonchalantly resting on his side. An interpreter of space, holding back for a ball that may break to him, unchallenged, in front of the Basel goal.

Seventeen years' experience on the pitches of Italy distilled into one moment of time, recorded for posterity.

III

The conductor of play appeared in his shirt of red and black for the last time on the following Sunday, 26th April 1908, back at the Arena, in a Dapples Ball game, fittingly against the old foe from Genoa.

La Stampa reported concisely that in front of a modest crowd Milan beat Genoa 3-0.

A lively game, with very good passages of play by both sides, the Milanese defence was superior, with Milan scoring twice in the first half and once in the second.

None of the Genoese players had lined up in the first games against Milan at the beginning of the century. They had been bested by a young, hungry team from

Milan, full of running.

Attilio Trerè, twenty years old (who this time kept his concentration and a clean sheet).

Adolf Zryd, twenty-four years old.

Marco Sala, twenty-one years old.

Guido Moda, twenty-two years old.

Andrea Meschia, twenty-two years old.

Carl Hopf, twenty-one years old.

Attilio Colombo, twenty-one years old.

Guido Pedroni, twenty-four years old.

Luigi Forlano, twenty-three years old.

Alessandro Trerè, twenty-four years old.

Herbert Kilpin, thirty-eight years young.

In the changing room after the game Kilpin received a silver hipflask from his teammates and wearing a tired mask of bonhomie he christened it on the spot, sharing his invigorating spirits with his brothers for a final time.

'My time is over. Now it's time to leave room for the youngsters.'

His teammates jokingly called him *'nonno'* – grandad – rather than the *'papà'* (dad) of the club and gave him a walking stick to go with his flask.

The rest of the team had changed and gone to the osteria for drinks before the celebratory meal with the Genoese, leaving Kilpin alone in the changing room as the shadows lengthened, shattered from his exertions and by the conflicting emotions he felt; of pride at what he had achieved, regret and despair at the circumstances in which he was finishing his career with his club torn apart by a senseless feud over nationality and, above all, apprehension about what he would do with his life without the all-consuming thrill from being in the thick of the action.

Sat in silence and darkness, striking a match to light a cigarette and taking another swig of Black & White from his shiny new hip flask.

This old devil was done. And deep down, he knew it.

IV

At first it seemed Milan didn't miss Kilpin. The team kept retaining the Dapples Ball. After their defeat to U.S. Milanese in early December when Kilpin had lain in his sick-bed, Milan made the trophy their own, winning eight and drawing one of the next ten challenge games, beating the old Genoese foe four times.

The team picked up cups all over the north, winning the St Mark of Venice Cup for the third time in a row and earning the right to keep it; the Chiasso Cup, Lugano Cup and Gold Medal of the City of Milan.

Then Milan Foot-Ball and Cricket Club hit a brick wall in the shape of the bright young things from Vercelli.

Sporting Union Pro Vercelli had only formed in 1903 as the football section of a long-established gym club but in 1908 Vercelli succeeded Milan as champions of Italy, winning the alternative, federal, championship set up for teams fielding foreign as well as Italian players. This turned out to be the only show in town that year as most of the main teams had shunned the official domestic championship in protest and it didn't even get off the ground.

The Vercelli players had chosen to take part in this competition even though they were all Italian, from the town or the surrounding countryside, to pit themselves against all-comers, supremely confident in their own ability. And well they might be, having prevailed in a hostile environment.

On the train line between Turin and Milan, Vercelli was famed for the rice cultivated in the surrounding paddy fields, upon which Kilpin had gazed every time he'd travelled back to Milan after playing in Turin just before the turn of the century.

In the hot, stuffy summer months the fields were flooded and Vercelli stood alone in its vast lagoon on the Padana plain. From the middle ages the malaria-infested, stagnant waters had brought both livelihoods and death to those who worked the fields.

Somehow in this fever-ridden hothouse a group of enthusiastic young men had got bitten by the football bug as its popularity spread from Milan in the first years of the twentieth century. With its economy based on the land, providing the bowls of risotto to fuel the workers in the expanding metropolis, Vercelli was no Milan; inward looking and conservative, not at all cosmopolitan or welcoming of new sports brought from foreign lands. The team had to overcome the prejudices and hostility of the political authorities, of the schools, churches and of the players' families. It was built on the indestructible bonds of youth.

In September 1904, the year after the club was established, Pro Vercelli had received an invitation to play in a tournament in Casteggio, seventy kilometres away, across the Po valley.

The eagerness of the Vercelli youths knew no bounds; they would go anywhere for a game to test themselves so the players had risen at dawn and met at the steps of the church on their bicycles before striking out across the misty flatlands. The centre forward Sessa had learnt how to ride a bike in record time to travel with his teammates but unsurprisingly he struggled to keep pace with the convoy as it charged the bridge over the Ticino River to avoid paying the toll. He paid the price for being the slowest across, collared by the old guard and forced to pay for the passage of the whole team.

One of Sessa's mates, Frova, found this highly amusing until he nearly fell off his bike as a wheel came out of place. Forced to walk to the nearest blacksmith's forge, he rejoined his teammates after they had eaten all the food brought for the journey. Famished and shattered from the ride, unsurprisingly Frova didn't give of his best during the tournament and that day decided football wasn't for him after all.

But despite the far from ideal preparation of an epic

bike ride the team excelled at the tournament, beating the hosts and only losing narrowly to the two-time national champions Milan, cycling all the way back to Vercelli in triumph. The tired, hungry and yet penniless Vercelli heroes returned home. The team's founder Marcello Bertinetti calmly walked into a trattoria, took a seat near the window, chose steak and potatoes from the menu but kept asking for more bread - free of charge with the meal - which he then casually threw out of the window when the waiter wasn't looking, to the famished Casteggio tournament runners-up, all crouching outside on the street.

In contrast with the cosmopolitan teams from the cities of Genoa, Turin and Milan, Pro Vercelli only let local lads into the team, one big, happy family, all for one, one for all. They had no trainer, instead following the lead of their captain, adopting a no-nonsense, athletic game that no one could match. They just got better and better.

In November 1908 Kilpin was now watching from the sidelines as the visitors came to challenge a Milan side that had lifted the Dapples Silver Ball on twenty-two of the last twenty-four occasions, in a sequence going back to April 1905.

Milan had already faced Vercelli earlier that year, before all the controversy over the championship on Sunday 9th February, when, for one day Italian football had descended upon the small textile town of Biella, nestling in the foothills of the Alps, to compete for the Eugenio Bona Cup. The local sports club CS Veloces had organized a tournament and invited the most prominent teams of the day to compete; Milan, Juventus, Torino, along with the lads from Vercelli who were causing such a stir. All had been attracted by the prize of a splendid silver trophy worth the princely sum of five hundred lire.

An overnight stay still wasn't within the budgets of most teams and by nine in the morning of the tournament only the ever keen lads from Vercelli had arrived in time for their game. They were supposed to play Milan, the champions of Italy, but their illustrious opponents were still on a train bound for Biella, having missed their connection in the town of Santhià, only arriving at the ground after the scheduled end of the game, by which time the referee had already awarded victory to Pro Vercelli by default.

Winners don't like losing, especially when they've never been given the chance to play, and when Kilpin and his teammates finally arrived at the tournament, they goaded the Vercelli players:

'You're afraid to play us!'

'Don't be daft. You couldn't even get here on time.'

'Prove it. Let's play the game now. Show us you're not going to hide behind the rules.'

The Vercelli lads gathered in a huddle and conferred, but not for long. They rose to the challenge, beat Milan 3-0 and went on to dispatch Juventus in the final to take the shiny new trophy back down the mountains to the paddy fields of the plains.

Now, nine months later in Milan and recently retired from the game Kilpin marvelled silently at this new force of nature, as Vercelli again defeated Milan, this time by two goals without reply, to end Milan's dominance of the Dapples Ball.

Pro Vercelli had learnt to play without instruction from others, assimilating everything as they outran and out-fought each team they faced. For entire stretches of games they took things slowly, passing the ball around, probing and sizing up the opposition before suddenly launching into all-out attack with a war cry, to devastating effect. The *'Lions'* in their all-white shirts were a dynamic machine, and no one had an answer to this group of young athletes who had grown up together, each precisely performing the role assigned to him.

Onlookers could see how effective it was to play as a collective rather than to rely on kick and run and the talent of a couple of individuals.

This gym team had assimilated the skills Kilpin and others had imparted to the eager youths of Turin and Milan. A team that out-kilpined Kilpin and reminded him of a team of kids dressed in red back in Nottingham a quarter of a century earlier.

Maybe Pro Vercelli had won a weakened league in their debut season in the top flight in 1908 but make no mistake, they were the real deal. Vercelli were the new Genoa; only harder, better, faster, stronger.

V

They say you should never go back. Kilpin played in a Dapples Ball game for Torino, but who wanted a clapped out thirty-eight year old, jaded after a three-hour train trip from Milan, collected from Porta Nuova station like grandad by a couple of teammates.

One of the Torino players at this time who had helped to found the club in a bar off Piazza Solferino in December 1906 was a young man called Vittorio Pozzo who had recently returned to Italy from abroad, having played in Zurich for Grasshoppers, after completing his education in England.

Finally Pozzo got to see Herbert Kilpin at close quarters.

'I'm pleased to meet you Mr Kilpin, I've heard so much about you.'

'Your English is very good, Vittorio, my compliments.'

'You're very kind. I've spent some time studying in Manchester and while in England I met some of your greatest players. You know of Steve Bloomer and Charlie Robert, no doubt?'

'I'm sorry, I don't. My current knowledge of the game in England isn't detailed, I came here many years ago and I haven't been back in a long time...'

Pozzo was surprised. Why would Kilpin have come to Italy if he was that good? Why hadn't he played for the professional clubs in his home city, for Notts County or

Nottingham Forest?

Pozzo watched closely as Kilpin turned out for his club that day. He certainly had positional awareness and read the game well. His stamina was impressive too, for a thirty-eight year old, playing with lads who could have been his children. But his technical abilities were not on a level with the players he had watched turn out for Manchester United during his stay in the north of England.

Was it just Pozzo who was aware of the gulf in class between the footballers he had seen plying their trade in England and those who were playing just for fun in Italy?

The Turinese players seemed oblivious, thrilled to have such an illustrious teammate, having no yardstick by which to judge this myth of Italian football.

But now Pozzo had seen Kilpin in action close up, his educated view was that the old man had feet of clay. Deep down Kilpin knew that Pozzo knew. That Kilpin wasn't and never had been quite up to the mark of his most skilled compatriots.

Kilpin had bossed the pitches in Italy for a decade but his strength was finally failing him. A diligent student, Pozzo had absorbed the latest tactics and techniques of the English game, which had moved on considerably since Kilpin had packed his bags for Italy nearly twenty years earlier. Signor Herbert was still playing the game of the last century.

Kilpin left Turin in darkness under the gaslights for the last time, returning to Milan a dejected figure. He had arrived in this city as a footballing pioneer seventeen years ago but was leaving it again as a *'has been.'*

But he didn't return to Nottingham after he stopped playing for Milan. Why would he? After more than ten years this city was now his home. He had spent most of his adult life in Italy, learnt the language, taken an Italian wife and gone native. What would he have done on returning to England? As Italian textile workers learnt more from him about how to operate the machinery powering Italy's belated industrial revolution, so he had less and less of a trade to exercise, rendering himself redundant. England's industry remained decades ahead of Italy's: what good would it have served Kilpin to speak Italian fluently back in the East Midlands, other than to chat with the travelling ice cream sellers and organ grinders?

No. Kilpin's life was here, working in textiles, mixing with the city's footballing fraternity and watching games every Sunday.

At first Kilpin stayed away from Milan's games and convinced himself, at least for a while, that now he had lots of time to spend doing other things, things he had always meant to do.

The problem was that he had been obsessed for most of his life by a game upon which, ultimately, not very much turned.

At weekends, spending time with Maria around the house, neither quite knew what to do. For the best part of a decade and ever since he had known her, Kilpin had maintained a frenetic lifestyle, fitting paid work around his passion, organising weekday football training, club meetings, making arrangements for fixtures and travelling all over northern Italy at weekends to play matches.

Suddenly, there was stillness on Sundays.

The stillness of the Easter mass to which he accompanied his wife, maybe for the first time in their marriage, causing excitement amongst the murmuring black-clad widows in the pews, who finally caught sight of the odd, foreign spouse of poor Signora Maria, left for years to attend church by herself while her ('protestant!') husband gallivanted on muddy fields around the city or in Turin, Genoa, Venice...even as far away as lovely Florence ('...and he didn't even take her!'), returning at some godforsaken hour and entering their flat with the stealth of the cat thief, while Maria slept all alone under the serene gaze of her holy namesake and a simple wooden crucifix.

The stillness of the midday hour at the weekend, reading the paper to learn of the latest news from the London Olympic Games of 1908 - of the woes of poor Dorando Pietri in the marathon, first across the line after a heroic effort but disqualified because race officials helped him back onto his feet on each of the five occasions he collapsed within sight of the finish - as his quiet, modest wife prepared the dinner or sewed by the apartment window, and the clock continued to tick, reminding him that time waits for no man.

Outwardly a picture of domestic contentment.

But then he stood up, walked over to the window past his wife, looked down at the children kicking a ball up and down the street, took a final drag on his cigarette before grabbing his jacket and making his way down to the bar for an aperitivo.

Like a demobbed soldier trying to re-adjust to civilian life that simply couldn't match the adrenaline rush of a proper game. Retired from his true vocation at the age of thirty-eight.

Maria was as relieved as Herbert when it was time for him to return to work on a Monday morning. For the sake of his sanity and their marriage, at her prompting he began coaching the youths of the local Enotria team and playing with the Milan veterans and for a time he even refereed games, but this prevented him from taking sides and he desperately missed the thrill of competition. Impartiality bored him.

Precisely because the time and energy he had spent in helping to create an entire league as well as a football club had been so great, the hole left in Kilpin's life was gaping when he was no longer organising, leading, playing week in, week out.

He'd departed the stage just at the time when football was gaining in popularity. Despite the downturn in the economy, Milan's population almost doubled in the first decade of the twentieth century to over seven hundred thousand. Kilpin kept his job but his services were nowhere near as much in demand as they had been when he'd arrived in Milan more than a decade earlier. Now he was only useful as a clerk, using his native English as Italian textiles found markets abroad.

No longer in control, his world shrinking as it had once expanded when he had moved to Italy, Kilpin had not planned for the future or schemed for career advancement and now he was a prematurely old man.

Even so he still managed to struggle on playing veterans' football until 1913 at the ripe old age of forty-three. Continuing to punish his body with exercise, as he punished it with cigarettes and alcohol. Using his vast experience to dictate his team's tempo, playing until he finally dropped or until they'd had to drag him from the field of play.

Raging against the dying of the light. And the light was indeed dying, not just for Herbert Kilpin, but for an entire generation.

VI

Filippo Tommaso Marinetti published the Manifesto of Futurism on 20th February 1909 in Le Figaro. It called for a new artistic and cultural value system based on the celebration of energy, danger, courage, aggression, speed, subversion and modernity. Article 9 stipulated: *'We want to glorify war- the only source of hygiene in the world - militarism, patriotism, the destructive act.'*

Nationalists couldn't promise paradise in heaven like the Catholics could, or the paradise on earth planned by the socialists, but why wait for either of those when there could be immediate, unbridled love for the Fatherland?

Although the Football Federation had backed down in 1909 and re-admitted foreign footballers into the championship following the previous year's furore, the governing body laid down a linguistic marker by removing forever the word 'football' from its name, emerging as the Italian Federation of 'calcio', harking back to the rough and tumble game played in the squares of medieval Florence.

But nationalists had their eyes on bigger prizes, back across the Mediterranean, towards the Dark Continent. Colonial conquest in Africa was the goal and war would achieve it and be the balm to heal the country's internal fractures, between rich and poor, devout and non-believer, northerner and southerner.

Italy had already had its fingers and a lot more burnt when it had played with fire in Africa fifteen years earlier in looking to build a colonial empire but the old frustrations about Italy's place in the world had resurfaced amidst the celebrations in the spring of 1911 marking the fiftieth anniversary of Italian unity. Fifty years old and what had Italy got to show for it? It had got by, but not much more. Still an upstart, a minor player on the European stage, more often just a member of the audience looking on glumly as the big boys carved up the rest of the world. What was a country to do about a mid-life crisis?

Most people got on with their lives as best they could but the attention of the chattering classes focused on the Turkish provinces of Libya in north Africa. With intellectuals and artists in the vanguard, nationalists began calling for war, claiming that it alone could arouse and rekindle the highest moral virtues and that ideals could scorch in a purifying flame a people that had grown corrupt in peacetime and been dragged into petty, narrow-minded interests.

Prime Minister Giovanni Giolitti was a moderate, sensible man. But those who had too much time to think didn't want sense or moderation and Giolitti was, above all, a pragmatic politician who reasoned that military success in Libya would bolster his position at home. His reluctant decision to go to war with the Ottoman Empire was greeted with excitement: the Church had large financial holdings in Libya and heralded the country's invasion as a new crusade against the infidel. Even some socialists thought war would provide land for Italian peasants.

On a wave of patriotic fervour Italy's expeditionary force landed on the shores of Libya in September 1911 to quickly take the main coastal towns. Although the invaders were the first to make military use of airplanes for reconnaissance and bombing they made no meaningful gains after their initial conquests and got bogged down in guerrilla warfare.

On 23rd October 1911 ten thousand Arabs and Turks attacked the Italian lines in the oasis of Sciara Sciat near

Tripoli, killing over five hundred soldiers, sewing up eyes and cutting off genitals, before nailing corpses to palm trees, in retaliation for sexual offences committed against local women. In response thousands of Arabs were massacred or sent to penal colonies. As a warning against further resistance Italian soldiers carried out public executions when locals refused to act as hangmen.

The peasant conscripts sent to Libya didn't understand why they were in north Africa, taken from their land just before the harvest. Under pressure from the industrialists, landowners, intellectuals, even from the Church, Prime Minister Giolitti had sent his countrymen to a promised land of vast spaces and opportunity. But the factory workers, shepherds and subsistence farmers didn't find a noble war in Libya, only a desert in their hearts and a stony wasteland all around them as they were turned into killing machines, holding the lives of Arabs as cheaply as slithering snakes, ending up staggering around without water or food, their boots shredded by the prickly undergrowth, feet wrapped in jackets, fingernails eaten by fleas, covered in sores.

This was a fight Italy had picked which it couldn't win, but it was given a way out. In south eastern Europe increasing unrest led to the outbreak of the first Balkan War in October 1912 pitting Serbia, Greece, Montenegro and Bulgaria against the Ottoman Empire. Unable to fight on two major fronts and valuing the Balkans more than Libya, the Ottoman Empire decided to end the war in North Africa and sued for peace with Italy, although thousands continued to die resisting the invader following the Turkish withdrawal.

VII

Lucy had been writing to Kilpin more infrequently, hardly inspired to continue to open her heart to a taciturn brother who only sent brief greetings home by telegram every once in a while.

But by October 1912 she was getting worried for her family.

Dearest Herbert

I write following the end of this year's Goose Fair. We took little Eileen and had great fun in the Market Place. There was so much entertainment, in particular Bostock and Wombwell's Menagerie and its Magnificent Zoological Collection ('Too Numerous to Detail', they say!) including a lion called Wallace.

But our delight was cut short by the news of a terrible incident at sea. One of our submarine boats has collided with a German steam passenger just off the coast at Dover. Our vessel was cut in two and fifteen

crewmen were lost at sea. There is a terrible argument with Germany over the incident and the Kaiser seems very keen to rival our navy.

I hear that trouble is brewing in the Balkans but also that Italy is no longer at war in Libya and I do hope that is the case. Do you know of men who have travelled to fight in North Africa?

I pray for you and for Maria. Please send me your news.

Lucy

All Lucy received back was the usual Christmas greeting, with an assurance that all was well with her brother who kept on going as usual while the politicians continued to bicker. He wrote a letter this time, finishing it off one Saturday afternoon at Milan's Porta Monforte Ground, as he watched the players training for the following day's game.

He looked up to see an argument developing on the far side of the field where a group of players were remonstrating with a couple of young men walking past the ground on via Castel Morrone.

Afterwards he learnt from the players that one of the passing men, a cocksure character who didn't sound as though he was a local, had goaded the Milan boys, telling them to stop indulging in effete activity and to get some proper exercise.

The man had eventually been pulled away by his companion who had been heard to remonstrate with him.

'Benito, the last thing you need is trouble at this time. Andiamo, lascia stare - just drop it.'

Kilpin turned back to his letter as the men walked off.

'...the politicans bicker, but so does everyone in this country and things still seem to work more or less, although I'm not quite sure how...'

The following year brought an economic crisis, with strikes beginning in the spring and continuing until the summer months.

Nationalists claimed credit for having pushed the government into invading Libya but denounced the prime minister for his slack prosecution of the war and many Catholics agreed with the nationalists, while the war provoked socialists into calling a general strike. The moderate government tried to placate everyone but ended up pleasing no one and in elections held at the end of October 1913 socialists, radicals, Catholics and Nationalists all made significant gains at Giolitti's expense.

After limping on for months his government fell in the spring of 1914. That June three demonstrators were shot dead by police in the eastern port of Ancona, beginning *'Red Week'*, during which rioting and strikes hit much of northern and central Italy. Churches were ransacked, buildings burnt down and barricades set up. Hundreds were killed in battles with the authorities and gangs were formed to protect private property as the country seemed to be heading for revolution. In Milan a young socialist troublemaker called Benito Mussolini whipped up the crowds into a frenzy and was nearly trampled to death after being struck to the ground in Piazza Duomo.

Although Italy was preoccupied with its own problems, all was far from well in continental Europe.

In this charged atmosphere the major powers were armed to the teeth and itching for a fight. The spark for the almighty bang came when a car engine cut out on 28th June 1914 as a twenty-nine year old chauffeur called Leopold Lojka took a wrong turn down a street in Sarajevo and stalled his car when trying to put it into reverse. In doing so Lojka made his own small, but telling, contribution to world history. His car was carrying Archduke Franz Ferdinand, heir to the crown of the Austro-Hungarian Empire who was visiting Sarajevo to observe military manoeuvres in Bosnia.

And a nineteen-year-old member of the Young Bosnian Movement called Gavrilo Princip who was standing outside Moritz Schiller's café with a loaded gun in his pocket when the car's engine cut out just couldn't believe his luck.

'Herbert, have you heard what's happened in Bosnia?'

'Why would I care, if I even knew where that was?'

'Because both your country and ours are going to get sucked into a lot of trouble. Austria are going to declare war on Serbia, Germany will back Austria and Russia, France and Britain are not going to stand by and let that happen. We may hang back for a while but it's only a matter of time before Italy will join in too...'

On the outbreak of war in Europe, the liner Duke of Genoa had been far out in the Atlantic Ocean, headed for South America and carrying Vittorio Pozzo's Torino team to a football tournament. The hostilities resulted in the requisitioning of ships and unexpectedly extended the team's stay in Brazil and Argentina but eventually the Turinese found their way back to Italy aboard the Duke of the Abruzzi.

On their return home the team watched from the deck as British battleships patrolled the waters for German boats. Italy hadn't joined the conflict...yet: in breach of its treaty obligations Austria had failed to consult its ally before declaring war on Serbia, leaving Italy free to announce its neutrality.

Many in parliament and in the country thought Italy should remain on the sidelines, but democracy was to be thwarted by those who shouted loudest.

On 26th October 1914 Mussolini agitated for intervention after deciding that involving Italy in a great conflict was the best way of bringing about a revolution. He left his post as editor of the newspaper *Forward!* and was expelled from the Socialist party the following month.

On Christmas Day 1914 along parts of the Western Front there was a truce between English and German troops. Soldiers collected their dead from no man's land before exchanging gifts, sauerkraut and sausages for chocolate, and playing a game of football.

The interest this story generated showed there was still an appetite for the diversion sport brought in these dark, uncertain times. The editor of *'Illustrated Sport'* told his staff to fill some space with light relief, to take minds off what might be coming around the corner and to provide a little comfort from the past.

One middle-aged journalist recalled some chance remarks in a bar that the founding captain of the original Milan football club still lived somewhere in the city. An odd name, similar to the English writer, Kipling.

Enquiries were made, an understanding reached and one cold, damp morning in February 1915 the journalist walked past the Galleria and the Duomo, pushing through the crowds assembled in the Piazza demonstrating for and against involvement in the war raging in much of the rest of Europe. The man turned down a dark backstreet to arrive at his destination, Birreria Colombo, the headquarters of Milan Football Club.

Kilpin had suggested this place and on entering the journalist soon realises it's the old man's patch. As they glide around the bar the *camerieri* share a quick smile and a few words with *'Signor Herbert'*, sat silhouetted with his back to the window, as people hurry down the street outside.

As part of his research the journalist has seen photos in the old papers. As he approaches the table he notes how thin and sharp-featured Kilpin has become; a ghost of the well-nourished utility player of the early 1900s.

Kilpin pulls himself up and stretches out his hand in greeting. The interviewer notices the Englishman's slightly worn overcoat and his yellow-stained, trembling fingers.

The journalist engages in a little small talk to try to warm up Kilpin.

Kilpin has been leading a quiet life with his wife since retiring from competitive football in 1908. He refereed for a time, coached the kids and played with the veterans until a couple of years ago. He misses the club.

The waiter comes to take the journalist's order (a coffee) and to bring another glass of whisky for Kilpin.

'Come sei bravo, Bruno - how good you are. Grazie.'

As the waiter departs, Kilpin starts coughing violently and quickly downs the whisky, spilling drops onto his coat and the tablecloth. The journalist pretends not to notice.

'Black & White, signor - the finest of whiskies and the only way to forget a conceded goal!'

He loves his adopted country, it's been good to him. It's given him his wife, his livelihood and some fine friends. Still employed in the textile trade, but work's harder to come by and at the moment he's been told to take some time off as he's not been feeling too well of late.

'So Signor Kilpin, can you tell me about the good old days, how it all began?'

Kilpin doesn't reply straightaway. Instead he leans back into his chair to extract a silver holder from his overcoat's inside pocket, puts a cigarette to his lips and strikes a match.

Suddenly someone has switched on the blinding lights and Herbert Kilpin is back by popular demand, centre stage one last time.

He takes the cue, stops nervously tapping his empty glass and unfurls his hands, placing his left one lightly on the table while in his right he waves his wispy cigarette with the grace of a conductor, as the pale face morphs into the greasepaint mask of…The Entertainer.

Ladies and gentlemen, we give you Mr Herbert Kilpin and…

The curious beginnings of Italian football through the recollections of a great champion of yesteryear.

Kilpin. A name that the new generation of footballers will never honour enough, a magical name that made the first crowds delirious for a great champion: a name that is almost everything in the first years of our football.

For a moment he pauses, smiling as the memories come back and then he begins speaking, little realizing his words will be preserved for posterity.

He talks of his childhood back in Nottingham, kicking a ball around the 'halfa crown round' at the Forest Recreation Ground, playing and winning with the Garibaldi Reds, and this triggers one episode after another…

A pioneering young lady of football

Among the most fanatical followers of the game was the Heyes family; father, mother and three children, two young men and a daughter who all donned football boots on a Sunday before heading off to the Trotter. Roller skates helped Mrs Heyes to avoid slipping around the outside of a muddy pitch as she watched her husband and sons playing the game, but her beautiful young daughter Marta played as well, if only just in the warm ups before games. She had a really strong shot and great courage, attacking the opposing halfback with the spirit of an accomplished player.

So she is to be rightfully included among the pioneers of football in Italy, despite being wrongly forgotten and ignored by everyone.

The lineman
with the umbrella

In Turin I refereed a match between Torino and Genoa.

For the first time linesmen were used and cheery Doctor Canfari, current president of the Referees' Association, was the official for Torino.

All of a sudden it begins to rain. What does Canfari do? He abandons the line and comes back shortly afterwards with an umbrella. And he shakes the open umbrella above his head whenever he wants to tell me that the ball has gone out of play.

I stop the game and go up to him.

'Please close your umbrella!'

'Why should I get soaked?'

'And I'm not soaked either? The linesman has to put up with rubbish weather as much as the referee!'

With great reluctance and still muttering away, the current president of referees falls into line and puts his umbrella down.

The referee who knew nothing about football

Milan once played a game against Andrea Doria in Florence. The referee came from Puglia and he evidently knew nothing about football.

Do you want to know how he began the game? He appeared with the ball under his arm, blew his whistle and then booted the ball into the air. Naturally I protested and explained that the players, not the referee, kick off the game.

And he replies: 'And you sir, how do you come into it? Am I or am I not the referee? You'll play how I like and you'll keep your trap shut, unless you want to be sent off.'

The singing footballer

A really useful footballer in those days was Knoote, a Dutchman who had come to Milan to study singing and who is now an opera singer at the Metropolitan in New York.

Knoote, good footballer that he was, was absolutely obsessed with the condition of his throat and would only play a game when the pitch was dry and the sun was shining. There was no way of persuading him to play when the weather conditions were humid, because he was scared stiff of catching a cold.

You need to appreciate that to have such a delicate player in your team was as good (or as bad) as not having him at all. You could never count on him.

On the Friday when we chose the team for the Sunday game, before committing himself to play Knoote would check the barometer in the Galleria.

Once, during a game, there was a sudden downpour on what had been, until then, a glorious day. As soon as the rain fell there were only ten of us - Knoote had vanished!

He had run off to the changing room and only came back when the sun came out!

Kilpin rounds off his reminiscences by telling the journalist about the kick up the backside he gave the snotty little street kid Renzo De Vecchi, currently the biggest star in the game, the youngest player to represent his country to date and on course for his first championship title that year with Genoa.

At first the journalist asks questions, encourages a dialogue but soon, in his wisdom, he shuts up, and just keeps writing in his notebook, ever faster, nodding encouragingly, only lifting his head to smile respectfully at Kilpin, as the narrator coughs or wheezes, pauses for breath and then sucks in another mouthful of smoke.

By the time he is done some colour has returned to Kilpin's taut cheeks. After mopping his brow he sits back and suddenly feels very tired and a little drunk.

'I hope that's enough for your article, signore. I'm afraid my memory's not as good as it used to be.

'I've enjoyed your company greatly but now I must be off. My little wife has ordered me to be home for one o'clock. Otherwise, the pasta will be in the bin. Please let me know if you need any more information once you've written your piece…

'…And I would be grateful if you would pass on my regards to your editor who was kind enough to publish a couple of my letters many years ago.

'Addio.'

Kilpin stands up, shakes hands, puts on his bowler hat and on leaving the bar steps back out into the hurly-burly, walking slowly back up the street towards Piazza Duomo.

The journalist remains seated, looking at the pages of his notes covering the table and the cold coffee he hasn't touched, watching Kilpin through the window before he disappears into the crowd.

He turns to Bruno who is taking away Kilpin's empty glass.

'I hadn't realised Signor Kilpin was so old. He must have played football until well into his fifties!'

'Impossibile, signore. He dropped by for a celebratory drink on his birthday a week or so ago.'

The journalist raised a quizzical eyebrow, inviting the waiter to continue.

'He's just turned forty five.'

VIII

Kilpin had retired from Milan's senior team in 1908 but then moved effortlessly from number one player to the club's greatest supporter. He rarely missed a home game in Milan, in the same way he had been an almost constant presence in the team for the best part of a decade.

On 21st March 1915 he was at the Velodrome, near his home, to watch the game against Novara, perched on the rail around the cycle track, staring intently at the pitch, watching his '*family*' play.

Not for him the agitation of the fans who don't accept

that the only battle should take place on the field of play, taken to the extreme the previous summer when rival supporters at a game by the seaside between Spes Livorno and Pisa Sporting Club had gone way beyond booing and whistling or even throwing stones and punches and ended up shooting at each other, jumping the starting gun for the war that had since engulfed most of Europe.

Ruddy-faced and tight-lipped, bowler-hatted and huddled in his great overcoat, Kilpin's hands remained in his pockets. Only his eyes moved, following the ball and the players. He willingly acknowledged all who approached him, his hand appearing from his coat in greeting and exchanging pleasantries, before returning his hand to its pocket and his gaze to the pitch.

Milan had not won a bean since 1908 but triumphed in that game against Novara, 2-1, under Kilpin's unyielding stare.

But by now he had been reduced to the role of spectator, no longer a player. Ill, sad and powerless, surrounded by the chaos of a divided nation on the brink of war.

Less than two weeks after Milan beat Novara there were two opposing demonstrations in Milan: one organized by socialists against the war and the other by interventionists led by Benito Mussolini.

On 12th April neutralist and interventionists clashed in Piazza Duomo and the killing of a worker by plainclothes police provoked a general strike two days later.

Two weeks later the Treaty of London was concluded

in secret. Italy agreed to enter the war on the side of Britain, France and Russia, in return for the promise of territorial gain in the South Tyrol, Trentino, Istria, Trieste and much of Dalmatia.

On 4th May Italy broke its treaty with Austria-Hungary and three days later a series of demonstrations was held in favour of intervention. On 19th May a crowd of fifty thousand rallied in Piazza Duomo.

On 23rd May, instead of signaling the start of games referees all over the country announced the suspension of the championship and the following day Italy entered the Great War.

Peasants were dragged from sowing crops on the land, put into uniform and sent to the Front in shock, guns thrust into their hands. They were unable to grasp what was happening, receiving no consolation from the knowledge that they were about to fight and die for the greatness of an Italian nation whose language many of them didn't even speak. They had been here before, less than four years earlier.

Italy engaged in its first significant battle with Austria on the Black Mountain, rising more than two thousand metres above the town of Caporetto, and took it on 16th June in a daring pre-dawn attack by Alpini troops from Piedmont. One of the three fatalities was Alberto Picco, a twenty-year-old officer, centre forward and first captain of his hometown team Spezia Calcio 06 from the port of La Spezia which had formed in 1912. Scorer of his team's first ever goal.

After the Novara game that March Kilpin had been seen less and less in public as rumours circulated of a terrible illness gnawing away at him. But people stopped talking about Herbert Kilpin, as the news filtered back to Milan from the Front of each set-back for the Italian Army fighting the Austrian Empire in the Alps and on the Carso plateau on the eastern confines.

Then just before the Christmas of 1915 Kilpin received a visit from an old friend, Guido Moda, a teammate from the championship winning side of 1907 and in the captain's last game for Milan at Easter ten years earlier.

'My dear Mr Fashion, how nice to see you,' smiled a frail-looking Kilpin, sunk into a frayed armchair and wrapped in a blanket.

'Ciao Herbie, the boys haven't seen you around for months so I reasoned that if you weren't going to come to see us then I'd just have to pay you a visit to wish you a Merry Christmas.'

'Guido, you are very kind. As you see I'm not in the greatest of health but I live and breathe and am still able to enjoy Signora Kilpin's exquisite cooking, when I have the appetite.'

Kilpin paused, then carried on in a serious tone, with sadness in his voice.

'I am very sorry for your great loss. I've heard about Domenico...'

'Grazie, Herbie. He tried his best to comfort his mother

in his letters home and the censors did the rest, but no one is fooled about what's going on out there. At least he cannot suffer anymore. We hear of the trench warfare in Flanders which is bad enough, but stuck in the mountains here in winter, on the dry Carso blasted by the Bora wind and with nowhere to take cover when the shells land....

'Those bloody generals don't know their arse from their elbow. What hope is there? They don't tell us that men are dying up there because no one bothers to tell them to keep their heads down when they reach the trenches. And if the Austrians don't get our lads, the typhoid and cholera will because of the incompetents who can't even dig holes for the men to shit in.'

'Far be it from me to criticise the leadership of the Italian Army, Guido, as it looks from afar as though the British generals are hardly covering themselves in glory either, but urging your troops to go forward, no matter how hopeless the odds, without proper equipment and expecting to overcome the enemy with 'daring' alone, that is no way to win a war. Willpower will never trump sound strategy and tactics, let alone machine guns and barbed wire.'

'You've heard about Attilio?' Moda asked.

'Yes, I understand they've brought him home from the Carso. Cut to pieces by shrapnel. He's a mess and won't kick another football.'

Kilpin paused and a smile flickered across his face and he continued.

'I can't help seeing his beaming face, five years ago,

when I went to Centrale to see off the national team for their match against Hungary. There he was, stumbling along the platform dragging his suitcase stuffed with salami and God knows what else that Mamma Trerè had packed for the train journey. They'd eaten the lot before they got to Venice. He came a long way after dropping the ball in my last game for Milan, goodness knows how many years ago now...'

'But at least, he'll live, God willing.'

'True, Guido, true. Unlike your poor brother... and Spencer and Canfari. You didn't play against either, did you? Not great players, but men of immense courage and integrity. Dead within a month of each other.'

'Didn't the papers mess up, writing Spencer's obituary weeks before he died?'

'A matter of mere detail, he'd already been mortally wounded, shot in the chest while tending to the wounds of an enemy German soldier in no man's land. He was the type who makes me proud of my countrymen, not the likes of Haig and Kitchener, who can all go to hell, along with that bloody Kaiser.'

Kilpin was getting upset at the thought of these distant figures sending his friends to a senseless death and started coughing violently. Moda reached out to pass a glass of water that Kilpin gulped down noisily, before catching his breath and continuing.

'You know what Spencer's motto was? 'Never hit a man when he's down.' Well, he lived and died by his creed, unlike the bastard who shot him. Genoa owe him a huge debt, and will surely honour his memory.'

Kilpin paused and his gaze strayed from Moda, out through the window, to some unseen point.

'You probably didn't know Canfari, either, did you? He and his brother and some friends started Juventus, on a bench outside their school, near their father's bicycle shop. Like me, Enrico came to Milan from Turin and we played together, in 1904, when we lost to his old team. We had some fun... he always had a smile on his face.

'A few years ago I was refereeing a game and he was the linesman. It started raining and he put up an umbrella and kept running the line with it!

'I heard that last month his mother received the dreaded letter from his second-in-command. Ordered to lead his men in a hopeless attack on an enemy trench, he was shot straight in the chest, falling without uttering a last word.

'Poor Enrico, scared of a little rain, but he didn't fear death when it came. ...'

Kilpin's words were cut short again by his rattling cough, shaking his bent frame as he cupped a skinny hand to his mouth.

Moda got up from his chair to offer the older man his handkerchief but without lifting his head Kilpin gently waved him away.

'No, no, that's quite all right, Guido, it can't be helped. Once upon a time the cigarettes fired me up but now they are taking their toll. Maria keeps hiding them from me and doesn't realise it doesn't matter now if I stop. I keep getting the son of Signora Maragno across the corridor to nip out and get me some more from the tabacchaio. Why should the condemned man be denied his last smoke or two, eh?'

With a knowing wink Kilpin lifted his blanket holding out in triumph a silver hip flask that had evaded the clutch of his fussing wife.

'Or a dash of petroleum to keep the engine going? 'Black & White', the finest Scotch whisky. Can I warm you with something a little more comforting than that coffee?'

'You're very kind, Herbie, but I must be going. The night is falling and I don't want to leave mamma alone with her thoughts for too long.'

It had been good to catch up with Herbert and to see that his memory and dry wit remained intact but he was a ghost of the man who had commanded the respect of a generation of footballers, not just in Milan but across northern Italy. He had been hard but fair, once even excluding Moda from training because he had forgotten to pay his subs.

Moda rose to leave but Kilpin grasped his arm with a surprising strength.

'Guido, a final matter. You know what it's like to be the best, but I hear Milan is no longer feared as we once were and people are saying we'll never win anything again - promise me you'll raise a glass to me when we do?'

'Herbie, of course, and I hope you'll be with me when

we do!'

Kilpin's eyes lit up with the kindness Moda had shown and went along with the lie.

'That would be very nice, Guido, very nice.'

IX

Lucy Kilpin wrote her last letter to her long-lost brother in September 1916.

Dearest Herbert

I write to you with no end in sight to this terrible war. When we think it cannot get any worse news reaches us of yet more casualties in the bloodiest of battles on either side of the Somme River in France. They say that on the first day alone twenty thousand men were lost or wounded and that three whole battalions of the Sherwood Foresters were lost.

We trust you are far from the battle in Italy but we hear Austrian planes have bombed some of your cities and I continue to pray for your safekeeping and that of your dear wife.

Herbert, I know you are not one for writing but please give us all the comfort of knowing you remain safe and well.

Your loving sister,
Lucy

The letter had laid open on the little wooden table next to Kilpin's bed since Maria had read it to him, with some of the medals her husband had won with Milan.

He lay alone in the double bed, shrunken and lost in its expanse. Maria was now sleeping on a mattress in the living room so Kilpin could lie in peace and she could grab some respite from her near-constant vigil.

She had left her crucifix on the wall above their bed to watch over her husband but Kilpin wouldn't have glanced up for solace even if he'd been able to raise his head. Instead he gazed with watery eyes at the medals next to his sister's letter, taking comfort from what had been, rather than from what was to come. After all, he was the most catholic of protestants, the founder of a team of devils who had usurped the cross as their emblem.

And so it came to this, in the cold autumn of 1916. Lying in his bedroom in via Giotto, coughing up blood and looking out of his window at the falling rain until it disappeared with the fading of the light in the early evening. Maria sat quietly in the other room, head bowed and clutching her rosary beads, wondering what she would do next, as the pitter patter of the unseen rain underscored the irregular wheezing of her dying husband.

X

On 25th October 1916 the weekly bulletin of the Lombardy Regional Committee of the Italian Football Federation came out as usual, despite the ongoing war.

News of the week

Banned: Amleto Malinverni [Hamlet Badwinter] of Vigor FC has been banned from playing for 15 days starting on the 25th October for offending the referee during the Saronno Cup match on the 22nd October at Busto.

But precisely what had Hamlet said or done to offend the referee? Had he been provoked by a ridiculous decision of the official and did he in turn decide that enough was enough and that he wasn't prepared to suffer the slings and arrows of outrageous fortune?

Reina Paolo of FC Saronno has been punished with an eight-day ban, beginning from the 25th October, for improper conduct towards an opponent during a game.

What did Paolo do? Had he in turn been provoked by Hamlet?

Alas, the reporter did not say, as the News of the Week moved straight onto details of the Tournament '*Val d'Olona*' Cup between Milan Foot-Ball and Cricket Club and Legnano Foot-Ball Club.

The Committee has heartily congratulated AC Enotria for the gold medal awarded to its glorious member Mario Giurati, who has died in battle.

And then, finally:

In memory of Mr Herbert Kilpin, exemplary teacher to many of our champions, who died on the 22nd of this month. The committee sends its deferential best wishes and warmest condolences to the Milan Club, which had the good fortune to have him as its founder, teacher and most worthy footballer.

XI

The following Friday morning Bruno Rossi was getting

ready for another day of serving customers in the Birreria Colombo. He had changed into his immaculately pressed uniform, checked that all the beer glasses were clean and was killing time before the arrival of a thirsty clientele.

He thumbed through the pink pages of the Gazzetta dello Sport and started at the sight of a photograph of Signor Kilpin under the heading *'The pioneer of Italian foot-ball has died.'*

Bruno was not keen on football, or calcio, or whatever they called it now. On his days away from work he liked nothing better than to escape the city on his bicycle and ride around the countryside or even to take it on a train into the mountains where he could push himself to the limit and set his pulse racing.

He had known Signor Herbert only as the reserved English gentleman who everyone respected and who had aged very quickly in recent years. He read the gushing words of the obituary, not understanding the meaning of all of them, especially the bit about the apostolic fervor with which Signor Kilpin had sacrificed his own personality for the sake of the cause, but *'uncontested fame'*, *'exceptional at his sport'*, *'the most perfect player'* and the phrase *'Herbert Kilpin was Milan and Milan was Herbert Kilpin'*, were telling him that as well as being a nice man signor Herbert had been an important one.

Instinctively Bruno glanced up at the near full bottle of Black & White whisky gathering dust behind the bar, a reminder that he hadn't seen Signor Herbert for many months, and wouldn't now see him again, this side of Paradise.

XII

This world's farewell to Herbert Kilpin was a short, poorly attended affair, towards the end of October, just before All Souls' Day.

He was buried in the vast cemetery in Musocco to the north west of the city in foul weather, cold stinging rain pelting down on the handful of mourners, drowning out all sound other than the crunch of gravel underfoot as the funeral party trudged to the chapel of rest, filing past row upon row of russet poplar trees.

A little black sparrow, Maria bade farewell to her husband after the service, as the others retreated in silence. Maria and Herbert had only had each other, solitary leaves fallen from their family trees. He, long gone from the land of his birth; she swallowed up by the bustling metropolis and as detached from her own family, who were no more than twenty miles distant in the town of Lodi. There had been very few family get-togethers in the twelve years of union with her husband, he always playing away (football), watching or refereeing games or telling others how to kick a ball properly.

Bruno had come to pay his respects and had waited for Maria at a distance and offered the widow his arm as she turned away from the grave. They walked slowly down the avenue of trees until they became a black speck in the distance.

Despite the effusive obituaries in recent days people were living in the present and fearful for the future; at this time of war the dead were buried without great fanfare as the living took care of themselves.

Kilpin was buried in the protestant part of the cemetery, marked an outsider, a *'diavolo'*, as he had so deliberately styled himself and his team of red and black.

No name was placed on the vault prepared for Kilpin and it said *'Alberto'* on the record card because someone had misspelt his name on the death certificate.

Dispatched with haste from this mortal coil as the dead meat kept on arriving at Musocco from the city, the priest checked his watch before the next service.

An unsentimental ending to a sentimental journey.

The vault door slammed shut and then there was darkness.

RESURRECTION

10

You can't bet a penny on your future if you don't know your past.

—— *Paul Valéry*

I

On the evening of Monday 4th October 2015 it was cold inside the Giuseppe Meazza Stadium and AC Milan were losing 0-3 at home. Piero Rossi sat glumly next to his friend Carmelo, watching the Napoli players take their time to return to their own half, celebrating in front of their travelling fans, after scoring from a free kick in the sixty-seventh minute.

'What a load of merda.'

Piero had hoped that joining the die-hard fans on the Curva Sud would give him more of a buzz than sitting in his usual seat on the third tier near the half-way line, but clearly this was not the game to cause an adrenalin rush at a quiet time of year, the summer long gone and not even the shopping channels daring to peddle Christmas this early.

Seeing not much was happening on the pitch, at least to interest the forty-odd thousand Milan fans in the half-empty ground that was getting emptier by the minute, Piero's eyes wandered around the Curva Sud where he sat, to his right at a hard core of youths in black bomber jackets, still banging on their drum and chanting, even louder now than at the beginning of the match in defiance of the result unfolding before them, Milan's worst home defeat for five years.

Turning to his left, a group of older men sat glumly in their seats shaking their heads. Maybe this was how those undeterred youths would turn out, after being worn down by another few decades of the fare being dished out on the grass for the spectators, feeling short-changed.

But no, some defiance still remained deep within even these men, as they unfurled a large banner in response to the occasional speculative forays by Milan into the Napoli half, trying to catch the wind behind their sail, before each move petered out and, once again, Napoli took control.

On the couple of occasions the banner came out towards the end of the game Piero spotted the caricature of an old-time footballer in Milan colours, sporting a moustache and a tassled cap above the words *'Banda Casciavìt Herbert Kilpin Firm.'* Under their jackets a couple of the men were even wearing T-shirts sporting the same image.

Piero turned to Carmelo and gestured in the direction of the banner.

'What's that all about?'

'They're Banda Casciavìt – *'the Screwdriver Crew'* – even you know the nickname of the working class Milan fans, right? They stopped letting off flares a long time ago, settled down, got jobs and started families. But they still turn up week in, week out, rain or shine, good results or... (looking at the pitch).. bad, reminding the rest of us what Milan is really all about - a rich heritage.'

'Who's the old player?'

'An Englishman called Kilpin who founded the club with a group of others back in the day. Ever wondered why we're 'Milan', not 'Milano'?

'I know one of the guys over there, Giuseppe, he lives in our block – come on, let's go over, nothing for us to see here.'

By now more red seats had appeared all over the ground, even the blue ones on the Curva Sud, and it was easy for Carmelo and Piero to step back a few rows and join the Screwdriver Crew.

Carmelo greeted his neighbour. 'Ciao Giuseppe, fancy seeing you here. I'll be glad when this rubbish is over.'

'You're not kidding. I can't wait for a nice hot chocolate at home in front of my Game of Thrones box set,' Giuseppe remarked, already regretting having renewed his season ticket at the cost of two weeks' silence from his wife who had wanted to go on a cruise.

Carmelo introduced his companion. 'This is my friend, Piero. Usually he sits over there,' gesturing to the west stand, 'but he thought he'd come into the Curva Sud for a bit of atmosphere...'

'Picked the wrong game for that, I'm afraid son,' piped up a little man (apparently, 'Franco') with a hangdog expression.

Franco didn't seem the sort of person to engage with if you wanted cheering up so Carmelo ignored his remarks and carried on talking to Giuseppe.

'Piero was asking about Herbert Kilpin, your specialist subject.'

'Seriously, you're a grown man and you nothing about The Lord?' grimaced Giuseppe.

Slightly affronted, having studied history at the University these past five years, Piero piped up. 'Our family has supported Milan from the time of my great-grandfather. I know the club started in 1899 as the Milan Cricket and Football Club – otherwise why the date on the badge, and that we've won the Champions League seven times...'

'Actually, it was the Milan *Foot-Ball* and Cricket Club, only three Champions Leagues and four European Cups...' added the doleful one.

'Whatever, Franco, why do you have to be so anal all the time?'

Franco had clearly been asked the question many times before, his reply pinging back quicker than any instant messaging ever could.

'Because we really were 'champion of champions' four times, when it actually was about the football and not about the money,' rubbing his fingers together in a gesture of disgust.

'Just be glad it's not that way anymore Franco; otherwise the limit of our ambitions would be the bloody Europa League every Thursday night...'

'Anyway, son...' continued Giuseppe, having heard all this banter before and clearly long bored by it, 'Herbert Kilpin made it all happen: the name, the badge, the red and black stripes. He was our first captain and won three championships.

'He's the spirit of this club, always was and always will be, whoever owns it. We never forget that - especially at times like this...' nodding towards the pitch, just as Milan scored an inglorious own goal from a Napoli cross, the defender's outstretched leg guiding the ball, bobbling, over his own goal-line.

This was the cue for more headshaking, sighs of exasperation and shuffling of sad feet heading for the exits.

'We've remembered Kilpin at important times, like when we last won the Champions League in Athens back in 2007.'

Here Giuseppe turned to Piero and asked him, 'Are you old enough to remember Kaká at the end of the game, all in white and on his knees, arms raised towards the sky, wearing his '*I belong to Jesus*' T-shirt?'

Piero nodded, pleased that these guys were now talking about stuff within his living memory, and Giuseppe continued:

'Well, none of all that would have happened without Kilpin. We left a little 'thank you' note at his resting place.'

'You went all the way to England, just to do that?' Piero asked, impressed by the dedication of these fans.

'No, son, just down the road to the Monumental Cemetery – he's buried there.

He was a proper character, smoked all his life like a chimney, drank whisky before and after games, to celebrate goals or to forget defeats. Still managed to play until he was forty-three though, even longer than Maldini.'

Well at least I've had a history lesson tonight, reasoned Piero, looking back to the pitch as the whistle ended the torture and the Milan players trudged off to the tunnel after sheepishly acknowledging the remaining fans in the ground, leaving the limelight to the buoyant Neapolitans and their manic fans dancing around the Curva Nord.

II

Piero thought no more about Kilpin and the Screwdrivers as he returned to his studies during the Autumn semester. Christmas came and went, Milan were climbing the table but hardly blowing teams away, as his dad constantly reminded him they once had, 'back in the day.'

Then one Saturday the following January Carmelo texted him, just after Milan had messed up again, although in a less spectacular way than against Napoli, surrendering a lead against Empoli twice and ending up with a draw that still left the club some way off the chasing pack at the top of Serie A.

Same old, same old! WYD. Casciavìt off to cemetery to wish Kilpin H-BDAY 146. AFAIC – shopping with Silvia. WDYT. Text Professor on 033 5227872. MTFBWU.

Carmelo was great but if there was one thing about him that irritated Piero it was his need to get down with the kids, when he really ought to know better. Piero couldn't work out what Carmelo was telling him so had to ask his younger sister Olivia, who explained that he was being invited to go and celebrate the 146th birthday of a football player in a cemetery.

Why on earth would Piero want to do that?

But then again, why not? Piero had been looking for an excuse not to finish the blessed thesis that would allow him, finally, to graduate. The problem was that he didn't know what on earth he was going to do when he did.

Sunday 24th January was a cold sunny day. Piero took the metropolitana to Porta Garibaldi station and headed in the direction of the Monumental Cemetery. He'd passed it in the car lots of times but had never had reason to stop and go inside.

Of course years ago at school he'd seen photos of oversized memorials to well-known or well heeled departed souls: cherubs, loving couples, angels, obelisks, and even a life size bronze depiction of Christ's Last Supper, for the Cinzano family, he recalled (but surely Jesus had drunk wine rather than an aperitivo with his disciples?).

Piero's feet crunched over the gravel towards a middle-aged guy in a leather jacket standing outside a side entrance and who was looking expectantly at him.

'Professore?'

'Ciao - Piero? That's my nickname but no one remembers my real name any more. Your friend Carmelo told us you would like to join us in wishing Kilpin a happy birthday.'

'Sure, why not?'

'Let's go then, the rest of the boys are already there.'

'So he's not in the main bit of the cemetery?'

'We should be grateful for small mercies. That's a story I can tell you later. The big fish who no one remembers can keep their fancy memorials.'

The Professor led Piero to a small group of men halfway down the corridor they had entered, who were grouped in a small alcove to the right. Piero recognised a couple of them from the game at the San Siro back in October, including that man of mirth Franco, who at least nodded back in recognition.

'Eccoci, we're all here.'

For a moment, standing there in silence with a group of virtual strangers on a Sunday morning looking at the vault of a man who had died nearly a hundred years ago felt a bit odd.

But on their day off and away from their families all these men had taken time to remember someone, to give thanks for something important this person had given to their grandfathers and which they in turn had passed down to their children. You didn't choose your club in the same way you couldn't choose your family. For these grown men this wasn't loyalty to a brand, carefully nurtured by expert marketing, but their birthright.

They'd brought flowers and left them leaning against the foot of the wall containing Kilpin's modest vault, on which someone had stuck a handwritten card: 'Happy Birthday Herbert from Banda Casciavìt.'

At least someone remembered Kilpin nearly a thousand miles from his hometown, thought Piero as he looked round at the score of other vaults, one on top of the other, adorned with cracked plastic flowers in commemoration or with no flowers at all.

The gathering lasted a few minutes. A little small talk and then the group zipped up their jackets and ambled back towards the entrance.

The Professor gently tapped Piero on the shoulder.

'Everyone's going to Bar Europa for a drink and we'll join them there. First I want to show you something else...'

At the exit Piero followed the Professor as he turned to the right, to the steps of the big black and white striped building facing the main cemetery gates to which the rest of the group was headed.

'Do you know what this is?'

'Looks like the Cemetery chapel.'

'Not quite. It's the Famedio, the Temple of Fame. Behind it, in the main part of the cemetery you'll find all the grand monuments for the wealthy industrialists, a family vault for the conductor Toscanini and somewhere in there is even Marinetti the Futurist artist, the guy who hated pasta because he said it sapped energy and made Italians poor fighters. All the more reason to eat lots of it, I'd say...

'But this here is the resting place for many of the city's most honoured citizens and which pays homage to those buried elsewhere.'

They were now inside the building, within a great

vaulted space below an azure ceiling studded with golden stars, and approached a big memorial.

'Before you ask, that's the mausoleum of Manzoni, the writer we all honour but only read at school because we have to...'

Straight ahead of them, slightly above eye level Piero caught the smiling gaze of a marble bust of Count Cavour, first prime minister of Italy. Then, a few steps further back, on the other side of a window facing out into the cemetery, that of Giuseppe Garibaldi.

Probably too close to each other for either's comfort (he recalled they had never trusted one another) Piero noted that both were in an elevated central position, unlike the dark bust of the other *'Joe'*, Giuseppe Mazzini, placed on a simple plinth at floor level, on the margins of veneration fifteen metres away; never really close to the action at the time back in the 1800s, even though not entirely forgotten.

The Professor beckoned Piero towards the side wall on the right, reserved for three large white marble tablets and pointed to the list of names etched in red on the first tablet.

'You're seen the latest roll of honour announced every year by the city council in the Corriere della Sera, no? Well, there's your hall of fame. Look towards the bottom of that list - at the class of 2010.'

Herbert Kilpin was there, towards the bottom, sandwiched between Gian Maria Gazzaniga and Chiara Lubich.

'There's a story behind that.'

Already used to the drill, Piero prompted the Professor to continue, 'Which is…?'

'Some fans gave the authorities grief for many years, pushing for Kilpin to be recognized by the city in some worthy way. Every Inter bugger seemed to get a nod. We share a stadium but they went and named it after Meazza who everyone knows as an Inter legend, even if he did play a few games for us when he was past his sell-by date.

'That's just one example: Inter bloody this, Inter bloody that.

'On the ninetieth anniversary of Kilpin's death we stuck a plastic plaque on his vault in commemoration and sent an open letter to the Gazzetta dello Sport to let everyone know, asking why Spensley, the founder of Genoa, or the Grande Torino team of the 1940s, had streets named after them in their cities but why still no tribute had been paid to the Lord of Milan.

'Still nothing happened, the council kept inducting the usual suspects into the Famedio.

'Time passes, the class of 2009 is announced – TV presenter, soprano from La Scala, sculptor, blah, blah, blah. No footballer though. No Kilpin, in the year of the one hundred and tenth anniversary of the founding of AC Milan.

'Basta! This city is *calcio*. Eighteen UEFA and FIFA titles for us (as well as a few for the other lot…).

'So one of our greatest fans, Luigi La Rocca, starts writing to the authorities, complaining about the lack of recognition of Milan heroes. A press conference is called to announce the launch of two online petitions to lobby the mayor and the council to enroll Kilpin in the Famedio and to inter his remains in a setting more in keeping with his place in history.

'Basically, it's a call to the streets to batter down the pen pushers' door and to do the right thing. Finally, in 2010, Kilpin gets in and there's the usual ceremony and Franco Baresi represents the club.'

This had really meant a lot to many people. So how come it had all gone under his radar - he a student of history - lost in the noise of the Champions League anthem and financial fair play and the minutiae of the lives of celebrity players in the gossip magazines?

'Time for an aperitivo, my friend,' the Professor advised, as he looked for a last time at the list of names and turned to head back outside.

'But why all the fuss in recent years, if Kilpin's been here for the last hundred years?' asked Piero.

From the smile that crept onto the Professor's face Piero had already guessed what was coming next.

'Ah, now there's yet another story. One of these days I should write a book, but for now I'll tell you all about it on the way. Andiamo.'

III

By the time they had rejoined the others in the Bar Europa less than twenty minutes later the Professor had told Piero the incredible tale of Herbert Kilpin's journey from the Cimitero Maggiore in Musocco to his last resting place in the Monumental Cemetery. It had all been due to the efforts of one man; Signor La Rocca.

Although he had worked his adult life as a customs expert, liaising with the customs and tax offices on import and export matters, on his headed notepaper La Rocca set out his true credentials:

Red and Black memorabilia.
Historic archivist.
Contributor to 'FORZA MILAN' (the official club magazine).
Ex MILAN Museum (stadio San Siro).
MILAN historian.

Since the early 1960s La Rocca had witnessed the club's successes at first hand, attending European Cup finals, watching great players in red and black win Serie A Scudetti time and again, a fan of one of the most successful club sides in the world.

He became the unofficial historian of AC Milan. On Sunday mornings, cigarette in hand, he trawled the flea market at the back of Piazza Duomo for brightly-coloured tobacco cards of footballers from the 1950s, seeking out old editions of sports magazines.

As a boy he had assiduously collected cards of his Rossoneri idols. Dario Barluzzi, the Milan goalkeeper who'd won the European Cup in 1963, signed his autograph for La Rocca on his Panini sticker for the 1965-66 season, which the young fan had treasured as the most precious thing in the world.

La Rocca was twenty-one when an ageing Gianni Rivera led AC Milan to their tenth Scudetto, giving the team the first *star* for its shirt. Enthused by reaching that landmark La Rocca conceived of a grand plan: to set out to retrieve as much of the history of the club as possible in time for its centenary celebrations in twenty years' time, raising the Knights of the Round Table, the players of the *'heroic age.'*

His idea was to collect biographical details and statistical data of every player, trainer and president of the club and of all the thousands of official games. He went about his business in a systematic way and, before the dawn of the internet, began by going through the telephone books for the whole of Italy to find contact details for former Milan players or their relatives, compiling a vast narrative of exploits on the field of play spanning the twentieth century.

La Rocca wasn't to be dazzled by the stars but had sought out the lesser lights. Players like Camillo Parisini, who at the age of twenty-one played on the left wing for

Milan Foot-Ball and Cricket Club in just one game, on 13th January 1907 against U.S. Milanese. At the end of the season Milan won their third championship and on account of his minutes on a pitch that day Parisini was a football champion of Italy forever more.

Unlike poor Francesco Soldera, a professional midfield player. All of five foot three inches, Soldera played over one hundred times for Milan over ten seasons between 1914 and 1924, winning nothing but his pay.

La Rocca recalled the thrill of tracking down Attila Kossovel in Monza in 1981, the year before the former player had died. In his youth Kossovel had been a striker for eight clubs in a fifteen-year career, including Milan in the early 1930s, before he managed a further nine clubs over a twenty-three year period. In all, thirty-eight years earning his living in the game all around Italy. But La Rocca didn't meet Kossovel by a swimming pool in a large mansion in leafy Monza, to have a leisurely chat over a cool spritz. The old man was running a petrol station in the town and recounted his footballing adventures in between filling up the cars of customers.

In the year Milan was on its way to winning its six-teenth Scudetto La Rocca trawled the libraries of the cities he happened to visit, wrote to registry offices all around the world, and bought and traded information with other statisticians before turning his gaze back home to scour the cemeteries of Milan with the intention of honouring the deceased players of Milan with a red and black rosette in the club's centenary year.

And then one day in September 1998 in the Musocco cemetery La Rocca struck gold. He came across a thin pink card marked with the precise coordinates of the location of *'Alberto'*, aka Herbert, Kilpin in the Protestant section behind an unmarked marble plaque, high up in a forgotten corner of a bank of vaults.

The last resting place of a legend, the founder of his club. Not someone who would stand a chance of gracing the great teams of AC Milan throughout the decades, but without whom there would have been no AC Milan.

But more than that: a figure fundamental to his country's footballing history, the father of Italian football.

A player as far removed from the wealthy, high profile players of the modern era as one could imagine.

Kilpin had been buried with the wrong name in haste in the middle of the Great War. But the unceremonial ditching of Kilpin's bones in a communal grave after a number of years had been avoided, maybe as a result of the re-publication in 1928 of Kilpin's anecdotes about the pioneering era of Italian football. For a brief moment the old champion had resurfaced in the public consciousness as he had done in 1915 and maybe this had struck a chord with someone from Kilpin's past.

Somehow Kilpin didn't disappear without trace and the flame continued to flicker, hidden in the embers, for another seventy years until La Rocca tracked down 'Alberto'. It hadn't been an easy search. Some people had helped him, others hadn't, but in the end his self-appointed mission had been accomplished.

As the centenary of AC Milan loomed La Rocca set about securing a final resting place more befitting its founder. At this point he enlisted the help of AC Milan, who paid for Kilpin to be moved from Musocco to the Monumental Cemetery, just in time for the club's anniversary celebrations.

And so, a hundred years after pounding the night streets of Milan Herbert Kilpin had finally been brought to rest in public view.

IV

'So, our little studente, are you now a fully fledged member of Banda Casciavìt Herbert Kilpin Firm? There's a little more to this club than mid-table mediocrity, no?'

The Professor looked sharply at Franco.

'That's very true, my friend, but Kilpin doesn't just remind us of all the success. We have a history, bad times as well as good, of falling short.'

Turning to Piero, he began his lecture. 'Your father may have told you about all the trophies and flowing football he saw when he was young, but life is shade as well as light.

'I bet you don't know that we won nothing official for over forty years after Kilpin had left the scene, right?

'When the club spilt in 1908 one of the players who went off to form Inter famously uttered a curse that Milan would never win another championship.

'We won the Federal Cup during the Great War but it was never recognised by the authorities, God knows why, maybe because they were all Inter fans...

'Well, anyway, the spell was finally broken in 1951. After the last game, when Milan had won the title by a point from Inter, the players were celebrating in the dressing room, the big midfielder Omero Tognon jumping around, yelling 'We've waited forty years - enough!'

'Suddenly this little old man comes out of nowhere to respond at the top of his voice, 'It's forty *four* years, forty four years of waiting *for me*, not for Tognon!'

'It turns out the old-timer who had dodged security and all the hangers-on was Guido Moda, past captain, coach and former director of the club, a winner of Milan's last championship alongside Kilpin back in 1907.

'You weren't born when we blew it against Verona on the last day of the season and finished second, but you're old enough to remember that 'Istanbul' came before 'Athens': winning 3-0 at half time in the Champions League Final and we still ended up losing on penalties.

'We have all the science in the world to prolong the careers of our best players, but even with his whisky and cigarettes Kilpin played on for Milan until he was thirty-eight, because he looked after himself, ate the right foods. They say that on icy mornings in winter he could be seen running around the Public Gardens near his home, and then up and down the stairs of his apartment block, all before work.

'But he didn't shout about it. He wasn't always angling for a move to another club, for more money, a faster car, a more beautiful wife.

'We watch these guys tap the ball around the San Siro on manicured lush grass – ok, at least it's in decent shape until Christmas - but we forget where we came from, that only a little more than ten decades ago we played a game in the Solcio Cup on a stony field with an old fig tree growing in the penalty area – behind which our attacker hid until the ball came close to him and he sprang out from his cover.

'Humility and a heritage. These are things money can't buy.'

Someone ordered beers, then a panino or two and the group settled down to chat about lighter things.

By now Milan were sixth in the league, at best looking to challenge for a Champions League place for next season's competition, consigned for now to watching the final rounds of this one on television. To rub salt into the wound, this year's final was going to be played at the San Siro, so the best in Europe would be coming all the way to Milan to remind them of that fact.

'Well boys, we won't be watching Milan in the San Siro on 28th May, but Nottingham here we come. You ever been to England, studente?'

'I went to London on a school trip one year. Why are you going to Nottingham?'

'And you need to ask? To celebrate the centenary of our dear Herbie's death. You've seen where his journey has ended but we're all going back to where it all began. We're flying from Bergamo for a few days in October. Want to come along?'

Now there was an incentive to finish his degree quickly. Would papà's pocket stretch to a couple of hundred euros if he suddenly found the inspiration to complete his paper ('*The Risorgimento made Italy, but what has made the Italians?*') and, finally, to collect his degree?

Suddenly Piero started to focus very hard on post-industrial Italian politics and social theory.

EXTRA TIME

We shall not cease from exploration
And the end of all our exploring
Will be to arrive where we started
And know the place for the first time

—— *TS Eliot, Little Gidding V*

I can't even spell 'spaghetti' never mind talk Italian.
How could I tell an Italian to get the ball – he might grab mine.

—— *Brian Clough*

I

It took Piero Rossi longer than he had hoped to complete his blessed thesis but it's amazing what you can achieve when you ditch all distractions and finish what you once set out to do, while barely remembering why you started it. He worked through all his original sources and came to the conclusion that foreigners had created Italy and Italians because those who actually lived there had been and always would be territorial.

Despite having celebrated one hundred and fifty years of unification Italians still struggled to defy Prince Metternich's dismissive description of their country as nothing more than a *'geographical expression.'* Loyalty was given first and foremost to the family, then to the neighbourhood and then, at most, to the town or city.

The nation was an illusion created for foreign consumption: the Leaning Tower of Pisa, singing gondoliers, a cheery rascal on a vespa screeching through the backstreets of Naples, pizza, pasta, Pavarotti. Nothing more.

Very cynical and hardly original, his tutor had remarked, but Piero scraped through, mainly because of the decent grades he had laboriously accumulated in the past five years and that was that, job done.

All that remained was for him to decide what to do with the rest of his life. Twenty-five years old, likely to live with mum and dad for years to come, no practical qualifications and entering the worst job market for young

Italians for more than thirty years.

Pazienza! At least Papà had coughed up as promised and here he was, just arrived in England on a Friday morning with a group of ageing AC Milan fans for a short break, before having to face up to reality back home.

The travellers had received odd looks at East Midlands airport and on the shuttle bus into Nottingham. Only he was under the age of forty and all were wearing red and black striped hats and scarves.

What were AC Milan doing in town? The pre-season friendlies with foreign teams had been and gone months ago and the chances of Forest or County playing Milan any time soon in the Europa League, let alone in the Champions League, were in the realms of pure fantasy. Maybe these guys had bought cheap flights to Nottingham en route to Manchester or London for a big game? But no, when they got off the bus at the coach station they didn't cross the main road to make for the train station but headed in the opposite direction towards the city centre. Maybe the black and red stripes actually signified the colours of Bournemouth? That would make much more sense, but weren't even they in the Premier League now?

After a ten-minute walk the Screwdrivers dropped their bags on the pavement and looked around the wide expanse of the Old Market Square they had entered, a modern water feature at one end and what looked like a town hall in front of them at the other. A big space, surrounded by some interesting old buildings but also a fair few uninspiring, modern ones. The Hollywood films of Robin Hood hadn't prepared them for this and there had been no guidebooks to Nottingham on sale in Milan, although they knew the old castle here had burnt down a long time ago and so weren't expecting its replacement to resemble the vast medieval Sforza Castle in their own city.

So this was it?

'It feels like we've landed back in Linate,' whined Franco.

'Stop moaning, mummy's boy, take your dummy out of your mouth and let's check into the hotel before we meet Gavin.'

Gavin was someone the Professor had made contact with over the internet. He worked for the city council and being a keen local historian seemed to be one of the few people in Nottingham who had heard of Herbert Kilpin. He'd offered to show the Milanese the sights and places connected with their hero.

They were to meet him at one o'clock, in just over an hour's time. They'd picked up sandwiches in the airport shop before catching the bus into Nottingham so headed to the edge of the square to drop their bags at the hotel and freshen up a bit before coming back to meet Gavin at one of the statues of a lion in front of the Town Hall, the left one.

'Gavin? Piacere - pleased to meet you.'

The Professor led the way, in his heavily accented but, as far as Piero could tell, very passable, English.

Gavin seemed amiable enough, a bit bookish and shy,

but everyone was pleased to see him and after a number of heavy pats on the back from complete strangers he started to warm to his new role of tour guide to this small group of football fans who had landed in the middle of Nottingham.

He suggested to the Professor that he lead them on a tour of places connected with Kilpin's early life in Nottingham. Piero caught the gist of the English explanation before the Professor translated for everyone else, heads bowed in concentration and stamping their feet on the ground to warm their toes, frightening away some inquisitive pigeons who had gathered around this huddled mass in the hope of some scraps of food.

The Professor's words of translation resulted in vigorous nodding of heads, murmurs of 'sì, sì' all round and an excited buzz followed Gavin as he headed off up Poultry, along the tram tracks, past curious shoppers who turned round to stare at the odd party.

Gavin ducked into Bottle Alley, next to a bookshop, and led them up the cobbles, away from the flow of shoppers.

Franco nudged Giuseppe.

'I tell you what, if there weren't all of us, I'd swear he was leading us up here to rob us!'

'Put a sock in it Franco. Don't worry, you'll soon be tucked up in bed by mummy when you get home.'

Wallets intact, they emerged on the tramline again, crossed it and entered a small square behind the street, to face a grand old building. Over its ornate entrance the letters *Adams and Compny* stood out in gold leaf against the stonework. (Piero wondered whether the Victorians couldn't spell or whether that was the nineteenth century equivalent of text messaging: he must mention it to Carmelo when he got home.)

Now Gavin was really getting into his stride. 'This is now a college of further education but in the nineteenth century it was a lace warehouse where Kilpin worked after leaving school and where (I believe) he met Mr Bosio who was responsible for bringing him to Italy.

'You may know that while Manchester led the world in cotton-working, Nottingham became a very important centre for the manufacture of lace during the second half of the nineteenth century. Thomas Adams was a wealthy lace merchant who looked after his workers. Unusually for the times this building had good lighting and heating, indoor toilets and washing facilities and even tea rooms.

'Apparently the façade of this building is similar to the Riccardi Palace built in medieval Florence built for the Medici family. A local newspaper described this wonderful building at the time as the finest erection in the East Midlands.'

The Professor was still translating as Gavin retraced his steps back out of the square in the direction of the Old Market Square and the Screwdrivers looked at one another before laughing in unison.

Gavin turned round with a puzzled look on his face as the men quickly recovered their composure, smiles disappearing in an instant, before once again following Gavin's lead. The flexi-time council worker had by now assumed the bearing of a seasoned tour guide in all respects, except for the absence of a raised umbrella which, considering the threatening skies overhead, might well turn out to be a significant failing, mused Franco as he brought up the rear of the pack.

The guide led the group back towards the Old Market Square.

'This could well have been the route Kilpin took on his way to and from work every day, in which case he would have passed this particular building many times. Here was the office of the local newspaper on which a Scottish writer called Barrie worked before he became a famous writer for the theatre. You will know him as the author of Peter Pan.'

They carried on and had almost completed a circuit, but just before reaching the Left Lion again Gavin beckoned the Milanese into Exchange Arcade within the Town Hall structure and waited for everyone to assemble under the glass dome.

'This building was erected (smirks all round again) after Kilpin had left Nottingham for Turin but I wanted to show you the ceiling because those four mosaics show four important scenes in the city's culture and history.'

'Ah, una galleria piccolina!' exclaimed Franco, who seemed to be cheering up.

The Professor explained to Gavin that Exchange Arcade with its upmarket boutique shops bore a passing resemblance to the somewhat grander Galleria in the centre of Milan. 'Except...' the Professor added, raising his hand gravely and knotting his brow in a frown, as a sign of qualification, '...in Milan we have a McDonalds restaurant at the end of our Gallery!' before the frown lines disappeared from his forehead and his mouth creased into a broad smile.

Gavin saw the funny side and joined in the general laughter and winking but his puzzled expression returned as he noticed Franco rubbing his right heel into the centre of the large compass on the Arcade floor directly below the decorated dome.

'What is he doing?' Gavin asked, concerned that Franco might be attempting to deface municipal property.

'In the Galleria back home we don't have this – circle – but instead there is a representation of a bull on the floor. Well, it's a tradition in Milan that standing on the 'testicoli' – how do you say?', at this point using an appropriate gesture, 'brings the visitor good luck. So Franco is trying to bring us fortune on our trip, no?'

Gavin was keen to move on. 'I see. That's an interesting story, thank you... Anyway, looking up you will see the Danish invaders taking Nottingham in the ninth century.

'The next mosaic shows William the First – 'the Conqueror' – ordering Nottingham Castle to be built on the Castle Rock in the year 1066.

'Then I am sure you will all recognise the figures of Robin Hood and his Merry Men. His great friend, Little

John (he's actually the big man) has the face of a famous old goalkeeper for the Notts County football team.'

Gavin paused for dramatic effect, before adding, 'That's Notts County, the club that gave your rivals Juventus their black and white stripes.'

The Professor continued to translate dutifully for his companions. Gavin had anticipated more than the mild, polite interest the group showed in this information.

'Have you not heard of the historic link between Nottingham and Juventus?'

'Yes, of course, but you must understand that Juventus are a team of, how do you say, *'parvenu'*? They have only won the European Cup twice.'

Gavin's expectations continued to be confounded. His dear mother had always told him he worried too much and his friends advised him to 'chill out, duckie.' He regained some semblance of poise as quickly as he could and pointed to the fourth frieze on the inside of the dome, depicting King Charles the First raising his standard in 1642, still looking to rally the people of Nottingham after more than three hundred and fifty years of trying, as the bell bonged once above the gathering.

'That is the chime of 'Little John'. Now, can I suggest we continue our journey back in time, to Herbert Kilpin's birthplace?'

The group suddenly regained its enthusiasm after the digression about Juventus. They left Exchange Arcade, passing the statue of a smiling Brian Clough, Gavin explaining how an eccentric northerner had first won the league title with nearby Derby County before later pulling off the incredible feat of transforming little old Nottingham Forest first into champions of England and then, twice in succession, of the whole of Europe.

The men listened with interest to the Professor's translation and their mutterings and facial expressions suggested approval and respect while the Professor added in English, for Gavin's benefit:

'Same as Juventus, but we are sure Nottingham doesn't keep shouting about it.'

The Rossoneri followed Gavin up King Street and then right towards a junction where they turned left to look up a busy street leading out of the centre, just like hundreds of others up and down the land.

Gavin announced, somewhat breathlessly, with a sense of anticipation:

'This is Milton Street, but just up there in the distance it becomes Mansfield Road!'

'Davvero? Really?'

Six middle-aged, overweight football fans were babbling amongst themselves, apparently overcome by the excitement of standing at the bottom of Mansfield Road on a Friday afternoon in late October, as passing shoppers wondered what they were missing out on, while a younger fan loitered awkwardly a few metres behind the group, a little embarrassed by the scene.

'Please follow me. It's a ten-minute walk up the road to

Kilpin's birthplace.'

They traipsed up the steady incline, past a big shopping centre on the right. The familiar brands and big shop fronts soon gave way to local delicatessens, kebab houses and pubs. Side roads leading off Mansfield Road interrupted the long terraced brick buildings lining the road uphill. After a few minutes the men reached a Mexican restaurant, with the number 129A on the door.

'Siamo qui, abbiamo visto questo ristorante sul web!' spurted out Franco.

The Professor turned to Gavin. 'We have seen a photo of this restaurant on the internet. This is the place, no, where Kilpin was born?'

Gavin broke into a knowing smile, feeling in control.

'Actually no, it's not. I'm aware that some of your compatriots visited Nottingham a few years ago and came for a meal here to celebrate Kilpin but the street was re-numbered in the 1890s after he had left England and his father's shop became number 191, further up the street, at the next bus stop – do you see, up there?'

The group picked up the pace again and fell silent as it reached the end of the pilgrimage, reaching a corner betting shop and then a Thai restaurant until Gavin stopped, turned to his companions and, with a flourish of his right arm, pointed to a building on their left.

'Is that it?'

Gavin could tell they were not impressed. And in truth he could understand why.

They faced an abandoned terrace, the brickwork noticeably worse for wear than the adjoining properties, the battered shop front secured with metal grilling. The Professor peered beyond the grubby glass window into the gloom of a shop space that clearly hadn't seen a customer's footfall in many years.

'The neighbours say it's been in this condition for a very long time. A couple of brothers ran a sweet shop here and there was a butcher's yard at the back.'

Cue shaking of heads and mutterings of discontent in a language Gavin couldn't make out. The Professor explained:

'Gavin, we understand that the building is empty but, more than that, where is the recognition that Kilpin was born here, that he grew up and lived here, before he left this place forever to bring us the gift of football?'

Gavin wanted to reply, but didn't feel that he could.

The party carried on to the top of the hill, crossed the road and walked past an old cemetery, where people were no longer dying to get in. Wonky headstones jutted out at all angles, dotting the sandstone hillocks of this holy ground like the irregular teeth of the village drunk. Thousands congregating in silence and hope, waiting for the Sermon on the Mount to begin again. Or maybe just the Last Judgement. A cemetery without fresh flowers, stones engraved with dead names: Walter, Elsie, Leonard.

Gavin led his charges back down Mansfield Road to the Lodge entrance into the Forest.

A big open space, bordered by landscaped trees on the slope leading down from the cemetery, hundreds of ordered chestnut trees silently watching locals walking their dogs, or letting their dogs do the walking while they took a breather on park benches. And at the far, western end, row upon row of empty cars parked on tarmac next to the tram stop.

But despite the car park, asphalted play areas, wooded slope and the constant traffic skirting its northern perimeter up and down a tree-lined boulevard, there was still a lot of grass, this Forest more a clearance than canopy, a green prairie under a big grey sky where the kids were no longer playing cowboys and indians but still came to run around, to ride their bikes and, predominantly, over one hundred and twenty years after Herbert Kilpin last booted a ball on this grass, to play football.

A couple of games were in progress, from informal kickabouts between boys using their tops and bikes as goalposts to refereed games between adults of all shapes and sizes.

The group watched three boys nearest to them decide who was going to keep goal as a man wearing a funny old hat wrapped up in a big brown overcoat and looking a little the worse for wear silently kicked the misplaced ball back to them.

One of the lads in a red Forest shirt picked up the ball, kissed it very deliberately before placing it on the still frosty grass (carefully avoiding any dog dirt) and turned to walk back five paces in the direction of the bare trees on the slope above the flat expanse.

He screwed up his eyes; branches stretched upwards to heaven silently urging him on to score, or perhaps in anticipation of a wild celebration.

Then he turned and ran to kick the ball...

II

Now it was dark. They were all cold and hungry and walked back down Mansfield Road, where they were to leave Gavin and get a meal near their hotel. But first they wanted to offer their guide a parting drink, and he had suggested they head back into town to a place he thought they might like.

On the way up the road an hour or so earlier the group had been excited and talkative, babbling on in Italian, asking the occasional question of Gavin which the Professor would translate. But now they all seemed a bit fed up.

'I bet you're all tired after such a long day?'

The Professor looked a little wistfully at Gavin.

'Not really, we're fine, even if we had no leg room on the flight and your weather's even worse than ours at this time of year. It's just...' and here the Professor prefaced his remarks by looking round at his companions, all trudging along, heads bowed, as they walked down Clumber Street before crossing Cheapside to enter Bridlesmith Gate, uninterested in the brightly-lit shop windows around them: '...we came to pay our respects to Herbert but we see no sign here that he ever existed. This is his home town, no?'

On hearing the Professor's disconsolate response Gavin quickened his pace, turning left off the street and leading his followers into a covered walkway towards a flight of steps at the end and shot back a question at the older man.

'Yes, but he left a long, long time ago and I understand Kilpin wasn't exactly a great footballer here. There has been the occasional article about him in the local paper and a short television programme, but that's about it, I think. What exactly were you expecting?'

The Professor didn't want to get into an argument with this kind gentlemen who had freely given of his time to show the touring party around Kilpin's haunts, so he changed the subject, noticing that the guide's steps were taking them away from the centre.

'Gavin, are we nearly there? We've passed many pubs and surely one of them will have good beer? We want to get back to the hotel before too long so we can have some rest before going out to eat.'

Gavin stopped and turned round as they all gathered at the top of the steps, gesturing to the building on their right.

'We are here.'

An old building looked to have been given a bit of a facelift, the stone cleaned and the brickwork freshly pointed.

They were all about to walk in when Gavin stopped them, a smile on his face, relieved that he could now reveal the secret he had struggled to keep all afternoon, before pointing up towards the glass above the door, spelling out the name of the pub.

The Herbert Kilpin.

The look on the faces of his guests had suddenly made it worthwhile Gavin having worked a few extra hours at the office in the last week to free up this afternoon so he could lead them on his little tour, which had now reached its end.

The Italians were all still quiet but no longer because there was nothing to say but because words could not express how happy they felt.

All together they rushed up to Gavin, hugging and kissing him as though he had just scored the first and most important goal in his career, as the regulars stood at the bar inside mused about how excitable these foreign football fans could get.

III

Several hours later, a large number of pints of Herbert Kilpin Pale Ale had been drunk and everyone was slumped in the comfy chairs on the first floor of the pub, looking out of the windows at the falling rain under the street light. Dinner had been overlooked and Gavin had realised that he didn't really have much to go home to. They had chatted about this and that and after quizzing him remorselessly about the pub had assured him it would become a place of pilgrimage for the '*tifosi*' back home.

The Professor was still in control, but only just. He was gazing up towards the vaulted ceiling, at the lights hanging down into the space above them.

Then suddenly he sat up in his chair, swept a mound of empty crisp packets to the other side of the table in front of him, on which he placed his half-empty pint glass, preparing to make a point and wanting to ensure everyone was listening, even though most of them wouldn't be able to understand him in English.

'Gavin, let me explain what Herbert Kilpin is to us, the reason we have come from Milan to Nottingham in October, spending all this money, having to explain to our wives and children why they are going to have to wait until Christmas for a new television and the latest smartphone.'

The Professor turned unexpectedly to Piero.

'And I also say this for your benefit, young man. I know you've finished university now – complimenti. I heard about the subject of your thesis and I don't know what your arguments were, but this is the right answer...'

'Gavin, you watch the World Cup, like everyone else, vero? I know it is a very long time since your country won it, before you were born, I imagine.

'You may remember the final of ten years ago, between France and Italy when their captain, the great Zidane, head-butted our poor, innocent Materazzi instead of looking for the ball...'

'Professore, how can you say that about Materazzi with a straight face?' butted in Piero, the only one of the group who had the faintest idea what the Professor was saying to Gavin but who had missed the sarcasm in translation.

Undeterred, the Professor continued, 'So, Zidane is sent off, with ten minutes of extra time to go and the game in the balance. As he leaves the pitch he has to walk past the little gold statute on a pedestal, quite unremarkable except for the fact that being given it means you're champions of the world.

'Right past it, so close that he can touch it. But of course he can't and he doesn't. Doesn't even look at it, but he knows it's there, all right.

'Can you imagine, getting that close and thinking you may have blown it, not just for you but for your teammates, for your whole country?

'Anyhow, they play on, until after two hours of deadlock the teams are still drawing. Time for penalties.

'You should know that six years earlier we have played France in another final, this time to decide the champions of Europe. We're 1-0 with one minute to go. We're that close to winning. Then France equalise and we're straight into extra time and the *'golden goal.'* They score again, so - finito - it's all over for us.

'So here we are again a few more years down the line in 2006, this time in Berlin. Back home we are in the middle of the biggest football scandal we've ever had (and believe me, we've had a few). Juventus have won the league but are about to be stripped of their title and relegated for the first time in their history. In Germany, not surprisingly, our national team starts badly in the tournament and the press are straight onto the players' backs.

'The manager decides to use all this bad karma and the team goes into lockdown. Won't talk to the press, to anyone. They stick together, start playing for each other, finding a way to win each game that comes their way and eventually they're in the final, after beating the hosts in a semi-final, right at the death.

'Now, it's sudden death again, against France, before 69,000 spectators in the Olympic stadium in Berlin and another 600 million people sat in front of their televisions back home or in a bar. Whoever wins the penalty shoot-out will lift the World Cup.

'I know these guys are loaded, overpraised, isolated from ordinary people like you and me, but you have to admit it takes coglioni to leave the chain of your team-mates in the centre circle and slowly walk thirty yards to pick up a ball and place it on a chalk spot, with a French keeper jumping up and down in front of you, trying his best to distract you.

'It's down to you. Nothing can prepare you for that moment, no matter how many times you practice penalties. You could score a hundred kicks in a row but it means nothing when you're under that amount of pressure.

'France go first, then Italy, and so on. Eight of the first nine penalties are perfect, the keepers don't get close to them. The other one is almost perfect, but not quite. It is hit well but bounces off the inside of the crossbar down onto the goal-line and stays out of the Italian goal.

'The first four Italians have done their job. Two were Roman. One came from Lecce...' here the Professor taps his heel, 'right down here, in the south, and the other two were from the north.

'One of the Romans, Fabio Grosso, walks up to the penalty area. He stares at some point in the distance, I've often wondered where. It's like he's not there, in front of all those eyes, but somewhere else.

'Then he runs up from the edge of the area, towards the ball. It doesn't look good. He's a defender, with too much time to think. The goalkeeper facing him is still jumping around.

'Next thing we know he's kicked the ball to his right, straight into the back of the net as the keeper dives the other way.

'Meaning we win the World Cup – for a fourth time.

'We stay up all night, going wild, driving around the streets making loads of noise, watching on the television the same scenes in Rome, Turin, Naples, Genoa...

'If I ask you who are Italian people and what is Italy, you'll probably say good food, *'bella figura'*, nice design, family, beautiful old towns and cities and maybe the Catholic Church.

'Ask an Italian the same question and he'll probably shrug his shoulders, struggling to give an answer about what defines him and his country, rather than his own town or region.

'But then, if he thinks about it, maybe he'll smile before telling you to just look at a map, at long-legged Italy kicking poor Sicily out into the Mediterranean Sea.

The Professor paused, looked around at the group and then back to Gavin, who was struggling to keep up. Then he sat back in his chair and with his left foot planted on the floor he raised and drew back his right leg, before kicking an unseen ball into space.

'Calcio.'

FULL TIME